the aRt of the SWAP

of the

Kristine Asselin & Jen Malone

ALADDIN
New York   London   Toronto   Sydney   New Delhi

⚜ALADDIN

An imprint of Simon & Schuster Children's Publishing Division
1230 Avenue of the Americas, New York, New York 10020
First Aladdin hardcover edition February 2018
Text copyright © 2018 by Kristine Asselin and Jen Malone
Jacket illustration copyright © 2018 by Julie McLaughlin
All rights reserved, including the right of reproduction in whole or in part in any form.
ALADDIN and related logo are registered trademarks of Simon & Schuster, Inc.
For information about special discounts for bulk purchases, please contact Simon & Schuster Special Sales at 1-866-506-1949
or business@simonandschuster.com.
The Simon & Schuster Speakers Bureau can bring authors to your live event. For more information or to book an event, contact the Simon & Schuster Speakers Bureau at 1-866-248-3049 or visit our website at www.simonspeakers.com.
Book designed by Laura Lyn DiSiena
The text of this book was set in Berthold Baskerville Book.
Manufactured in the United States of America 0118 FFG
10 9 8 7 6 5 4 3 2 1
Library of Congress Cataloging-in-Publication Data
Names: Asselin, Kristine Carlson, author. | Malone, Jen, author.
Title: The art of the swap / by Kristine Asselin and Jen Malone.
Description: First Aladdin hardcover edition. | New York : Aladdin, 2018. |
Summary: When twelve-year-olds Hannah and Maggie switch places, Hannah must prevent a famous art theft in 1905 and Maggie must cope with modern life until they can switch back.
Identifiers: LCCN 2017030041 |
ISBN 9781481478717 (hardcover) | ISBN 9781481478731 (eBook)
Subjects: | CYAC: Mystery and detective stories. | Impersonation—Fiction. | Art thefts—Fiction. | Mansions—Fiction. | Museums—Fiction. | Time travel—Fiction. | Newport (R.I.)—Fiction. | Newport (R.I.)—History—20th century—Fiction. | BISAC: JUVENILE FICTION / Mysteries & Detective Stories. | JUVENILE FICTION / Historical / United States / 20th Century.
Classification: LCC PZ7.1.A88 Art 2018 | DDC [Fic]—dc23
LC record available at https://lccn.loc.gov/2017030041

For all the strong, smart, persistent girls out there, and to one special one in particular, Katie, who sparked this story idea

Chapter One

Hannah

S O, IF YOU EVER NEED THE PERFECT setting for a life-size version of the board game Clue (you know, Miss Scarlet in the conservatory with a lead pipe?), look no further. It's my house. Because we've *got* a conservatory. And a ballroom. Hall? Dining room? Library? Check, check, double check. Kitchen? Obviously.

Plus, if you want alternate murder locales (not real murders, just board game varieties), there are forty-two other room options. Like one devoted entirely to making ice, called—wait for it—the ice-making room. No, seriously. An entire room devoted to . . . ice.

There are also sunken gardens with teahouses, and

statues, and murals painted right onto the ceilings, and walls covered in silk, and marble floors, and sitting rooms, and carriage houses, and an underground railroad track from the street into the basement, and columns, and arches, and so much gilded gold, and, and, AND!

I live in a mansion.

(Which definitely doesn't suck.)

After slipping my shoes off when I hit the back terrace, I tuck my fingers through my sandal straps so that they dangle from my right hand while my left pushes open the glass door. I step into the hallway. The ceiling is so high, three other me's could stand on my shoulders and still not reach the top . . . and I'm pretty tall for twelve.

Tiptoeing across the marble floor, I head for the grand staircase, but I hear a voice in one of the nearby rooms that I just can't ignore, no matter how many times I've been told to please, please try. I should keep walking. I know this.

But I don't.

"And of course, here we have the ballroom," the voice is saying, in a kind of snooty tone. "Step inside, step inside, everyone. This is the largest room in the home and was host to glamorous evenings of high-society entertaining. You are standing in what was considered *the* most fashionable house on *the* most fashionable street in *the* most fashionable resort during America's Gilded Age."

I creep behind a woman in a red sundress who raises her hand.

"How many people would this space accommodate?" she asks.

Oh, um, I might have forgotten to mention that our house is sometimes open for tours. What with being *the* most fashionable house on *the* most fashionable street blah, blah, blah. I don't mind. It's pretty cool to show off the amazingness I get to live among every single day.

"Hundreds," Trent answers. He's my least favorite of the docents. He has silver-white hair he is forever smoothing down with a palm he licks first, and he stands way too straight for anyone who's not a statue.

"When the home was completed on August 30, 1902," Trent says, "Mr. and Mrs. Berwind played host to more than a hundred guests for a seventeenth-century cotillion. Two famous orchestras performed, and there were even monkeys scattered about the gardens."

Okay, once again, I know I shouldn't do this. I know, I know, I know. But it's like one of those mischievous monkeys is sitting on my shoulder, poking me. I clear my throat, and then . . . I do it.

"Ahem. Excuse me? Trent? I don't mean to interrupt your tour, but I'd like to clarify a few things you just said. The house was completed on August 30, 1901, not 1902. Cotillions were an *eighteenth*-century formal ball. Also, there were more than *two* hundred guests who attended, and actually the monkeys were really over-the-top for the Berwinds. I don't want anyone on the tour to think that was a typical occurrence. Although, the Berwinds did entertain a lot. Like, A LOT a lot."

Trent stares daggers at me. Then he remembers there are people watching and forces a smile that doesn't quite reach his eyes.

"Ladies and gentlemen, please pardon the interruption. We have a young history buff here." His words are pleasant, but he says the words "history buff" the same way I might say "we're having sauerkraut and undercooked liver for dinner." If he feels that way about the past, maybe he shouldn't be giving historical tours. Just saying.

He adds, "Allow me to introduce Hannah. She's our caretaker's daughter."

Oh. I might also have forgotten to mention that. Although technically speaking I do live here inside this mansion, called The Elms, I sort of left out the part where my dad and I have our rooms upstairs in the former servants' quarters/current caretaker's apartment. Which, I guess, doesn't make us that different from servants, only we don't really serve anyone so much as keep the place looking perfect for all the visitors who roll through here every day to admire how the mega-super-rich used to live back in Newport's heyday. The state of Rhode Island might be extra tiny, but the "summer cottages" around here are anything but.

Visitors go home at the end of the day. And me? Well, I get to stay and hold cotillions of my own in the ballroom. Who cares if my ball gown is really a nightgown and my dance partner is my stuffed bear, Berwind, aka "Windy." He's surprisingly good at spinning.

I also get to read the books in the library. (Yes, I had to get special training to handle them and they are a hundred-plus years old and therefore smell like dust and mothballs, but I suffer through that part because it's thrilling to think that the Berwinds—or maybe one of their glamorous houseguests—turned the very same pages!) And I splash all I want in the fountains or sunbathe on the rooftop anytime I feel like it. It might not *technically* be my house, but it basically is. It's the only home I've ever known. I've explored every square inch of this place, and

I know the Berwind family history probably better than any Berwind ever did. I kind of, sort of, consider them my family too. I would give *anything* to have lived back then and known them for real.

"Where is the famous Margaret Dunlap portrait?" a man in a Red Sox cap asks.

Trent turns and gestures for everyone to follow him into the adjoining drawing room. He points at a large gilded mirror. A smaller—but still pretty big—painting hangs from long wires right in front of it, almost like the mirror is forming a second frame around the first one. (It was a style back then.) "Obviously, that is the age-old question, isn't it? Here is the commissioned reproduction of the now-famous painting. As most of you know, the original was stolen in a renowned art heist on the evening of its scheduled unveiling in 1905. The room was full of high society turned out in their finest. . . ." Trent pauses for effect, and I try not to roll my eyes. "But no one ever saw the portrait hanging. When they removed the silk sheet covering the portrait . . . the painting was gone!"

The art heist is Trent's favorite part of the tour. And I get it. It's one of my favorite things about the Berwinds' history too. A mystery for the ages. The priceless portrait was painted by famed artist Mary Cassatt and commissioned by Mrs. Berwind to mark the occasion of her beloved niece Margaret's thirteenth birthday. But even though the police determined that a kitchen boy named Jonah Rankin stole the work of art, he disappeared before he could be arrested. No one has ever found the missing art.

Many have tried.

"If the picture was gone before the unveiling and wasn't ever seen by anyone, how was it able to be re-created here?" the guy in the Sox cap asks, gesturing at the painting of a serenely smiling Margaret (whom I secretly call Maggie, because I read once that her close family called her that) in a daffodil-yellow gown that billows around her as she sits with her hands folded in her lap. Her eyes twinkle like she has a secret for only me. I'm positive that if I'd lived back then, we would have been best friends. I can just tell.

But I live here and now, with a pretentious docent shooting me glares when he thinks no one will notice. Sigh.

"There was exactly one photograph of the painting, taken over Mary Cassatt's shoulder during the last portrait sitting," Trent says. "Of course, cameras were still new then—and only accessible to the upper class—so it wasn't the best image, but—"

Don't butt in, Hannah. Don't butt in. Remember how upset Dad got the last time the docents complained about you.

I know that should be incentive enough to turn and run away, but Trent always messes this part up, and I can't stand here and let people learn the wrong version of history. I just can't. Besides loving The Elms enough to care that our guests are getting the right information, I also can't help hoping that one of these days the docents will realize I'm more than some bratty kid who's always underfoot, which I swear is how they treat me. I guess not *all* of them are that bad. I mean, Trent's my total nemesis, but some of the others aren't outright dismissive. Yet they sure aren't outright accepting of me as their peer either. It sucks to be judged by something I can't control. If I could make myself older, believe me, I would.

Maybe this is gonna sound all humble-braggy, but I'm pretty used to being decent at things. Okay, maybe even a little better than decent. And I'm also kind of used to being recognized for that. Take the soccer field, for example. Everyone knows that if the ball comes my way, I'm most likely gonna block the goal. Or at school. Let's just say I get by pretty well and I have the awards to prove it, especially when it's anything related to my favorite subject: history. But somehow no one else seems to accept that I know my stuff when it comes to The Elms. I'm not expecting a trophy for it, but a teeny tiny bit of acknowledgment—or, God forbid, some encouragement—wouldn't be the worst thing in the world, would it?

But no. Never. Not when I was the one to notice that someone had nudged one of the chairs in Mrs. Berwind's bedroom, so that a corner of it was getting hit with light from the window. (Daylight is public enemy number one for antique fabric.) Not when I stayed up all night helping my dad patch a corner of the roof in the middle of a rainstorm, before any water could drip down onto the fresco in the dining room. (Actually, maybe water is public enemy number one . . . for antique *anything*.) It's so annoying. I wish that just *once* I could get some respect around here. Plus, these people are taking the tour to learn the facts, and it's only fair that they get the right ones.

I take a deep breath. I'm crossing a big line here by butting in on Trent. I know he actively hates me (as opposed to the other docents, who mostly just ignore me) and I really should just leave his tours alone, but it

KILLS me that these guests are getting the wrong information. I keep crossing my fingers that if I can get away with correcting him long enough for guests to mention all his errors on their comment cards, he'll be reassigned to the gift shop or something. Then every future visitor will leave with the accurate version of The Elms' history. I know it's just a house, so what difference does it make if some tours get a slightly wonky version of things that took place here more than a hundred years ago? But I can't help it: *I* care. It's *my* house, and even though the history isn't mine exactly, I still feel connected to it.

Last chance to reconsider, Hannah.

"Actually, about half the households in the country had a camera by 1905," I say.

Trent takes me by the elbow, and his fingernails dig in way more than necessary. Way more. I try to wiggle free, but he tightens his grip as he says, in a fake-cheerful voice, "Oh goodness, thank you *so* very much for illuminating us on the origins of photography, young Hannah. I'm only sorry you won't be able to join us for the rest of the tour. Ladies and gentlemen, if you'll please look up, I'm sure you'll marvel at the elaborate painted murals on the ceilings."

Under his breath he hisses, "Your father will be hearing about this, young lady! It might even be time to get the Antiquities Society involved. Dear old Dad's job can go away like that, you know." He snaps his fingers, and now his creepy smile makes him look like the Grinch. "And put some shoes on. You look like a street rat. Although, maybe that's appropriate, since that's exactly where you may end up, once I've had my say with your father's bosses!"

Epic sigh.

Mansion living is mostly amazing.

High and mighty docents who get half the details wrong more than 80 percent of the time and still think it's okay to get mad at *me* for basically doing *their* job are super-annoying.

Still, once my dad hears about this, I am extra dead.

Chapter Two

Maggie

"ISS MARGARET." THE VOICE SOUNDS stern, but there's a hint of mirth under the frustration. "Your aunt will have my head on one of her silver platters if she discovers I've allowed you to be anywhere near the servants' staircase again, let alone come this far into the kitchen by yourself."

If she's this annoyed at me for simply standing in the kitchen, I can only imagine Mrs. O'Neil's outrage if I had slid down the banister, the way I'd wanted. Sliding down banisters is beyond strictly forbidden, even though I've seen Cousin Peter glide down every one in the house. Aunt would be livid just knowing I'd imagined doing it. I close my eyes, hoping the head housekeeper will be gone when I open them. But the impatient tap-tap-tapping of her left foot on the tile doesn't stop.

I count my blessings that I haven't been caught by the butler, Mr. Ernest Birch. He wouldn't waste time speaking to me; he'd simply march me by the ear to the breakfast room, where Aunt is finishing her tea. I'd rather avoid that particular sensation this afternoon. I'm sure my aunt does not fully understand and appreciate that *I have never* acted on a spontaneous impulse, no matter how much I might wish to. In my mind's eye I can picture her saying, "Maggie, darling. Young ladies should be able to control their emotions and behavior."

And I am Miss Margaret Dunlap, daughter of Mr. and Mrs. Sallows Dunlap of New York City, and niece of Edward J. and Herminie Berwind. I always follow the rules.

"I . . . I was just—"

"You can forget your excuses. I heard Miss Colette dare you over breakfast to come down here. By the by, since when have you stooped to her taunts? You should have more self-respect, if you ask me. You know she's only trying to get your goat." Mrs. O'Neil sighs. "Anyway, I can look the other way when you use the servants' staircase as a shortcut if it means you can manage to get to tea on time and spare me your aunt's rants. But land sakes, walking bold as brass into the kitchen . . . at your age! I simply can't allow it."

I clear my throat and try to speak like my aunt, Mrs. Herminie Berwind, the mistress of The Elms, the most extravagant summer cottage in all Newport, Rhode Island. The corners of Mrs. O'Neil's mouth turn up, as if she's trying to prevent a smile, and my resolve to stay strong wavers.

"My dear Mrs. O'Neil . . ."

The twitching of her lips as she stares me down causes me to lose my train of thought.

"Your aunt is correct, of course, in advising you to stay upstairs. It is not becoming of a young woman of your stature to be trifling with the help, Miss Margaret. It's 1905, and this house has amenities. You know that if you need something, you need only to use the call button, and the bell will ring in the kitchen." She gestures at the elaborate bell system on the wall. "One of the maids will bring it to you."

She wouldn't believe that I'd rather not have a maid do things for me that I'm perfectly capable of doing myself, so I don't bother to explain it to her.

She taps her foot a few more times, but she doesn't

make any move to push me out of the kitchen. Other servants have stopped their activities, and while no one is overtly staring, I can tell they are all waiting for my next move.

It's true my cousin Colette dared me to show my face down here. For a moment I consider taking something to prove I went through with it. But someone would be punished if an item went missing, and I refuse to stoop that low. I hope that just coming down here will keep her at bay for a few hours, at least.

I clear my throat and start again. "My dear Mrs. O'Neil. As the grand ball tomorrow evening is in honor of my portrait unveiling, I feel it is my duty to inspect the goings-on in the kitchen." I clasp my hands to stop them from shaking as I raise my voice and hope she believes me. "I would also like to procure a table setting, so that I might practice."

She must allow me this one small indulgence. Even with years of practice at tea parties, I am so afraid of making a ninny of myself at the ball by using the oyster fork for my hors d'oeuvres. Aunt doesn't seem to be worried, but she's *used to* hundreds of guests staring at her while she eats. I'm not.

I smooth down my dress and wait for Mrs. O'Neil's

reply, hoping she doesn't call for my aunt. I'm supposed to meet with Mademoiselle Cassatt today to view the finished portrait, and Aunt will not be pleased if I'm late. Uncle E. J. was my mother's favorite brother, and I'm treated accordingly, but there is a limit to how far I'll risk pushing my summer hosts.

Mrs. O'Neil stares me down. "Haven't you spent hours preparing for this, Miss Margaret? I'm sure you're more than capable of maintaining your manners." She softens her tone. "You should relax and try to have fun at the ball."

Between boarding school, a constant rotation of nannies, and my always-traveling father, I am constantly reminded to be good. Someone is always watching, ready to admonish or correct me. I have to mind my manners and act just so. All the time. There is precious little fun in my life. The ball is in my honor, but the last thing it will be is fun. At least during my summer at The Elms, there are people who seem to care for me. Back in the city my father is so busy, he barely says good morning when he's home. I might not even see him before I return to school. Even so, I don't want to seem ungrateful. But I can't stop myself from blurting, "There's nothing fun for a young woman of my stature." I sound whiny and childish, but

I don't care. "All that is allowed of me is to be still and silent. And to mind my manners."

I don't really expect Mrs. O'Neil to answer. But the shadow of a smile fades into a small frown as she turns to face me. "Miss Margaret." Her voice is drawn and tight. "The alternative is to be tired and invisible. As much as you don't want to be still, it would do you well to remember that others"—she makes a vague gesture to the girls behind her—"don't have the choice to sit at all." The scolding from Mrs. O'Neil washes over me. She's right. There are girls just a bit older than me back in the dark, hot kitchen. None of them are permitted to be seen upstairs. And no one is throwing a ball for any of them.

I wish I knew how to respond.

She turns away, leaving me to watch the staff go back to work. I've delayed their afternoon, which means they won't finish with their work until late this evening. I feel horrible. Also, she hasn't given me a table setting, and unless I want to involve Aunt Herminie, I'm not going to get one.

As I head back up the stairs, a noise catches my attention and I peek over the railing. A boy dressed in a starched white shirt and plain black pants stands quite still in the kitchen foyer, looking like he's waiting for some sort of instruction. Suddenly sounds from dinner preparation crescendo as someone drops something onto the slate floor—voices, and the pounding of feet, and the clatter of dishes. It's a noise I'd never hear from the main part of the mansion. I always think of the basement level as being like the steam engine of a train—it's loud and messy and you're not supposed to see it, but it keeps the rest of the cars happily moving down the tracks. It's an especially appropriate analogy, considering there are real train tracks down here that carry the coal from the street to the kitchen. I usually forget about the people who make the house run smoothly every day.

Mrs. O'Neil's skirts swish as she strides into the hall. "Jonah, what are you doing there? You should be taking the waste from the lady's tea to the compost."

"Yes, ma'am." The boy nods and retreats into the kitchen.

"Lord help me," Mrs. O'Neil says under her breath as she starts up the steps for what I'm sure is at least the tenth time since lunch. I briefly wonder what it's like to climb eighty-two steps ten times a day. Before she gets to the first landing, I hear her mutter, "What am I going to do with willful heiresses and disobedient kitchen boys? As if I didn't have enough to deal with."

As I rush up the stairs before she catches me, I remember an overheard conversation from last summer. My aunt was gossiping with her neighbor Mrs. Alva Vanderbilt Belmont from Belcourt Castle, one of the mansions down the street. "Can you imagine being born into a life of servitude, Herminie, dear? To spend your days elbow-deep in someone else's unspeakables?" Mrs. Belmont chuckled behind her gloved hand.

To her credit, my aunt didn't laugh. But neither did she defend the hardworking staff, from whom she demands an impeccable work ethic. I asked her about it afterward. "There's nothing to be gained by disagreeing with Alva Belmont, Maggie. You should remember that. She'd have the whole of Newport society against me." And then Aunt walked away to inspect the evening table settings for a dinner party.

I sigh and head toward the part of the house where I belong, feeling awful that I'm glad I wasn't born into a life of servitude. As the niece of the owners of the The Elms, the most magnificent summer cottage on Bellevue Avenue, I was born into a life of privilege. But for me, that privilege sometimes feels like a burden.

Such is life here. The servants have their own staircase, and I'm not allowed to be anywhere near it *or* the kitchen *or* the attic, where the thirty-five full-time servants live. During my first visit here, when I was ten, I was allowed to play with some children visiting other cottages for the summer. Now, at thirteen, I am considered almost a woman, so there's no fun anymore. Just manners. And of course speaking only when one is spoken to. And sitting quietly for portraits. And holding still. Constantly. Then there are the things forbidden for girls: sliding down banisters, of course. Also: walking without a chaperone, running, or doing anything that might result in perspiration. Aunt Herminie says it often, as if we're likely to forget. "Young ladies must not, under any circumstances, perspire."

I wish there were something more for me to look forward to than debutante balls and high-society parties.

New century, my foot; for a girl, there's nothing progressive about living in the twentieth century.

Chapter Three

Hannah

I POKE MY HEAD AROUND A GINORMOUS marble statue in the conservatory and watch the last of the day's guests make their way across the back lawn and over to the parking lot. Departing guests don't usually make me jealous, but right about now, skipping out the door and down to Newport Harbor for the night sounds a whole boatload better than an evening of dusting—my punishment for interrupting Trent's tour.

Especially after an entire afternoon under strict orders to stay put in the attic. Okay, that isn't actually the "Cinderella locked up by the evil stepmother" scenario it sounds like, since we converted the servants' quarters up there into an apartment for me and Dad, and it's really bright and airy, not dusty and dark like most attics. Plus, it has access to the amazing roof deck. So not exactly a prison sentence. But still.

I hate being told that I have to stay in one place. I'm usually given free rein to roam about all I want. But no. Not today. And all because palm-licking Trent went straight above my dad's head and complained to the president of the Antiquities Society about my butting in on his precious tour. I tried with the damage control, but this is maybe the thousand-millionth time my dad has warned me to stay out of the docents' way when they're giving tours, and it turns out the thousand-millionth time is Dad's breaking point. Who knew?

At least they didn't fire him, so there's that. I guess I'll have plenty of occasions to "reflect" on my actions while I spend the next month on extra dusting duty. And I quote: "You're going to get every painting in the ballroom, from top to bottom. Yes, all the way to the top. I don't care that you need the ladder."

I tried to tell my dad that Trent was giving the guests the wrong information, but all I got was a sad headshake and, "You forget, sweetie. I work for the Antiquities Society. They allow us to live here, but it's not because it's a requirement for the job. They could just as easily house me in an apartment downtown." And, "The Antiquities Society likes to use esteemed locals as docents as much as possible, and Trent comes from a very old Rhode Island family."

Blah, blah, blah. People (even kids!) who come from lesser-known Rhode Island families can have just as much to contribute. Just saying.

When I hear the front desk manager turn the bolt on the door, I jump into action and head for the drawing room. The stepladder hides out behind heavy curtains draping one of the windows, where guests won't see it during tours. I carry it over the carpeting, being extra careful not to drag it and damage a bazillion-dollar Oriental rug. Then I adjust the ladder in front of the sideboard below my favorite picture—the one of Maggie Dunlap. If I have to endure death by dusting, I'm at least gonna start with the best part of the room.

Even though I'm super-annoyed with Trent, I would never take any of that anger out on the house or its artifacts. As much as I might pout to Dad about the docents, I love everything else about being here. There's something about living in the middle of history that makes me feel like I'm part of something way bigger than me.

I gaze up at Maggie's portrait. It hangs above this

really elaborately painted sideboard. People back then (or at least the people who owned the Newport mansions) were pretty cool to hang their paintings in front of giant mirrors, because the backs of the frames get reflected, so they look kind of 3-D.

Maggie's picture doesn't even need that trick to feel lifelike, though. She seems ready to walk right out of the frame. I stare at her, like I always do, wondering what it would have been like to be her. Or even to be friends with her. I'll bet she was amazing. I'll bet she never felt halfway in her own time and halfway caught up in the lives of people who lived a hundred years ago. Why would she, when her own day and age must have been magical?

It's not that I don't love my dad and my friends and my life, but I'll just bet everyone who knew Margaret Dunlap respected *her* and treated *her* like her opinion mattered. What would that feel like?

I study her hands, folded neatly in the lap of her butter-yellow dress. They're so delicate. I'll bet they were soft. I'll bet she never did a day of dusting in her life. I'll bet *she* wouldn't have gotten in trouble for adding an entirely appropriate and accurate anecdote to a tour!

But this is my life, not Maggie's, and I have a punishment to live out. Even if it means spending the next two hours wiping down places that no guest will ever even see, let alone touch. Ugh. I climb up the stepladder and catch my foot in the hinge, almost toppling onto the wide lacquered top of the buffet sideboard.

"Oooopf." I grab the scalloped edge of the priceless piece of furniture that dates practically back to the days of the Pilgrims. An ancient Chinese vase to my left wobbles once, twice, three times before I can steady it with shaking fingers. Phew! If I break something . . . But that thought is way too horrible to even finish thinking. I would seriously be extinct, and Dad would totally lose his job.

This is going to be waaay harder than I thought. I whip the folded feather duster out of my back pocket and open it, but even fully stretched out, I can reach only the bottom of the gilded frame. Although, this is still tons closer than I usually get to the painting. Looking up, I can see more detail than I ever could from the floor. From this angle I can practically see into Maggie's eyes. Forget her eyes. I can basically see up her nose!

For a second I wonder if maybe Dad had ulterior motives when he dished out this punishment. He knows getting up close and personal with the artifacts is my favorite thing in the world. I just love how these objects that meant so much to people so long ago can still affect people today. I know they're just *things*, but they make me feel like the people who came before me are still talking to me through them. Ugh. That sounds super-cheesy.

"Do you think I'm loony tunes, Maggie?"

So, yes. Sometimes I talk to a painting.

She stares back, but her eyes are so friendly, I decide she doesn't think I'm crazy at all.

I sigh. "It must have been so unbelievable to live when you did. All those balls, and parties, and to-die-for dresses. I'll bet everyone treated you with respect. I'll bet you got to do anything your heart desired. *You* were an American princess, after all."

As I chat away, I use my duster to get into the tiny crevices and swirls carved into her fancy gilded frame. I don't usually pay close attention to the mirrors behind the paintings—they're just your basic ones, except for the extra-fancy frames, and cleaning all that glass is someone else's job, thank God!—but this time something catches my eye. Most of the mirrors around here have what I call age spots, little blobs of black discolorations that reflective glass gets over time. Nothing out of the ordinary about them. But *this* blob's shape looks exactly like an old-timey skeleton key, and I never noticed that before. I mean, I know sometimes people claim they see the face of Jesus in the burnt parts of their toast, but a key?

That's . . . different.

I can't make out the very right edge of the age spot because Maggie's portrait is hanging over it. I try to tilt the frame away from the mirror, but it's too dark behind there to see much.

Do I dare?

I look around to make sure I'm alone. What I'm considering doing is sooo not allowed. Taking a priceless artifact down from its hanging spot? Frowned upon. In a BIG way. As in, my dad would have an aneurysm. Then again, this *is* only a reproduction, so it's not exactly priceless, right?

Gently—so, so gently—I lift the frame off the hooks. I sway a little under the weight. Who knew frames were so heavy? Bending at my knees, I lower it carefully to the sideboard, where I lean it propped against the mirror. I straighten back up so that I'm eye level with the age spot blob. Now that I can see the rest of the design, it is unbelievably amazing how much it looks like the outline of an old-fashioned key. Which is the weirdest thing.

I reach my fingers up to touch it.

Chapter Four

Maggie

THE FOYER IS MY FAVORITE ROOM IN the cottage. There is so much promise in a room that welcomes you to the rest of the residence. The marble columns, the tapestry with the dancing unicorn, the urn from the Ming dynasty—they all beckon to guests to experience the rest of the magical house. Unfortunately, lingering in the foyer is another thing not allowed (unless you are a guest, waiting for the mistress).

My meeting with Mademoiselle Cassatt is supposed to take place in the conservatory. It's an odd relationship. I've spent so much time with her while sitting for the portrait, but she's always speaking in French to her assistant.

I have taken French lessons for years, but they speak so fast, and often in whispers I can't hear. Every time I try to ask a question, I'm told to sit still and keep quiet.

I long to be able to ask questions and get answers.

I pass through the ballroom into the drawing room, toward my appointment, and something catches my attention. A flicker in my side vision. I glance up to see my favorite Newport seascape perched over an ornate mirror. Something in the corner moved, I'm sure of it. I glance toward the conservatory, half expecting Aunt to emerge. Looking back at the picture, I see it again— movement in the corner of the mirror. Do I dare investigate? I would do anything to stall for a few more minutes, but what I'm considering is definitely against the rules.

Sometimes I catch Aunt looking at me with sad eyes. I think it's because I remind her of my mother, her sister-in-law, and I hope those tender feelings will help her to forgive me for what I'm about to do.

I know where Mr. Birch keeps the step stool for dusting the high mirrors, and it takes only a quick minute to drag out. I feel a thrill at doing something so . . . unexpected. Climbing up onto the sideboard over which the painting and the mirror backdrop hang, I admire the brushstrokes in the seascape. The harbor looks so beautiful in the painting—like I can almost reach out and touch the wispy clouds. Sometimes I wish I could escape into this seascape instead of being cooped up in the house, being obedient. I can almost feel the wind on my face. It's a shame this painting will be replaced by my portrait. I wonder where this one will go. Maybe Aunt will let me hang it in my room.

Then at the edge of my vision—between the painting and the mirrored glass underneath—something moves again. Like a shadow. I carefully push the painting, which is hanging from hooks in the ceiling, aside as far as I dare, bracing for a giant spider to be the culprit. Aunt Herminie will not be pleased if she catches me touching the artwork, let alone climbing on the furniture, but I lean closer. There's something there, a smudge, a shadow of some kind. I glance behind me to scan the room. When I look back at the section of the mirror, I get the shock of my life. Someone is looking back, like through a window. . . .

And it is not me.

Chapter Five

Hannah

OH. MY. GODDESS.

I'm squinting into the mirror, and, yes, I'm still looking at the same ballroom behind me.

And there's a girl staring back at me in the mirror, all right. . . .

But she's *definitely not me*!

In fact, she looks like a spot-on, dead ringer for . . . Margaret Dunlap. She's wearing the same dress from the painting (except it's green, not yellow, which is hardly the strangest thing about this scenario).

Mirror-Maggie blinks in surprise and cocks her head to the side as she looks into the glass. Wait, *can she see me*?

"Great, first I talk to inanimate paintings, and now

I'm having visions. Crazytown, here I come," I mutter. "Does spicy bean dip ever cause hallucinations? Because if so, I'd better lay off any more of Dad's. Going loco is *not* going to help me get all this dusting done."

"Pardon? I . . . Are you speaking to me?"

Omigod, Mirror-Maggie is talking! To me, I think!

I . . . This . . . What . . . ?

No. Way.

Mirror-Maggie has a forehead that's as scrunched up as mine must be. She reaches a hand out slowly, hesitating before laying it on the mirror right on top of the key shape. I can't help tilting my head in the opposite direction as my own hand comes up. I place my fingertips right against hers, and . . .

Chapter Six

Maggie

S I SIT UP FROM THE PARQUET FLOOR, it takes a moment for me to realize I have fallen off the sideboard in the drawing room. I scratch my head, trying to remember what happened. I was trying to get a better look at the painting being replaced by my portrait. I rub the bump on my head again, hoping there's no bruise that will show.

I thought I saw something. Someone. In the mirror. But no, that can't be right.

I don't remember slipping, but that's the only explanation for being down here, staring at the underside of the furniture.

When my head clears, I get shakily to my feet. Aunt

Herminie expects me to report to the conservatory to meet with Mademoiselle Cassatt presently, but first I notice a framed painting tilted dangerously against the mirror above the sideboard.

"What in tarnation?" I slap my hand over my mouth. If Aunt hears me swear, I'll really be in trouble. Especially the day before the big ball to unveil my portrait.

My hand still covering my mouth, I stand on tiptoes to see the painting. It looks exactly like the one I've been sitting for with Mademoiselle Cassatt. Except . . . except my dress should be green. Not that horrid shade of yellow.

Why in heaven's name would she change the color of my dress at such a late date? And why is the portrait here and not in the conservatory, where Aunt and I are supposed to be seeing it in its finished form for the first time? I specifically remember Mademoiselle Cassatt preferring the light in there for the occasion of our first glimpse at it.

Out of habit I reach to touch my lucky locket as I sink back to the floor. It's not hanging around my neck. For a terrifying second I'm afraid I've lost it. I must have left it on my dresser. But something else isn't right.

The neckline of my dress feels strange.

A wave of fear flows over me, and gooseflesh emerges

on my forearms. I didn't notice before, but now, looking down at myself, I see that my entire wardrobe is wrong. First of all, I'm wearing trousers. Trousers? I once saw a picture in a book of a woman wearing trousers, but it's not proper. It's indecent. I feel the fabric. Denim? The only people I've ever seen wearing denim are the cowboys in the Wild West show that Father took me to when I was ten, and those men were dusty and dirty. This denim is light blue and soft. My blouse is soft too, with words written on it. It says, *Well-Behaved Women Seldom Make History.*

I rub my eyes. "How hard did I hit my head?"

Chapter Seven

Hannah

I SIT UP ON THE FLOOR. WHOA. I DON'T remember falling off the stepladder, but I must have kicked it out of the way as I crashed, since there's zip, zero ladder in sight. I rub my eyes. The early-evening sun is still strong because it's summertime, and it streams through the windows. Wait. What happened to the velvet cording that ropes off the furniture in the middle of the room so that none of the visitors try to plop their butts onto priceless antiques?

"There you are, young lady."

I turn my head to see a woman bustling into the room. Her hair is drawn up away from her face in a superelaborate arrangement of curls, and the long skirts on her fancy dress swish as she glides toward me. As far as I can tell, it's a spot-on, early-twentieth-century Edwardian-period costume. I rub my eyes again. We have character actors in the mansion only a few times a year, and I'm one thousand percent sure there are no events like that scheduled for months. What the heck is going on?

"We're waiting for you," the lady says, stopping right in front of me with her hands on her hips.

"Well?" she asks when I don't answer.

She drops down to her knees. "Are you feeling unwell, my dear?" She reaches out to touch my forehead. "You look a bit flushed. Did you have a fainting spell?"

A what? Who has fainting spells anymore? Who *is* this woman? She looks an awful lot like pictures I've seen of—but no. Not possible.

"I . . . I was trying to get a closer look at that . . ." I gesture to where Maggie's portrait usually hangs. "I thought I saw . . ." I shake my head at the memory. "And then I fell."

"Goodness, what were you thinking?" the woman asks. "Did you use Mr. Birch's stool to— Now, I know for a fact that you've been raised to conduct yourself in a manner more becoming of a lady. Climbing is for monkeys and little boys! Whatever possessed you?"

"I . . . Huh?"

"Come now." The woman stands up and holds out her hand to help me up. "We mustn't dawdle. We have an appointment that I, for one, am quite eager to keep. We'll discuss this behavior later."

I grasp her hand and wobble to my feet. It's only then that I realize that I'm wearing a sea-foam-green calf-length taffeta dress with more ruffles than the bed skirt in the Rose Room on the second floor. My feet are covered from my toes to past my ankles in dainty leather boots. In July.

And they don't feel like my feet. My hands don't even *look* like my hands. Since when have I been able to grow actual fingernails without biting them down to stubs? Since never, that's when. And I swear I got shorter.

Say what?

What is happening here?

Chapter Eight

Maggie

I HAVE ONLY BEGUN TO PONDER THE strangeness of my situation, when my hip bone buzzes. It's like an electric shock of some kind! I stumble into the grand ballroom as I scramble to find the source of the buzzing. There's a small device in the pocket of my trousers, unlike anything I've ever seen. I turn it over in my hand. A picture of a man and the word "DAD" appear on the glass. I shiver. My uncle has all kinds of new electronic thingamajigs in this house. But I've never seen someone's likeness reproduced in vivid color—and mounted on glass like this. It's as though I could almost reach into the device and touch the man's face, it looks so real.

The device buzzes in my hand, until I drop it and it slides under the gilded grand piano in the corner, where it continues to vibrate.

I must be in some sort of fugue state where I changed my clothing and don't remember. It's the only explanation. But it doesn't explain the strange device. And how am I aware of it? If I were in a fugue state, I wouldn't think I'd be alert enough to know.

I turn in a circle. The ballroom has not yet been set for the ball, but it looks the way it often does for summer entertaining—with chairs set in several groupings for casual conversations. I take in the elaborate mirrors that dominate the room, the Louis XV–style paneling my aunt loves so much, the full-size portrait of Lady Elizabeth Drexel Lehr and one of her dogs. . . .

Wait. I don't remember that portrait. I step closer. It is most definitely a glamorous portrait of Elizabeth Lehr, the mistress of the cottage across the street from The Elms. Why would Aunt put that in such a prominent location? A placard on the ornate table beneath it proclaims the artist to be Giovanni Boldini. Aunt loves to showcase her art collection, but I've never known her to advertise the artist in that manner.

I stumble away from the portrait and shuffle out of

the ballroom, through the drawing room, and cross into the conservatory. (On top of everything else, I'm not even wearing shoes. Aunt Herminie will be scandalized when she sees me!)

I marvel at thick velvet ropes that seem to delineate a walking path through the rooms. That's strange. I don't recall them being there before; maybe Aunt has just added them to remind the servants not to walk on the carpet?

Ignoring one of the ropes, I flounce onto the cushion of a chaise longue. Flouncing works so much better in my regular clothes. I close my eyes, hoping this is some sort of dream from which I'll awaken. Mademoiselle Cassatt is nowhere to be seen. She is usually set up and tapping her foot, waiting for me.

A few minutes later I crack open one of my eyes. It's no good; no matter how I try, I'm still lying on a chaise in the conservatory. The white marble floor gleams. All the cherub statues are in their places, and yet there's something not quite right. A card game is set out on a glass-topped table. Aunt Herminie would be horrified; she hates it when guests set up bridge games in such a public spot in the house.

And I'm still extremely aware of wearing trousers. This isn't a fugue state. As much as I don't want Aunt

Herminie to see me in bare feet and trousers, there's something very wrong with me and I need to find her. I push myself off the chair to go in search of help.

"Aunt?" I call, walking back through the large rooms of the mansion, recalling that the last time I saw her, she was in the breakfast room, instructing Mr. Birch on the proper care of a new tea set.

I have to pass through the dining room, and as I do—ignoring the fact that it is not yet set for dinner and there are no servants in sight—I notice a small device on the ceiling flashing a red light. More of Uncle E. J.'s fascination with electricity, but I've never noticed that before. Incredible. This new century is certainly a time of rapid technological developments.

Up till now I have managed not to panic. Aunt will know what is happening to me. I just need to find her. But as I feared, she is not in the breakfast room. I dash into the pantry and then back through the dining room and out into the foyer.

I stand there, absolutely still. There is no sound. The house is silent.

"Aunt Herminie?" I run up the grand staircase, marveling—even through my growing panic—at how easy it is to move in trousers. Aunt insists that proper young ladies do not run; she never minds when visiting children run on the grounds, but even so, she says I'm "getting to an age." Right now I don't care. I just want to find her so she can tell me this is all a nightmare.

There's no one. Anywhere. There are a half dozen guests staying here this weekend and several more in the guesthouses on the other side of the estate. And at least forty servants preparing for the ball tomorrow night. But all the bedrooms are empty. And they all have that strange rope across their entrances. And the smell. Or really, no smell. Instead of the fragrant hint of Aunt's favorite roses, there is a distinct lack of smell. Like these rooms are not occupied at all.

Taking a deep breath to stall the hysteria bubbling up inside me, I resist the idea of going to bed in my own room. This horrible nightmare started in the drawing room when I looked at the mirror behind the seascape, so I decide to go back downstairs. I scratch at the spot on my head where a bump the size of an egg has blossomed.

That's it.

I hit my head when I fell, and this is just a dream. Clearly that is what is happening. I must be dreaming. Maybe if I go back downstairs, I'll wake up and all will be right. I need to see that mirror again.

Chapter Nine

Hannah

SOMETHING THAT *FREAKY FRIDAY* MOVIE I watched at my best friend Tara's sleepover last winter neglected to hammer home: walking around in someone else's body feels super-weird.

That's about the extent of what I've been able to piece together about this crazy-whoa-I-don't-know-what that's happening right now, but it's the only explanation that makes any sense. Because how else could I explain why I'm suddenly shorter and paler, with hair that's way curlier than mine has ever been? Speaking of eyes, whoever belongs to this body should probably see an optometrist about this nearsighted thing she's got going on. Plus, she must have had a *whole* lot of water to drink recently, since I'm getting pretty uncomfortable here. I'm trying to hold it, because using the bathroom in someone else's body feels like it would be a huge violation of her privacy, but . . .

Like I said, it's all pretty weird.

Something else I've figured out all on my own: corsets = barbaric torture devices. No wonder no one is smiling in old-timey pictures.

My brain is working overtime as I trail the lady in the long dress into the conservatory, where another woman is hovering over a framed painting propped against an easel. It's turned around so that the back of the picture is facing us.

"Ah, *c'est bon*! You have arrived! I am so eager for you to see the finished result. I pray you will be more than satisfied. This young lady was a wonderful subject!"

She lays a whopper of a smile on me, and the other lady pats my arm gently, before saying, "We're thrilled that you accepted our commission. It will be quite the honor to have your work hanging in our home."

If it weren't for the whole "I think I'm in someone else's body" thing, I would easily be able to convince myself that I somehow got mixed up in a TV show filming here at the house. Maybe one of those *Downton*

Abbey rip-offs. It would make perfect sense. The Elms has been used as the setting for bunches of Hollywood stuff. Once they even shot a Victoria's Secret commercial in our boiler rooms, only Dad wouldn't let me hang around the set because all the models were in their underwear and he didn't think it was "appropriate."

But there are no video cameras and no directors, and these people don't seem like they're acting. And of course, there's the whole "not my own body" thing. Which puts a wrinkle in every theory I have, except for the super-weird ones. For now I'll play along as best I can until I can figure out what the heck is going on.

So I curtsy. The dress I'm wearing seems like one someone should curtsy in.

Both women smile, and the lady next to the easel picks up the frame and carefully turns it to face us.

I gasp!

It's the portrait of Margaret Dunlap!

And everything about it matches the one I've visited every day of my life, except for the color of the dress. Which is not daffodil yellow but sea-foam green. The same sea-foam green of the dress I'm wearing right now. The same dress *entirely* as the one I have on now.

Does that mean . . .

"Oh, Mademoiselle Cassatt! It's breathtaking!" the lady next to me exclaims.

Mademoiselle Cassatt? As in Mary Cassatt?!? As in the artist who painted Maggie's portrait?

"Maggie, pet? Are you going to gape with your mouth open, or do you have some words for Mademoiselle Cassatt about your portrait? Do you simply adore it, as I do?" The woman nudges my arm, gently at first, and then with more force when I don't respond immediately.

"Um, yes. It's, er, wowza!" I manage to sputter, because my brain is tripping over thoughts now.

The woman by my side scrunches her forehead and whispers, "Wowza? What in the heavens kind of expression is that, Margaret, and whomever did you pick it up from?"

I open and close my mouth like a fish, thoughts still whirring.

Finally one clear thought floats out of my brain muck: *You're Maggie Dunlap.*

I'm Maggie Dunlap?

I'M MAGGIE DUNLAP!

Chapter Ten

Maggie

WHEN I GET BACK TO THE DRAWING room, the first thing I notice is a small stepladder next to the sideboard. Disregarding the fact that it is not made of wood, as it should be, I climb up to where the seascape is supposed to hang. But instead it's that portrait of me—which isn't to have been unveiled yet—off its moorings, leaning against the mirror it should be hanging in front of.

I crawl onto the sideboard to get a better look, and almost fall off the edge again at the sight of a girl staring back at me from the glass. She's got *my* face and she's wearing the clothes I remember putting on this morning.

But she's not me.

"There you are!" she exclaims. She seems to be trying for a whisper, but it comes out a good bit louder. "OMG . . . finally! I've been crossing fingers supertight that you'd come back to the mirror! You can hear me, right?"

I sit up straighter. "Of course I can hear you. This is my dream, is it not?"

"What?" she asks with a nervous titter. But then she looks around with a panicked expression. When she turns back, she seems relieved, but she's no longer laughing. "Quickly, before your aunt comes back. You *are* Maggie Dunlap, right?"

I nod. "No one except Aunt Herminie and Father calls me Maggie. But yes. And who, pray tell, are you? And why are you talking with my face?"

"This is so whackadoodle." The odd girl shakes her head. She looks as bemused as I feel. "*You're* talking with *my* face. Did you know?" When I don't answer, she continues. "The only thing I can figure out is that somehow we've traded places. I live at The Elms with my father—in the twenty-first century. We're the caretakers, and it's a historical museum maintained by the Newport Antiquities Society."

"That's preposterous." Although, with all the strange

happenings, this is an explanation that makes as much sense as anything else I've thought of.

"I know, right? But I think we, like, time traveled. You've zoomed forward. I've jumped backward." The girl with my face looks around again as though she's nervous about being caught.

I perk up at the mention of something I recognize. "You mean like that wonderful story by H. G. Wells? *The Time Machine* is one of my favorite books. But that's just made up."

"Believe me, I thought the same exact thing. But how else can we explain how *I'm* here and *you're* there?" She lowers her voice. "I dunno how it happened; I just touched that black spot on the mirror, and presto bingo, I ended up here."

"I remember now!" I shout at her, and then instantly cover my mouth with my hand before saying more quietly, "I thought I saw something flicker in the mirror behind the seascape, so I moved it to see better—then I saw you looking back at me! I tried to touch you, but then I fell!"

The girl nods. "Yep, same for me. Okay, your aunt will be back in a sec, so listen up. I don't know about you, but I've dreamed my whole life of seeing this place when it was actually lived in. I was even wishing it right before we switched. So, I mean, when fate delivers, you gotta embrace that, right?"

I can barely process her words. What is she suggesting?

"I—" I begin, but she talks right over me, as if she's never had an etiquette lesson in her life.

"I'm just saying, this had to have happened for a reason, so I say we go with it for a day before we swap back, ya know? You can totally explore the future and I can see if your time is everything I imagined. Perfect, right?"

I'm not feeling perfect about this at all, but I'm so taken aback, I can only nod.

She grins. "Okay, so from here on out, you have to be me and I have to be you, so no one suspects a thing. My dad will probs be calling you for dinner soon. Then we usually watch TV till we crash. Just go with the flow. Let's meet up here at . . ." She pats at the pockets of her—no, *my*—dress. "Man, it sucks not having my phone."

Did she just call me a man? She gazes over at what I'm sure is the clock on the mantel on her side of the mirror. "Meet me here at seven a.m. It's gotta be before the house opens for visitors." She smiles. "You look like me, but you sure don't talk like me. Just try to keep your head down and stay out of trouble until we can chat again."

Just then she gasps, says "Gotta go," and jumps off the sideboard.

She's gone. I don't even know her name.

She said to keep my head down? How is that going to help? And what in heaven's name is TeeVee?

I slide off the sideboard and spin around in a circle, taking in the antique Chinese vase, the crystal chandelier, the expansive parquet floor, the marble-topped sideboards, the winged cherubs on the ceiling, the seventeenth-century furniture. It looks exactly as it should, so my first impulse is to believe that I am still having that same dream and the girl in the mirror is just some sort of figment of my imagination. She said it was the twenty-first century. One hundred years into the future. Can it be true? As much as I love Mr. Wells's book about time travel, I can't believe it. It's just foolishness. Maybe the clams in Chef's chowder at lunch didn't agree with me.

But then I remember the ropes and the red light on the ceiling and the emptiness of the house. And the device I found in my pocket and tossed away. I run back into the ballroom and glance under the piano; it's still there. It's not ladylike, but I don't care about what my aunt would say right now; I crawl underneath to retrieve it and misjudge how much space I have. I bang my head on the exact spot of the bump. Is it possible that the new body I'm in is taller than my own?

Tossing that thought aside, I crouch under the piano with my elbows on my knees and turn the object over in my hand. It's about the size of a deck of cards. Where did the picture go? When I touch the glass front, it lights up again in full color. With shaking hands I stuff it back into the pocket of the trousers. Twenty-first-century technology isn't something I can manage right now. I have a sudden need to find a person. A real, live, in-the-flesh person. As though the universe hears me, a voice booms from the foyer.

"Hannah!"

I freeze. The girl's name must be Hannah. She mentioned her father. This has to be him. Do I dare pretend to be someone else? I consider my options. If this is a waking dream, what does it matter? On the other hand, if I have really traveled forward in time and look like Hannah, pretending to be her might be my only way back home.

"Here I am." I crawl out from under the piano just

as the man enters the ballroom. He kneels down so we're at the same level. His soft brown eyes remind me of Uncle E. J. His blouse is the same fabric as the one I'm wearing, and the words across the front exclaim, *Life Is Good.* He's also wearing denim trousers.

Do all people wear denim in the twenty-first century?

"You all right, Bug?" he asks, a small smile lighting up his face. When I don't answer, he continues, "You know how much I hate to punish you."

He leans forward, trying to make eye contact. "I just need you to promise me you'll stay away from the tours. Even though we both know you could be a better docent than some of them. Do we have a deal? You'll keep away from them? Promise?"

This sounds like an apology, but I can't make any sense of his meaning. So I don't say anything. He's waiting for a reply, though, so I smile back and nod my head slightly. Hopefully it will be enough.

It seems to do the trick.

"Tell you what!" He slaps his thigh, which makes me startle, and he jumps up, holding out his hand. "I'm commuting your sentence for the evening. We'll do delivery. I'll order a giant pie from Nikolas Pizza. The regular? Half cheese for you and the other half Hawaiian for me?

And your favorite Greek salad, dripping with olives? We'll settle in for the night and watch some *Doctor Who*."

He is speaking English, I know that. But I have no idea what he means by "delivery." I do understand "pizza," however. I had a slice last fall when Father took me to the World's Fair in Saint Louis. I loved it.

"That sounds delightful." I take his offered hand and stand up, brushing myself off. "But why do we need to see a doctor?"

Hannah's father laughs, a deep throaty one that makes me smile despite my confusion. He tousles my hair. "Fabulous, buddy. Just wonderful. But I think you need to work on your British accent. C'mon!"

He leads me through the foyer and down the hall toward the servants' staircase. When I grab the smooth wood, I cringe at the memory of Mrs. O'Neil's scolding just a short time ago.

We continue past the butler's pantry and still we climb, past the second floor, where my bedroom and all the other private quarters are located.

I've never in a million years dared use this stairwell to go all the way to the third floor, which is strictly off-limits, so when we start climbing toward the upper floors, I have to hide my surprise. Normally at this time of day, this corridor is bustling with lady's maids and valets going up and down from the kitchen to the living spaces to help the guests dress for dinner.

We finally emerge in a simple hallway. I know this is the servants' quarters, though I've never been this high in the house. Hannah told me the mansion is a museum in the future. The caretaker and his daughter work here.

Oh my goodness. Am I a servant?

Chapter Eleven

Hannah

FOR AS LONG AS I CAN REMEMBER, I'VE daydreamed about what it would be like to live at The Elms during the Gilded Age. I've endured endless teasing from my friends for my obsession with all things early twentieth century, and I've watched every movie and read every book set in this time period. I pick Theodore Roosevelt for every school project we do on presidents. Last Halloween I trick-or-treated as his wife, Edith, which was cool even if no one could figure out who I was. So, now that I'm actually here, I'm for sure going to make the most of it.

Of course, it would be a lot more enjoyable if I were having tea on the terrace with the Berwinds, whom I at least know tons about, so I could fake it till I make it with them. Instead they're off dressing for some musicale (this gathering at someone's house where everyone stands around and listens to people play or sing), and I'm stuck hanging out with Maggie's cousin Colette and our nanny. I know absolutely nothing about either of them from my research into the family. Ugh.

My strategy is to keep as quiet as possible. Can't bust me if I don't speak, right? Luckily, Colette seems to want nothing to do with me. She's annoyed about some kind of dare, but I can't ask about it, because I'm sure Maggie would already know, and I have to *be* Maggie. Colette can't be that much older than me—maybe fifteen?—but I'm getting the distinct impression that she and Maggie aren't exactly the Taylor Swift and Selena Gomez BFF power duo of their time.

I play copycat, though, and lift my teacup to my mouth the same way she does, with my pinky finger out all fancy-like. It feels sort of weird to just sit here and look out over the lawn, while none of us are also scrolling through Instagram on our phones. Also, tea? Let's just say it's no caramel Frappuccino, even with all the sugar I dump in whenever the nanny turns away.

"Are you excited for the ball tomorrow, Miss

Margaret?" the nanny asks in her formal British accent.

Am I? I mean, *I* personally am *beyond* . . . but would Maggie be? Or is attending balls something she does every other night of the week? "Um, yeah, totally," I mumble.

The nanny gives Colette a weird look, and Colette just smirks back. Something tells me this woman came from New York with Colette and not with Maggie. She's treating me like I'm mostly a stranger. Which actually works to my advantage; maybe she won't notice how un-Maggie-like I really am.

I swipe at my sweaty forehead with the back of my arm, and the nanny gasps.

"Manners, miss!" she scolds.

What? It's mega-hot out here, and it's not like the AC is blasting inside either. Plus, between my dress with a billion layers underneath it and its long sleeves AND the white gloves I have on, it's a miracle I'm not melting into the stone terrace. I sigh and pretend to be realllly interested in my tea while Colette and the nanny start gossiping about some couple who tried to pass themselves off as members of the Four Hundred—which I know is the term that the "best of society" call themselves—at a horsing event and got super-busted by someone who actually was a member, and now the couple are social pariahs, whatever that means.

Ick. But at least they're ignoring me, so now I can spend some time thinking. The thing I can't get out of a loop in my head is *How did this happen?* And not just how, but *why* did this happen? Am I here for a reason? Like, in the *Freaky Friday* movie, the mom and kid switched bodies so they could learn to appreciate the other person's perspective and stop fighting so much. I know I might sometimes chat at Painting-Maggie, but I've never, ever raised my voice at her. I mean, please. Last winter Dad and I had an eighties movies day, and we watched *Back to the Future*, his favorite movie from when he was my age. That kid had to make sure his parents met and fell in love, to guarantee he'd eventually be born. But no one in my family tree even lived in Newport in 1905. So, what, then? Am I just here to see what life was like, the way I wished, or is there more to it?

I start by making a mental list of everything I know.

It's 1905. In the history of The Elms, this year is famous as the one when the painting of Maggie is stolen.

I landed in not just the same year but on the same *weekend* as the heist. That canNOT be a coincidence.

If it's not a coincidence, what does it mean?

I know when the painting is stolen, so I could stop it from happening.

WAIT. I'm so stupid. Of course, that HAS to be it.

That's why I'm here! That's what I'm supposed to do! It has to be, because it would be way too big a coincidence otherwise, and I don't believe in coincidences. (I also didn't believe in time travel before today, but whatevs.) I'm right—I feel it in my gut.

"Are you planning to sit like a bump on a log all evening, or do you intend to join our conversation?"

With Colette's words, I snap back to reality. Or, you know, this whackadoodle version of reality I'm currently stuck in.

"Huh?" I ask.

She cocks her head at me. "What on earth is 'huh'? You're acting entirely bizarre, Margaret." Colette practically spits my name.

"Huh? Oh, um, yeah, sorry. I mean, uh, what? Um, excuse me?" *Jeez, Hannah. Get it together. You know how people talked back then. Or would it be "back now"? Either way, you know how formal things are, including language.*

The nanny squints her eyes at me. "It's true; you're not acting yourself at all, dear. Shall I fetch you some cold water and some crackers?"

"No thank you. I'm sorry," I mumble. "I—I think it must be the heat."

"It is quite warm," she says. "Perhaps you should lie down for a spell inside."

"Perfect idea!" I say, springing up from the table.

Both of them shoot me a weird look.

Whoops. Maybe that was a little too enthusiastic, but now that I've figured out my goal, the next day and a half is all laid out in front of me like a giant adventure. I only hope Maggie is going to be okay sticking around in the future, because I *have* to do this. Even if no one in my time will ever know, because to them it will be as if the painting was never stolen in the first place. It doesn't matter. *I'll* know. And it will feel amazing to not just learn about history but to take part in it, in a real way! Glory will be mine . . . just as soon as I get my inner Nancy Drew on and solve this theft.

I wonder if I can make this a permanent gig, traveling through time to stop heists from happening. I've always wanted to see the Ming dynasty. We have a vase from that time period in The Elms. It's never been stolen, that I know of, but I'll bet something from back then was.

This is the coolest.

Really, it should be like stealing candy from a baby,

since I already know exactly who did it. All I have to do is stop this Jonah guy from being in the same room as the painting during the ball . . . and I have a plan for that already. I'm gonna find him and stick to him like glue for the entire day. He won't get within ten feet of the painting. Easy peasy lemon squeezy.

I ignore the little voice in my ear that whispers, *But, Hannah, you never believed it was Jonah who stole the painting.*

I mean, sure, I've always had my doubts about that particular theory put forth in all the history books. It's true he was the prime suspect, because he skipped town the morning after the heist and was never heard from again. Neither was the painting.

But if you read all the eyewitness accounts—and believe me, I have—every single person interviewed who knew him said they could never imagine someone as quiet and sweet embarking on a life of crime. No one could figure out how he'd have access to enough money to disappear so completely. Or who he could have been working with.

And then there is the kicker. Jonah was young. Not young from my perspective, because I happen to believe twelve-year-olds are capable of greatness as much as anyone else (and I'm not at all biased). But. Even I have to admit, twelve is pretty young to be the mastermind behind a huge, complicated theft and cover-up.

But he's the best—the only—lead I have, and I plan to investigate for myself.

As soon as I excuse myself from the World's Stuffiest Tea Party and am out of sight, I skip down the hall and veer right at the staircase. The room where Maggie's staying is most likely on the second floor by the Berwinds', but I'm not headed there. Nope. I'm going to trust that the nanny will be too busy continuing her gossiping to check on me anytime soon, so instead I point myself to the basement level, where the servants prepare meals. Where the kitchen boy works. Luckily, the coast is clear, because I'm guessing that fraternizing with the help might be frowned upon.

Obviously, I know Maggie wouldn't spend much time here, but in the movies the president is always sneaking into the White House kitchens for a midnight snack, and in those British upstairs-downstairs dramas I'm obsessed with, the lord and lady of the house slip down to visit the servants from time to time. So hopefully my showing up won't be a giant big deal or anything. I'm sure Maggie must come here sometimes, because, just going by her eyes in the portrait, she doesn't seem like someone who'd get all caught up in class differences or anything. I mean, I know it's not her fault that she lives in this day and age, when servants are totally treated like, well, servants . . . and I can't imagine Maggie being like that.

"Miss Margaret!" A woman wearing a black dress with a white collar and a cardigan sweater gasps loudly when she sees me. "I thought we talked about this!"

Um, okay, so maybe Maggie doesn't do the whole "just popping in to say hi" thing on a regular basis.

"Hello!" I say, nice and cheerfully. "I'm, uh, I'm just looking for . . . for . . ." *Think, Hannah, think. What would Nancy Drew do?* "Well, the thing is, I need someone strong to help me with . . . with . . . moving a desk in my room, and I've heard there's a guy named Jonah who works down here and might be able to lend some muscle to the job."

The woman turns pinker than that Zombie Pigman in *Minecraft*. "Beg pardon, Miss Margaret, but I don't believe it would be appropriate for Jonah to accompany a proper young lady such as yourself into your chambers."

Oh, ugh. Didn't think that one through.

"Heavens no!" I say, trying to sound positively scandalized. "When I said 'my room,' I really meant the hallway outside of it, of course."

A kid about my age steps out from behind the stove, a wrench in his hand and dirt on his face. "I'm Jonah, miss."

This is Jonah? I mean, I expected him to be young, but not so shy and timid. He looks like the kind of person who'd rescue spiders instead of squashing them. His hair is floppy and nearly covers his eyes, which are soft and quiet and very *un*-criminal-like.

I stretch out my arm for a handshake, and he blushes about ten shades of red before wiping his dirty palms on his pant legs. He stares at my hand and hesitates, then finally ignores it and gives a little bow instead.

"Pleased to make your acquaintance, miss."

He shuffles his feet and glances at the woman in the apron, who gives him a small smile and a nod. Then he exhales and begins turning the wrench over and over in his fingers, like I make him nervous or something.

I am having a really tough time believing that the history books got this one right, but I force myself to be objective. Just because someone seems shy and very, very normal doesn't mean they're not hiding a devious side.

And it's up to me to discover it.

Once again I ignore the little prickle on my arms and that whispery voice in my ear. The one that's saying, *But, Hannah, what if the history books got it wrong?*

Chapter Twelve

Maggie

A HALF HOUR LATER, AFTER A YOUNG man delivers food to the back door (Hannah's father handed me some money and sent me back downstairs to pay the boy for the food—imagine!), we are seated on a comfortable divan in what he calls the living room. The twenty-first century is odd; my father would never in a million years imagine sitting with me so informally and eating without a proper place setting.

"May I have one more piece, please?" I ask, dabbing at the corners of my mouth with my paper napkin and returning it delicately to my lap. At least I can maintain some pretense of manners.

He furrows his brow as I fold my hands, waiting for his answer. "Well, I'm not the maid," he says finally with a chuckle. "Help yourself." He points to the box holding the pizza on the low table in front of us.

I pause, but since he's right—there are no servants in sight—I reach for another piece of the pizza. This time I feel brave enough to help myself to a slice of the other side, the one with the pineapple and cubes of ham.

A bemused expression crosses the father's face. "Since when do you like Hawaiian pizza?"

When I don't answer, he frowns. "Are you feeling okay? You've been awfully quiet tonight. And your manners are shockingly impressive." The tiniest of smiles plays on his lips, but I'm not sure if he's making fun of me or if he's serious.

I stop, slice of pizza poised in front of my mouth, still wondering what he means by "Hawaiian." He can't possibly mean this pizza comes from the new United States territory in the middle of the North Pacific.

Blast it!

Hannah must not eat this type of pizza. My brain scrambles for a reply. I think about something Aunt said to me on our tour of France last summer, and it seems appropriate.

"It's important to try something new every day." My voice goes up at the end of the sentence, like I'm asking a question. Of course, Aunt meant it in the context of trying caviar—fish eggs—for the first time, not meat-laden pizza.

"Okay." He nods. "I like your new attitude." Then he laughs again. "I guess you were hungry too! This is your fourth piece."

Maybe it's a symptom of time travel, but land sakes, I feel like I haven't eaten in a century.

I swallow my mouthful of cheese before I speak. "It's delicious, thank you very much." Aunt would disapprove if she could see me sharing a meal with a strange man, but she'd be proud that I haven't forgotten my manners. "Even better than I remember."

I freeze, realizing a moment too late that I've said the wrong thing.

But he only nods. "I know. This is definitely better than the pizza we had down on the pier last time."

He stands up and gestures to a piece of black glass framed on the wall. "So, what'll it be tonight? Are we going with a classic *Who*, or something more recent?"

I adjust the napkin in my lap as I pretend to think about the question, which makes no sense. So I say the only thing that comes to mind. "Why don't you pick?"

"Fair enough." He seems to ponder the issue but then jumps to attention, like he's changed his mind about something. He sits back down. "Sweetheart, before we watch the show, I wanted to have a talk. You know I was very angry with you earlier." He pauses, as though he's expecting me to react, but continues when I don't.

"I hope you understand that it's not because I don't want you to be excited about history or this house. I'm thrilled that you love living here. I've been waiting for the right time to surprise you, but this might be the perfect way to cheer you up."

I nod because it seems like the proper thing to do. "I do love surprises. Who doesn't?" I say, before taking another modest bite of pizza.

Hannah's father takes a breath and then speaks again. "You know how the house is going to be shut down for a couple of weeks when the art historian does the restoration work on the murals? Instead of laying low and hanging out, I thought maybe we'd use the opportunity to take that trip to Los Angeles we've been talking about. We leave Tuesday morning!"

The glass I'm holding drops to the ground, splashing milk everywhere. If not for the carpet, the glass would have shattered. A half-eaten morsel of pineapple is lodged in my throat, and I can't swallow.

After a momentary bolt of panic, I catch my breath and swallow my food. I don't need to worry about leaving on Tuesday. I'll be back home before then; Hannah assured me.

"I know you're excited, but try not to break stuff." He rushes to the kitchen and then sprints back holding a towel. "What's up with you tonight, anyway? Everyone says the teen years are unpredictable, but you're not even thirteen yet." He picks up the glass and starts blotting up milk with the towel. "Please tell me this isn't what the next seven years have in store for me. Give me some warning at least, will you?" He stops to gauge my reaction, looking like he's not sure himself if he's joking.

"Are you going to say anything?" he asks.

I'm thinking how lovely it is for Hannah to be taking a trip with her father, but I keep my mouth closed.

"I thought you were dying to see the Hollywood sign and the Walk of Fame." He frowns, standing with his hands on his hips and staring at me. "We could drive up to San Francisco once we land, I suppose, if you'd rather. We can talk about going anywhere you like; it just has to be on the West Coast. I bought the tickets for the flight with last month's paycheck." He tousles my hair as he moves the empty pizza box to the floor next to the table. "But we don't have a choice. We have to vacate for two weeks." He sighs. "I expected you to be happy to have two weeks taken off your month-long dusting duty."

"That sounds . . . fine." I think about my own father, busy with his law firm. He travels from New York to San Francisco by train often, but even before Mother died, he rarely took me on trips. He relies on Aunt Herminie and Uncle E. J. to introduce me to faraway places. "Wait. Did you say 'flight'? Do you mean you're going to fly?"

I know men have experimented with flying machines; Uncle was excited the summer before last about some brothers in North Carolina managing to get their machine off the ground. But I'm not daft; the only ways to get to California from Rhode Island are by train or steamer ship sailing around the tip of South America.

For the first time, I imagine Hannah living in my body and wonder if she's having as hard a time adjusting as I am. I wonder if Aunt has noticed that her speech is different from mine.

Hannah's father chuckles, but this time his laughter is accompanied by a confused look. "I can tell I surprised you," he says slowly. "And I'm sorry. We can talk about this in the morning. Let's see what our favorite Time Lord is up to." He picks up a small device from the coffee table and points it at the wall on his way toward the kitchen with the towel and glass.

Light and color and pictures come alive in the frame, and for a moment I forget everything else. It is moving pictures—like a window into another world. Is this what Hannah called TeeVee? An instant later there's sound. Someone singing about constipation, of all things. Then a bunch of people dancing around a red-and-white bull's-eye while loud music, such that I've never heard, plays. I'm horrified and enthralled at the same time as I get up to examine it further. It looks like I'm watching real life through a window. More and more, I feel as though I'm in a fantastical novel—I wonder if Mr. Wells knows about this invention.

"Sweetheart?" Hannah's father catches me peering behind the screen when he comes back into the room, holding a giant bowl of popcorn. He looks at me strangely. "What are you doing?"

My heart thumps hard as I return to the sofa and sit stiffly on the edge. "Just not feeling quite myself tonight."

He sighs. "Oh, honey. I know you're upset about what happened with Trent earlier. I'll deny ever saying this, but Trent is a . . . well, he's a swampdragon."

I don't believe that particular animal has been discovered yet in my time, but it sounds as if he means it as an insult, so I raise my eyebrows and nod.

"And," he continues, "I understand how badly you want to be treated like the docents' equal. You *know* I'm on your side here, and I wish they could see the same mature young woman I do, but, Bug, some of this is going to take time. You just have to be patient. Besides, no growing up too fast. As your dad, I forbid it."

He leans over and kisses the top of my head before dropping next to me on the couch and reaching his hand into the popcorn bowl.

Of course I haven't the faintest idea what he's talking about, but I do understand the part about things being forbidden, and part of me sympathizes with Hannah a little more. It's quite odd to have this stranger thinking I'm his child (even if he seems perfectly nice and caring), so it takes a bit of time before I relax and start watching the pictures.

I ascertain that *Doctor Who* is a serial about a time-traveling alien. The pictures are so lifelike, it's almost like he's in the room with us.

Every time Hannah's father gets up to retrieve a

snack or to answer a communication on his little device, I move closer to the TeeVee to see if I can figure out how the machine works. All I know is that it's plugged into the electrical circuit.

Uncle E. J. is proud of the electricity that runs through the mansion—he even has an electrical icebox. But I've never seen anything like this.

"You're not dusting behind the TV, are you?" the man says as he returns from the kitchen. Then under his breath, so I just barely hear, he mutters, "Who are you, and what have you done with my daughter?"

I jump back quickly, my heart pounding. He suspects I'm not her. What do I do?

"I know how much you were looking forward to dusting all the portraits." He laughs as he says this, and I gather from his tone that Hannah likely does not enjoy dusting at all. Since I've never tried it, I wouldn't know. "But let's give you a break tonight."

I stand stupidly in the middle of the room, not sure how to proceed. I'm not doing a very good job of pretending to be her.

Before either of us speaks again, Hannah's communication device (her father calls it an "I-phone") buzzes on the end table. Words appear on the screen this time, instead of a photograph like before. Is it possible that telegrams in the twenty-first century appear this way, rather than by courier?

I glance at the words. The name Tara Lopes appears above them.

Will be at Elms tomorrow. R you around before the game?

"Aren't you going to answer her?" Hannah's father pops a piece of popcorn into his mouth and looks from the device to me, and back again.

"No, thank you." The machine intrigues me, but I have no idea what the message means. It's almost like it's in code.

He looks troubled as he sinks back into the sofa. "It's not like you to ignore your best friend. Did you guys have a fight?"

He thinks something is wrong. I can tell. What if he's worried that Hannah is sick? Or insane?

I stifle a yawn, sitting on the edge of the sofa and folding my hands in my lap. Not insane. Just not his daughter, which might be hard for him to understand. "I think it's time for me to go to sleep."

I suddenly feel as though I've been awake for a hundred years. The twenty-first century is exhausting.

After I wander down the hall and arrive in what must be Hannah's bedroom, I turn in a circle slowly, trying to understand everything I'm seeing. Affixed to the wall is a huge photograph of five young men with their arms thrown casually around each other, laughing at something behind the camera. They are all wearing very tight-fitting shirts. I wonder what the words across the bottom mean: "The Five Heartbeats." The image is so clear and colorful. It looks like they could just step out of the picture. I think they must be friends of Hannah's, but it shocks me to see men so indecently dressed hanging on her wall.

A shelf full of books with colorful bindings catches my eye. I pluck one that looks interesting: *Harry Potter and the Sorcerer's Stone*. Flipping the pages, I spot my aunt's name, spelled slightly differently. Hermione. It makes me miss her. I put the book on the desk; it's a shame, but I won't have time to read it.

A pink stuffed toy bear leaning against Hannah's pillow is soft and worn. It makes me think of my own Teddy Bear, all furry and stiff-limbed. My aunt thinks the Teddy Bear fad will fade after President Roosevelt leaves office. But considering that he inspired the trend by refusing to shoot a real bear, I'm glad it hasn't diminished yet. Aunt hinted that he might make a surprise visit to The Elms later this summer as a favor to Uncle E. J. I curl my body around the toy and close my eyes, thinking how exciting it will be to meet the president.

Lying with my eyes closed, I marvel at the last several hours. Hannah and her father are servants in this house, but they have more electric machines than Uncle E. J. The wealth in this century must be universal.

I don't remember falling asleep, but I roll over when light streams through the curtains. For a moment I forget where I am—but a device with bright-red lights reminds me I'm not at home. It must be some sort of timepiece, because it declares a series of numbers—6:15—but it doesn't look like any clock I've ever seen. I sit up, taking in my surroundings in daylight. There's no chance of falling back to sleep, and Hannah expects to see me looking back at her at seven o'clock, so I wander out of the room and down the servants' staircase to the drawing room, and spend some time marveling at how much this part of the house looks the same. This place is so odd; I do not understand how I came to be here, and I cannot wait to get back where I belong.

Chapter Thirteen

Hannah

THERE ARE THINGS I'M FULLY confident about and things I'm a little less sure of. In the "Not So Much" column I'd definitely put my freckles, my ability to spell the word "rhythm" without using spell-check, and the likelihood that I'll get my acceptance letter from Hogwarts. (Two years late is still fine by me, Dumbledore!)

In the "Why, Yes, Of Course I've Got This" column, I'd put my knowledge of all things Newport, The Elms, and the Berwinds; the way my face looks when I laugh; the fact that I can block nearly any shot that comes at my soccer goal; and the very strong possibility that Ethan Grimes likes me.

But my having the skills to prevent a heist from happening in ONE SINGLE DAY?

Um . . .

*May*be?

Step one is getting Maggie on board with my plan for me to hang here for another day. She has to agree. HAS to. Even if there weren't an art heist to foil, the thought of switching back now is . . . No. Just no. Especially since last night was kind of a bust in terms of experiencing 1905 awesomeness, because the Berwinds and their houseguests went out for the night, and I had to spend most of my time avoiding bumping into evil Colette and trying to convince a lady's maid that I really and truly did not need help bathing or dressing for bed. Yes, I got to explore the house a little on my own, but given that in my time it's set up to look exactly like it does in this era, that wasn't exactly earth-shattering. So I'm determined not to miss one single second of today, which is why I'm awake even earlier than I ever am on a school day, much less a morning during summer vacation.

It's so super-weird to wake up in the Rose Room. I've spent my whole life looking at the pinkish-striped walls and the elaborately carved white wooden bed, but I've never experienced it as an actual living space. I mean,

I've always felt like I have the run of The Elms after-hours, and we do get to treat the museum parts as our home in a lot of ways. Like opening presents Christmas morning under the ginormous tree the museum staff sets up for the holidays in the foyer, instead of under the kind-of-sketchy artificial one in our own quarters. Or swimming in the fountains on scorching-hot mornings, before the grounds open to visitors. I've even hosted epic sleepovers for ten friends in "my" mansion. But we slept on the roof deck, NOT in the antique bed with fancy silk curtains draped over its headboard. I've never even plopped my butt onto this mattress, much less climbed under the sheets.

I blink in the early light at the completely familiar, yet somehow also totally strange, surroundings. It feels so much more *real* with Maggie's hair in the silver brush on the marble-topped bureau and her dog-eared copy of *The Wonderful Wizard of Oz* propped open on the dainty round nightstand.

The whole house even smells different. Lived-in. Alive. And it sounds different too. There were fewer echoes from the tall ceilings and more muffled footsteps and swishing of maids' skirts last night as I drifted off to sleep.

Although, at the moment it's perfectly quiet. On this level, at least. The servants are probably all downstairs already, and the other residents are still sleeping, I'd guess. There was a musicale last night at Arleigh, the mansion where Harry Lehr and his wife, Elizabeth Drexel Lehr, stay. A painting of her hangs at The Elms in my time. It's so Crazytown to know that these famous high-society people I've grown up reading about are RIGHT ACROSS THE STREET at this very second, 100 percent alive! Even the building is "alive"—in my time Arleigh has been replaced by a nursing home.

I heard the Berwinds and all their houseguests coming in way, way late, so I'm guessing they won't be up for hours.

I have to squint into the morning shadows to make out the time on the clock centered on the fireplace mantel. Obviously, it is *not* digital with lighted numbers, like mine at home. In fact, it's small and round and mounted onto a pedestal that has three spindles wrapped in gold roping connecting it to a base. That's because society is just coming out of the Gilded Age, and *everything* is, well, gilded. Plated in gold, to show off the owners' Daddy Warbucks–level mega-wealth.

Finally the hour hand creeps close enough to seven

that I figure I can make a run for the drawing room and (hopefully) Maggie. I push open the door just enough to slip through, then creep down the staircase, keeping an eye out for any servants who might spot me.

I head straight for the sideboard and climb onto it. As soon as I nudge aside the painting to expose more of the mirror behind it, Maggie's peering face comes into focus.

Her whole body relaxes when she spots me. "Where have you been? I've been waiting ages! I was positive we said seven a.m., not eight."

I scrunch my nose. "We did. It *is* seven. At least according to the clock in your room and . . ." I pause and glance down at the mantel. "This one too."

She holds my iPhone up to the mirror to show me the display. The numbers read 8:01.

"But that makes no sense," I say. "I traveled a century *plus one hour* into the past? It doesn't—" And then it hits me. "Yes, it does! Daylight saving time! The United States doesn't begin using it until—"

I catch myself just before I blab the words "World War I." Maggie doesn't need to know she's less than ten years away from half the planet going to battle. Instead I mumble, "Sometime next decade."

She's still looking baffled, so I give her a quick run-down on setting clocks forward and back, and she visibly relaxes. "I spent the entire hour fretting that the mirror didn't work anymore and I'd be stranded here forever. I mean you no offense, but—"

I hold up my hand. "I get it. I would have been really freaked too."

Literally no one else on earth could get how weird this entire experience is, except the two of us, and we share kind of a bonding smile over it. But then she leans in again and gasps. "Land sakes, what are you wearing?"

I glance down. "Um, your nightgown? Is that not okay? I kind of figured we were going with the 'what's mine is yours and what's yours is mine' idea. Speaking of which, please tell me you wore my night guard last night. You might not have to worry about braces in your time, but I just got mine off, and I'm pretty desperate to keep them that way."

She blinks at me a few times. "I . . . What?"

"Never mind. It's not that important, I guess. Wait, why are you still looking at me funny?"

"You're—you're rather indecent to be wandering about. If Aunt sees you or—or, oh heavens, if Uncle E. J.—"

"No worries. They're snoring harder than Geppetto in *Pinocchio*. Oh, wait. You haven't seen that movie, so of course that won't mean anything to you. Actually, you haven't seen *any* movie, have you? So weird. And what do you mean, 'indecent'? This nightgown reaches my wrists *and* my ankles! Plus, it's kind of stiff. You're soooo gonna love fabric softener, whenever *that* gets invented."

Maggie continues to blink at me even worse than before. Hmm. It's possible she is not rolling with this whole time-traveler thing as well as I am. Which I guess makes sense. I never lived in this time, but I've grown up learning all about it and surrounded by reminders every day. She probably feels like she's been dropped into a whole new world, instead of just a whole new century.

"If you want, I'll go grab a robe or something," I offer.

Maggie shakes her head quickly. "No. I don't know how much time we have. With the ball taking place tonight, the staff is surely up and about already, even if Aunt and Uncle are not. And I think I heard your father stirring as I slipped downstairs. We should hurry and switch back."

She raises her hand and presses her fingers to the age spot on the mirror. When I keep my arms by my side, she tilts her head and says, "I believe we both have to do it at the same time."

My eyes find hers. "Um, but I thought last night we agreed it would be good for both of us to have time to explore, since we've been given this crazy opportunity."

Her eyebrows shoot up. "It was all happening so quickly, and I was trying to process the situation. I don't— That is, I assumed we'd swap back first thing this morning."

I sigh. Not how I was hoping she'd respond. I make my voice soft and pleading. "Okay, so hear me out here. I'm not asking for much longer. Just today."

She gasps. "Oh no. No. No. That's simply not possible. Tonight is the ball, and I must be there. My portrait is being revealed to all Newport society."

I scrunch up my nose. "I only need the day. We could switch back before the ball starts. But about that reveal . . . Sorry to be the one to tell you this but, not so much. Your portrait is stolen on this day in history. In a matter of hours, actually."

She gasps again, and I'm quick to add, "Only, I'm not going to let that happen. That's what I wanted to tell you. I think I figured out why I'm here—to solve the heist!"

"Whatever do you mean?"

I fill her in on exactly what's about to go down at the ball tonight—or at least the version I know from the history books—and she clutches her throat. "Heavens!"

"I know, right?"

"I glimpsed that Jonah boy only yesterday. Just before . . . just before this all happened. I'd not seen him prior."

"Yeah, well, I met him yesterday too."

"Met him? You talked to him? But he's—he's a kitchen boy. I'm—*we* are not permitted in the basement." She narrows her eyes. "Please tell me that you did not enter the servants' area. After Mrs. O'Neil expressly forbade me! Where did you see him?"

Uh, exactly where you'd expect to find a *kitchen* boy? Only, I don't say that to Maggie, of course. One, because even though I know a whole lot about 1905, I'm not sure how sarcasm worked then, and I don't want her to think I don't like her, when I'm actually totally thrilled we're talking like this, even if it's under super-weird conditions. And two, because I'm not entirely sure she won't fall off her version of this sideboard if she finds out I went down to the staff area of the house.

"Oh, just . . . about," I tell her. "To be honest, he seemed really nice. And young. I—I actually thought he was pretty cool."

"Cool? I don't understand. You felt his skin?"

I bite my cheek to keep from laughing. It's not her fault she doesn't know our slang. I have to remember to dial it down, but half the time it just slips out. "No. Sorry. I just mean I thought he was sweet. And shy. Not at all how I would picture a criminal mastermind. Although, I can't say I've encountered all that many criminal masterminds, so maybe more of them have dimples and hair that won't stay smoothed down than I realize."

Maggie looks scandalized, like she just found out about the existence of bikinis or something. But she definitely aced etiquette school, because I can literally see her face rearrange itself into something more bland and ladylike right before my eyes.

"Or perhaps he is not the thief?" she suggests mildly.

I can't help jumping at her words, because they're so exactly what I was thinking yesterday. And last night as I was trying to fall asleep. And this morning when I woke up. Maybe the reason no one ever found the painting is what I always suspected—because they were looking in the wrong direction. Or at least for the wrong person. If I stick like glue to Jonah all day—to prevent him from getting close to the action—and it turns out I'm right that he's NOT the thief . . . then what's been the point of all this? If the real culprit steals the painting instead . . . why was I ever here? No matter who ends up being behind the theft, I have to solve it one way or another.

Maggie is patiently watching as the wheels turn in my head, waiting for me to get back to her.

"Okay, so what if he's not?" I finally say. "That means it could be anyone. Wait. You probably have some insider information! Quick. Who else would want to own a priceless piece of art?"

Oh, ugh. That's kind of obvious; the answer to that is "almost anyone."

Maggie shakes her head. "But the portrait of me isn't priceless. Of course, Aunt has ensured a lovely souvenir of my thirteenth year. And she does hope to impress Newport society with its unveiling . . . but Mademoiselle Cassatt is not Renoir. She is just a woman."

"'Just a woman'? *Just a woman*? Maggie! I can't believe you said that! We need to get you up to speed on Girl Power. Where you are now, girls can do anything boys can do. We can command military troops, design skyscrapers, run for president." I want to shake my fist at her. If she's gonna hang in my day and age, she'd better start flying her feminism flag higher than that.

Maggie's gasp is about as loud as a hurricane. "You have a female *president*? Of the *United States*!"

I drop my grin. "Well . . . not yet. But we got super-close. And we will again. I have faith."

"Goodness," she breathes. "I can't even imagine men allowing us to vote, much less that men would trust us to run the entire country."

I sigh, then mumble, "*Some* do. There, um . . . there might still be some ground to cover, although we *do* have the right to vote. People are always telling us girls we can be and do anything, and we can. It's just that I guess we don't always get the same respect guys do. Most of the time women get paid less for doing the same exact work. Or, like, girls will read books about boys no problem, but lots of boys refuse to read books with girls on the cover and stuff like that. So now it's more like we have equal rights on paper but we still have to earn them in people's hearts. I dunno." I shake my head and laugh. "Wow, that got heavy. Yikes."

"Still," Maggie says. "I can't begin to imagine what it would be like to dream of a career and know it could actually happen. Or to even be permitted to have an actual say in things, instead of just going along with anything my future husband wants me to."

"Wow, I guess I never thought about it like that. And on the bright side, we might not have a female president *yet*, but there are already women governors and representatives and senators. Plus brain surgeons. And CEOs of companies. And rocket scientists. You should Google some of them. I mean, if you agree to stay for the day." I cross every finger and toe.

Her forehead crinkles. "Beg pardon?"

Oh, right. If her mind is blown by the idea of a woman running for president, just wait until she discovers the Internet and endless hours of "baby hedgehogs getting massages" videos. It's a shame I can't be there to witness it.

Although, technically she hasn't agreed to let me hang here for another day yet, and even though I could just completely refuse to put my fingers to the age spot, I'd prefer not to, like, steamroll all over her or anything. One, because I'm not an evil person, and two, because the girl is currently occupying my body and what if she gets revenge by chopping off my hair with toenail clippers? For now I plan to plow ahead until she screams "Stop!"

"Okay, let's circle back to Girl Power later," I say. "Just in case it might be someone other than Jonah, I need you to tell me any possible person who might have a motive to steal your portrait, or who might have it out for your aunt and uncle. Or you. Anything you can think of, big or small, could help. If the ball starts at ten p.m., I have to use every last hour to solve this thing."

She seems a little dazed, but she nods. Wait. Does that mean she *is* agreeing to this plan? Officially? I try to stay all casual, even though I'm doing internal jumping jacks. "Suspects?" I prod.

She takes a deep breath and looks me in the eye. "Well, there are the Gilmores. Only the other afternoon at Bailey's Beach, I heard Mrs. Gilmore whispering to Mrs. Lehr something nasty about Aunt being 'new money.' As if more than half of Newport doesn't share the same distinction. She's merely jealous that her houseguest chose to accept the invitation to our ball, rather than accompany her to Saratoga Springs this afternoon. Although, now that I puzzle it out, if she's to be on a midday train, then of course she isn't going to be able to steal a painting in Newport tonight. I suppose I would only make a note to keep an eye out for her appearance, should her plans change."

I nod. "Gilmore. Got it. Who else?"

Maggie grimaces. "Colette. My cousin. Did you cross paths with her yesterday?"

I make a face. "Ohhhhh, yeah. What's with her, anyway? She's, like, the biggest 'mean girl' ever."

Maggie sighs. "She resents how Aunt favors me."

"Got it. Adding her to the list. Can you think of anyone else?"

Maggie closes her eyes, concentrating hard, but soon opens them. "I'm afraid I really cannot. Aunt is a darling of society and charms all who know her. The household is highly regarded."

Yup. I know this from all my studying up on them too. "Okay, well, at least I have some starting points. Not sure how things are gonna play out on this end, but let's plan to meet back here at six tonight. Six in *1905* time. Seven in yours. Although, I'm guessing they'll be setting up in the ballroom by then. Do you think it would attract attention if I shut the door between the two rooms?"

She blinks at me. "Of course not. I often close it when I read in here. You'll be left alone."

Right. Just because it's permanently open in my time doesn't mean it would be in hers. This is a home for these people, not a museum.

She's chewing on her lip, though. I hope she's not reconsidering.

"Um, is everything okay?" I ask. I really don't want to

bully her into this. She may not know it, but I've considered Maggie Dunlap a friend for practically forever. Even if it was just a painted version of her. The last thing I want to do is mess things up with the real-life person. What if we could keep meeting in the mirror to talk after we swap into our own bodies? Or maybe even switch again sometimes, just for fun!

"I'm considering," she says, and my heart sinks. She's gonna insist we trade back right now. But then she continues, "If we meet at six your time to trade places, it *should* still give me ample opportunity to dress for the ball."

"Oh, right. That takes hours, doesn't it? Don't get me started on crinolines. It's like wearing ten skirts on top of one another. Medieval torture devices, if you ask me."

"I agree," Maggie says. "I'd love to know when those become passé. I've not seen one in your closet alongside all the denim items. Trousers are far more . . ."

She seems to be struggling for words, so I help her out. "Comfy cozy?"

"I was going to say 'practical,' but yes. Whatever you said likely sums it up quite well."

"Hang in there. You've got less than two decades before flapper dresses, which look super-chill and breezy."

Her eyes grow wide. "In my lifetime? I can hardly imagine."

"Don't go getting too excited. Gloves are around for waaaaay longer. Which, what even is the point?"

"Perfectly white and smooth hands, of course. All proper ladies must possess those." I catch her glancing at her (well, but really my) hands, with their ragged, bitten nails and midsummer tan. Her eyes widen, but she's polite enough to zip her lips.

"Yeah. That's not really as important in my time," I say.

She nods. "I haven't even ventured *outside*, and I'm gobsmacked by all that has changed."

Speaking of venturing outside, I wish I could have time to explore all of Newport. I'd love to see it with horses and carriages clogging the streets, instead of tour buses. But no way am I pushing my luck, considering how cool Maggie is being. My only focus is solving the heist, and then I won't even complain when it's time to switch back later today. Much.

In the meantime I say, "If we had more time, I'd tell you everything, but we should probably skip the part where I fill you in on every single thing that happens between our two lifetimes. I can give you the CliffsNotes, though. Don't sail on the *Titanic*. Grab your money out of the stock market before 1929, but when you get back into it, remember these three words: 'McDonald's,' 'Disney,' 'Apple.' Oh, and also 'Hitler' equals 'Very Bad Man.' If you could manage to get a message to any and all of your German friends about that sometime before the end of the thirties, that would be extra amazing."

Maggie is doing the whole blinking thing again. Oh, man. I've totally overwhelmed her. To her credit, she rolls with it pretty well, because a second later she recovers.

Except then her face falls. "Only . . . well . . . what is it I'm to do while I am here?"

"Have fun! Explore! Party like a rock star! Just don't go too crazy wild and get me grounded for life or anything, because then I'd have to find a way to get back here again and strangle you."

When I catch her expression, I say, "Kidding. Totally kidding. I always imagined we'd be best friends if we lived at the same time. Us getting to talk like this? It's seriously giving me life!" I'm quick to add, "I love it!" just in case she wasn't following along. I know I could probably dial down on the slang—and I'll be way more careful when I'm trying to pass as her rest of today— but I'm so excited to be talking to Maggie that I don't want to have to censor myself around her. I just want to be the same way with her that I would be around any of my friends.

She gives me a small smile but then goes back to biting her lip. "Explore. Yes, that would be logical. I mean, I suppose you think I'm crazy for not leaping at the chance. *You're* brave enough to jump straight into solving a crime, for land sakes. But . . . girls in my position are not encouraged to be the exploring type. We are trained to act quiet and peaceful and to follow the expectations laid out for us."

I know all this from studying the history of this house so much, but hearing the wobble in Maggie's voice when she says it makes the reality hit home. I mean, I just took for granted that my dad would give me two thumbs-up when I told him I wanted to start a YouTube channel of coding tutorials for kids. And that, instead of rolling his eyes at me when I announced out of the blue that I wanted to give up meat, he'd go to town on an awesome veggie chili recipe. So yeah, maybe I get to do a bunch of things I want to do, without having to worry about scandalizing society. But does that make me brave? I don't know about that. If I'm being honest, I haven't even let myself think through any of the details about actually foiling a criminal, because when I start to, I get this acidy taste in the back of my mouth. But a part of me really likes that she sees me that way, and I don't want to change her opinion of me.

Besides, if she thinks I'm brave, maybe I can use that to convince her she needs to act that way too, to keep everyone believing she's me.

"Look, I get it," I say. "Girls in my time are raised to have a totally different mind-set from what you're taught. Everyone tells us we can do anything. Maybe you could just adopt a whole 'when in Rome' approach."

"'When in Rome'?"

"It's an expression. 'When in Rome, do as the Romans do.' I don't even know where it came from, but just . . . just pretend you've been told your entire life that you can do whatever you put your mind to, and then . . . act accordingly."

She looks pretty doubtful, but at least she's stopped biting her lip. She even smiles a little. "All right. I will endeavor to do that. Wish me luck."

"Luck!" Then I toss in one other thing. "Little tip, though. If you *really* want people to buy into you being me, maybe skip using the word 'endeavor,' huh?"

"I shall endeavor to. I— Oh! That is to say, I shall do my best."

"Great!" I tell her, trying my hardest to look extra encouraging and supportive. I briefly consider mentioning that she should slash a line through the word "shall," too, but I skip it. She'll probably decide to lock herself away in my room if I make her too self-conscious, and she deserves to soak up this experience too. Even if it means I have to run a little damage control when I get back.

After all, how badly can she mess things up for me in one measly day?

Chapter Fourteen

Maggie

"HANNAH. JORDAN."

The man says Hannah's name in a clipped tone. Almost like he's done it that way before. It makes me wonder about what sort of trouble the real Hannah gets into.

But I'm not her. And they can't blame me. I've been trapped in the future since yesterday, and the last hour is the only time I've spent in the pink bedroom with the carved headboard and silk drapes that Aunt Herminie keeps for me. Me! Not anyone else.

Even though I promised Hannah I would endeavor to be brave, I needed to find a place to think. I just want to shut out everything that is not from my own world.

I pray to be back at *my* Elms. Not this strange version. Prayer doesn't seem to work, though.

I think about what Hannah told me earlier from the other side of the mirror. The portrait Mademoiselle Cassatt has now finished painting of me—stolen and missing for more than a hundred years. And Hannah seeking to speak to that boy in the kitchen! If she's caught, Mrs. O'Neil will have no choice but to tell Aunt this time. But I certainly wouldn't want someone blamed for a crime he didn't commit. If there even is a crime. Oh, mercy! I just want to hide in my room and pretend like I am back in my own time. I pull the musty coverlet over my head like I did as a small child when Father was cross. But back then Mother was around to comfort me and make things right again.

"Hannah Jordan!" the voice says again. "This is the last straw. You know you are not allowed to touch the furniture."

I open one eye and peer at the man framed in the doorway. His short silver hair sticks up at odd angles, as though he's run his hands through it several times. A group of people stand behind him, looking at me like I'm a canary in a cage. His glasses are askew, and his face is the color of beets. A stray bit of spittle glistens at the edge of his lips.

With a sigh I stand up and smooth down my dress . . . er, trousers. There is no one here to comfort me. I need to be brave, like I promised Hannah. If I don't pull myself together, these people will think I'm hysterical, and then who knows what might happen. "I'm sorry, sir. You're right. I just couldn't help myself. I do love this room." I step over the red rope and bow my head, hoping it will be seen as apologetic. "I meant no disrespect."

"Well, uh . . ." He runs his hand through his hair, making it stick up that much more. "Um, I—I guess I can overlook it this time, but—but don't let it happen again." He stammers like he can't think of what to say or doesn't know how to react to an apology.

"Thank you, sir." I am tempted to curtsy, but I sense that girls in the twenty-first century have lost that particular custom. I push past the tourists and run away from him as fast as my legs will go—even though it is against all the rules. At the grand staircase I pause, before bounding to the bottom. Suddenly the house is stifling, and all I want is to get outside. I know the perfect place for some fresh air to help me breathe and consider my options. I skip across the marble foyer and out the front door, almost crashing into a girl and four adults.

"Watch it," one of the men says, grabbing the small

girl and pulling her out of the way. A gasp escapes my lips. Never in my life have I ever been so rude to anyone, and it feels wrong. But pretending to be someone I'm not, in a time I don't understand, feels worse than being rude. I can't pretend for one more second! I turn and run down the concrete steps. I need to think—and I don't care how impolite it must look. Skirting around another small group of visitors, I run the length of the mansion to the back of the house. What greets me stops me in my tracks, and my heart sinks even further.

The gardens! And the trees! The elm trees are all gone. The spacious back lawn is supposed to be lined with elm trees. They're what give the house its name, The Elms.

Why would someone remove all the elm trees? There *is* a row of nondescript trees lining the space between the drive on my left and the vast expanse of green lawn, but they don't feel right. And then I spot it. One large tree, separate from the others, at the far edge of the lawn, just in front of where I hope the sunken gardens still exist.

It's here. *My* tree.

I breathe a sigh of relief and make a beeline across the massive expanse of grass for the giant weeping beech, almost falling in my haste to find something familiar. I duck under the canopy of branches that skim the ground. It's bigger than I remember, but it feels as right as my bedroom. As I sweep aside the soft curtain of leaves, I say a prayer of thanks that no one is under here.

Normally I sit under the canopy and think or read against the tree. Aunt Herminie has no idea that I sometimes come here, and as long as I keep it secret from Colette, Aunt won't ever find out. Sitting outside isn't expressly forbidden, but it is not exactly proper. I look up, wondering if I dare. Climbing a tree would be firmly on the list of things a girl of my station should not do. But . . . maybe girls in this century are encouraged to climb trees? If what Hannah said is true about what girls can do, then I don't even have to feel guilty for breaking the rules. My heart gives a little thrill as I grip the tree and begin to climb. Higher and higher I go, hoping to reach a place where no one will find me.

About ten feet from the ground, there's a sturdy limb. I tuck my feet close to me and hug my knees to my chest. At first when I look down, I'm a bit dizzy and I can't quite believe what I've done. But after a few minutes I get my bearings, and it's amazing. From this vantage point I can watch people entering the clearing below me, but I don't think anyone can see me up here. I close my eyes and consider my options.

How did I end up in this time? How is it possible that I've traveled so far into the future? I think about my aunt and uncle and the things I love—my pony, all my books, the smell of the rose garden in the morning. But being able to climb trees, and run, and get dirty? I think of all the things I'm not ordinarily allowed to do, and wonder how many of them girls are allowed to do in this time.

Out of nowhere, something catches my attention, and I glance up. Between the top branches a small spot of blue sky is visible. I see a sight that almost causes me to fall from my perch. An object that is not a bird soars far above my head. It is glorious. Spectacular! A miracle of technology! Now I understand how Hannah and her father will fly to California. Uncle E. J. would be thrilled to see this.

I have one day in the twenty-first century. I will be back at *my* Elms by evening, enjoying the ball given in my honor with Aunt Herminie and Uncle E. J.

I can do this. I can pretend to be Hannah for the day. In fact, it might be informative to see what the future has in store. Though if a giant flying machine is any indication, I may need to brace myself. And, it occurs to me, I might find out what girls are allowed to do in the twenty-first century that I can't do in 1905. And maybe I'll experience a few of them for myself.

Finished with feeling sorry for myself, I rub my eyes with the back of my hand. *It is refreshing not to have petticoats impeding my legs,* I think as I scramble back down. I jump the last five feet and stumble at the landing.

"There you are. I've been looking everywhere for you." A girl about my age stands with her mouth open, incredulous at my sudden appearance from above. "Are you okay?"

I brush the dust off my trousers and shrug. "Yes, I am. Thank you. It is amazing what a little tree climbing will do for the heart and soul."

She scratches her head. Her skin is tanned brown, and her curly black hair is cropped very short. Her clothing is strange. She's wearing short pants like my cousin Peter wears, and across her front are the words *Newport Girls Soccer.* Her socks come up almost to her knees, and she's holding a white-and-black-checkered ball. "Um. Sure. Whatever you say." She looks up at the tree branches with a smirk. "You know the director of buildings and grounds would kill you for climbing one of the antique trees."

I feel myself go pale at the thought of such violence

over climbing a tree, but I tell myself she must be exaggerating. "Well, of course. But I was just checking to make sure no one had already gone up there and broken the rules. Someone has to do it." I give her a small salute and turn on my heel, wondering if I've misunderstood the extent of things girls are permitted to do.

"Wait. Hannah." The girl trots behind me, out from under the canopy of the tree, back onto the great lawn, and into the sun. "It's not like my mother's rules have ever stopped you before."

I don't slow my pace. Now that I've decided to take advantage of this situation, I've got no time to lose. "Your mother?" Because of the way she's dressed, I assume this girl must be a servant, and for a moment I cannot for the life of me understand her informality. But then I remember, Hannah is a servant as well. I stop to let her finish.

"What do you mean?" The girl's smile falters, like she's not sure if I'm joking. "Wait. Are you still mad? Is that why you didn't text back last night? I said I was sorry about the thing with your phone. You have to be kidding." She looks like she's about to cry.

I'm such a ninny. This girl is probably a friend of Hannah's! I try to remember seeing her face in one of the photographs in Hannah's room.

"I'm not mad at you. Why would I be kidding?" I ask, walking around the side of the house nearest the kitchen. "What did you do?"

She laughs nervously. "Now you're teasing me. I was just joking around. You know, my mother took my phone for a week, so when you left yours at practice the other day, I just thought I'd have some fun. I wanted to apologize when I got mine back last night, but you didn't answer my text."

I don't understand what she did wrong. But she seems sincere. "Well, then. I accept your apology. I was going to take a walk. Would you care to join me?" It suddenly occurs to me that having a guide from this century might help in making sense of all this.

She looks around as though perhaps I'm speaking to someone else. "What are you talking about? We have a game today." She nods at the ball she's carrying.

"A what?" I stop to stare at this strange girl.

"Soccer . . . Duh. Are you sure you're okay? Why aren't you changed yet?"

"Oh, how fun!" I clap my hands. I have no idea what "soccer" means, but the chance to play a ball game is almost too good to be true. Apparently girls play ball games in the twenty-first century.

Now that I really think about it, her outfit puts me in mind of the boys who play baseball in the dusty field near the harbor. My aunt won't let me anywhere near their game, but I've seen them walking home sometimes. They are usually covered in dirt and muck, but they always sound like they've had the most fun. I can only imagine being covered in dirt, since I'm not allowed. If Aunt—and my father as well, for that matter—ever caught me climbing the weeping beech, I'd likely be sent to bed without dinner. The only sport I'm permitted to play is lawn tennis, because Aunt considers it a socially acceptable activity. But only if I don't exert myself more than necessary.

And what fun is a game like that if one does not exert oneself?

The girl tosses the ball, and it bounces off me.

"Ouch. Why did you do that?" I rub my arm.

She rolls her eyes. "Sheesh, Hannah. I'll help you get your stuff." After picking up the ball, she grabs my arm, drags me into the servants' entrance, and practically pushes me up the stairs to the apartment.

What am I thinking? I have no idea how to dress for her game, let alone play it. As much as I want to make an effort, I don't want to look foolish. I try the ruse that sometimes works with my aunt when I don't want to accompany her on a social visit. "I'm not feeling well," I say, putting my hand to my cheek at the first landing. "Look, I'm all flushed. I can't possibly play."

"Not good enough. Coach will throw you off the team if you bail today." We enter the bedroom, and she scans the floor. "Here's your bag! Now get your uniform on and let's go."

The girl, whose name I don't even know, leaves the room and closes the door. I notice she has a large number twelve on the back of her shirt. It seems like I do not have a choice. So, as Hannah said, "When in Rome." I dump the contents of the bag onto the floor. A shirt and short pants, identical to the girl's—except this shirt has seventeen on the back—fall out. Even though Hannah told me to pretend to be her, I cannot believe I'm going through with this. But I vowed to myself that I wasn't going to let this opportunity pass. I pick up the shirt between my forefinger and thumb and sniff. "Girls play sports in the twenty-first century," I whisper to the bear sitting on the bed.

I cannot believe I am about to break all the rules of civilized society. My aunt thinks any sort of exertion will damage me in some way. She has never been specific, so I'm not sure what she thinks will happen. But when I perspire too much—even if I'm just sitting on the terrace drinking lemonade—she rolls her eyes and tells me that no man will want to marry a woman so immodest.

The uniform isn't terribly hard to figure out, so it takes me only a few minutes to change. It's incredible. There are no fasteners, so I don't even need any help. I open the door to show the girl, hoping I've dressed correctly. "What do you think?"

She laughs. "You look like you always do." She runs into the room and grabs the bag. "You're out of it today! You'll be in big-time trouble if you forget your cleats."

"Of course. Lead the way." Feeling proud of myself, I link my arm through hers and drag her back down the stairs. At the bottom I remember that I don't know her name, but I take a chance. "You're Tara," I say tentatively, remembering the name that appeared on Hannah's device the night before.

She furrows her brow. "That's my name, don't wear it out." She dips into a low curtsy and then holds out her hand to shake mine, but then pulls it away before I have a chance to grasp hers. She mutters under her breath, "I said I was sorry. You don't have to drag it out."

"Please accept my apologies as well, Tara." I sigh, not

even trying to make up an excuse. "It has been a sort of long morning. I'm not really feeling like myself."

I can't tell if she's mad or not. I hope she thinks Hannah is just teasing. She sort of winks at me as we come out of the building onto the sidewalk.

I'll have to figure out some way to make it up to her. I'm lost in thought when we reach the sidewalk, and for a second I lose my bearings. I have to contain the gasp that threatens to escape my lips. Automobiles like I've never seen line the street, whizzing past faster than anything I've ever imagined. No horses. No buggies. A few people walking, but they do not look like the ladies I am accustomed to seeing in the coach parade every afternoon.

How on earth am I going to be able to go through with this?

Chapter Fifteen

Hannah

*L*ITTLE TIP TO ANYONE CONSIDERING time travel: it's super-helpful to be a total history buff on the exact era and location you land in. Super-*duper*-helpful.

For example, I know just how to skirt around the Berwinds and their houseguests for now, because I have a pretty good handle on exactly how their day will shape up. It will probably be the same as almost every day, for almost every member of the Four Hundred who spends the summer season in Newport.

It would normally start with breakfast at eight. Though, after their late night, and judging from how quiet it is in the house, I think the Berwinds slept through this today. I'm also guessing no one went out for the hour-long horseback ride that would usually follow, but I'm not taking any chances. For now I'm holing up in my—*Maggie's*—room until I'm sure the coast is clear.

After the ride, if they end up going for part of it, they'll change out of those clothes and into their day dresses so that they can catch a horse-drawn carriage to the casino for lawn tennis or a public reading or maybe a play.

Then they'll change *again* into swimming costumes (seriously, these are like wool from neck to toe, and it must be like wading into the ocean in blankets) and head to the beach. The private, only-our-snooty-kind-is-allowed beach, called Bailey's.

I'm pretty sure I'm totally off the hook about taking part in any of this, because they don't drag their kids around to these things. Or anything, really. Children are usually just foisted off on the nannies and tutors, except for maybe an hour or so every day when they *might* get to hang with their parents (if Mom and Dad aren't off traveling or doing something more interesting or important than actually, you know, parenting their offspring). I can't even imagine if that were normal in my time. Dad would basically be a stranger. But that was pretty normal for every kid in Maggie's class.

Anyway, it means no forty-seven outfit changes for me. But I'm guessing that British nanny from last night has something up her sleeve for me and Colette today, and I need all the unsupervised solve-an-art-heist time I can get. Hmm . . . I think I might be feeling a little *cough, cough* under the weather.

Most likely the Berwinds will head off to someone's yacht from noon to two for a luncheon (meaning another new dress), and then to the polo fields from two to three to watch a match from their carriage. Then another change of clothes so that they can all promenade up and down the streets in their carriages and leave calling cards for their neighbors. I never got the point of that one, to be honest.

From there on out I'll have to be more careful to keep to the shadows for my lurking, because they'll probably be back for tea on the terrace at five, and then into their bedrooms to switch dresses (again) for the ball.

(I'm pretty sure that if anyone asked any of these people what they did for a living, they'd have to answer, "Change clothes.")

I need to quit "regrouping" and find Colette. The

sooner I can figure out if Miss Hoity-Toity hates Maggie enough to steal the portrait, the sooner I can work through my list of suspects.

I creak open my bedroom door again. The house is still almost as quiet as it was earlier this morning, but I can hear the far-off clinking of silverware from the dining room below and light footsteps from the servants' quarters above. My throat closes as I picture the top floor the way I know it—as my home. In the here and now it's filled with enough beds for a good percentage of the forty-three people responsible for keeping this household running like clockwork for eight weeks of summer. It still kills me that this crazy-fancy house will just sit empty the other ten months of the year. Maybe I should sneak in a talk with Mrs. Berwind about that before I swap back. (Or maybe not.)

I tiptoe across the hall. I'm guessing Mrs. Berwind would put her weekend visitors in the three guesthouses on the property, but since Colette and I are family and are here for the whole summer, I'm assuming Colette also has a bedroom on this floor. There are *only* seven to choose from. Sigh.

Although, Mr. and Mrs. Berwind's (separate) bedrooms count for two, and then, obviously, I'm in one.

So that gives me a one-in-four shot. I start around the corner from mine, as far as possible from the Berwinds' suites. The Green Bedroom is empty, its door wide open. The Van Alen Room across the hall is decorated way masculine, so I doubt that would be super-girly Colette's first pick. And if those are her snores coming through the closed door, more power to her, but I'm thinking not so much. I creep to the door of the Satinwood Room and lean my ear against it. It's mostly quiet, but I think I can make out some rustling inside. I give a tentative knock and immediately hear "Enter!" in reply.

Yaaaassss! Colette is sitting at her dressing table, peering into the mirror above it. In the reflection she catches my eye, and then she claps her palm to her chest as her focus widens.

"Your hair!"

On instinct I raise a hand to my head and run my fingers along my ponytail. It's probably pretty droopy, considering I had to use a scrap of ribbon in place of a cute elastic (it's the littlest inventions I'm missing the most!), but it can't be so bad that it's clutch-your-heart-worthy.

"What about it?" I ask, trying not to sound defensive.

"It's up! What are you playing at now, Margaret?" she asks in a voice dripping with snarkiness. "You know quite well that only women of age are permitted to wear their hair off their necks!"

Oh, right. I remember reading that. But, um, seriously? I have so, so many questions about this, but I can't exactly ask them, because I'm Maggie and these are things Maggie would already know. I'm here to see if Colette is acting suspicious, not to make *her* suspicious of me.

"Of course. I only tied it up for a second because I was feeling a little . . . flushed."

Colette squints at me, then rolls her eyes. Ha! I guess being eye-rolly has been a thing forever.

"I don't know how you expect to find a suitable husband if you can't be bothered to conduct yourself like a lady," she finally says when her eyes get back from their trip around her sockets.

Husband? *Husband?* Um, hello. I'm TWELVE. Any wedding of mine is, like, decades away. *If* I even decide to get married; I might not. I know most upper-class girls at the turn of this century got hitched at eighteen, but even that's five long years away for Maggie, who is just turning thirteen. Why would she have to be worried about husbands now?

I try to hide my true feelings and keep it to a simple, "Mmm."

Colette ignores this and goes back to running her brush through her perfectly straight hair. It's clear she doesn't have anything more to say to me, but I'm here to get my sleuth on, so probably I should ask some questions myself.

I start to say "um" at the beginning of my sentence and cover it quickly with a cough. Colette's look says, *Girl, you are acting cray-cray.*

"So, do you have anyone in mind for a . . ." I pause to cough. It's so weird to ask a kid this question. "Husband?"

"Of course you know I don't. Though, I do think this is the summer I will begin laying some groundwork with Theodore Willory. He's heir to a railroad fortune, and his mother seems lovely. She admired my embroidery last year when she was to tea."

I nod. This whole conversation is surreal. Colette can't be more than fifteen. Sixteen at the most.

She keeps right on yapping. "Mommy said I can go with Auntie to Paris next spring so I can begin to scout out which shops I'd like to order my debutante dresses from the following year. I can hardly wait! Not that you'd understand. You're such a child still."

Exactly! That's why this hubby talk is so super-strange. Time for a subject change anyway. I smooth my skirt and say, all prim and proper, like people spoke back—well, now, "What are your plans for today?"

She snorts. In a very unladylike way, I might add.

"Same as yours, obviously. Nanny is taking us to Providence for the day for some shopping."

"Right. I don't believe I'll take part in that."

She blinks a few times and then crosses her arms. "*I* don't believe that's up to you to determine."

"It's just, I—I'm feeling a little . . . off. Nothing too serious." I don't want to say I'm *too* sick, because, once we switch back, I don't want Maggie to have to miss out on the ball. "It might just be nerves about the unveiling, but I still think I'd better lay low and conserve my energy for tonight."

Colette does that one-eyebrow-up thing, then shrugs. "I suppose I shouldn't attempt to dissuade you as it would mean more attention at the stores for me."

Gee, nice to know she's so concerned about Maggie's well-being. But Colette's being self-centered works perfectly for me in this instance. I exhale. I've laid the groundwork for my "get free from supervision" plan, and now it's time for a little intel gathering on my first potential suspect.

"We got to see it yesterday, you know. The finished painting. I can't believe how perfect it is!"

Colette doesn't perk up or get shifty-eyed or do anything to indicate any interest whatsoever. In fact, she yawns.

"Mmm. That's nice. Of course, Mommy and Auntie have already plotted out my debutante portrait. Auntie says she's spoken to John Singer Sargent about a commission. Can you imagine? He's only *the* most famous portraitist of our time. Though I'm sure Mademoiselle Cassatt's painting will be quite serviceable."

Serviceable? Really? The woman's work is taught in classrooms the whole entire world over, but whatever. Although, I guess it does take a while for Mary Cassatt's talent to be appreciated here in America. At this point in time she's probably only famous in France, where she lives. John Singer Sargent's fame, on the other hand? Gobs bigger.

If it's true that he's all lined up to paint her, and if she's going to be in Providence for the whole day, she'd have zero reason—or chance—to steal Maggie's portrait. The disappearance would only increase interest in it, and I'm guessing Colette would way rather have Maggie's gift unveiled, only to fade into the background entirely.

That would let hers make the biggest splash of all.

Which means odds are extra high that she didn't have anything to do with the heist. I'm thinking I can cross her off the list.

Except, unless the Gilmores bag their trip to Saratoga Springs, that means I'm down to just one suspect again: Jonah.

Chapter Sixteen

Maggie

WE ARE OUT OF THE GATES AND A block down Bellevue Avenue before I realize I don't know where I am and I struggle to get my bearings. Things don't look right, and I pace back the way we came a few feet.

"Wha—" I can't even form a sentence after I notice the building across the street. It's a low, brick structure that spreads across the entire block. Just yesterday I was in the parlor of Arleigh, the mansion where my aunt's neighbor's dogs nipped around my feet. They are the most irritating little creatures, but the thought of them dead for a hundred years makes my eyes tear up more than anything else so far.

Arleigh is gone. I run down the sidewalk, but I get only a few yards before my shock turns to agony at yet another sight. Villa Rosa, the mansion closest to The Elms on the same side of the avenue, has disappeared as well, replaced by an ugly two-story monstrosity. I can't keep a groan from escaping my mouth. I cover it before Tara notices.

I realize it is going to be harder than I thought to maintain the pretense that I am Hannah. Since The Elms still stands, I assumed that all the houses on the street did as well.

I lean over and try to get control of my breathing. I've seen houses razed by fire or by vanity, and new structures blossom from summer to summer, but realizing that so many of the cottages I know are gone— modern buildings in their places—it is almost too much. It's all familiar, but not—like there's a layer of gauze covering the real Newport. It appears as though there was a feeble attempt to match the approximate style of the properties on the street, but the modern replacements are just faint imitations. They lack the grandeur and spectacle of summer cottages like The Elms and The Breakers.

Is this what time travel means? You get to see how

future generations replace everything you love and care about?

After a couple of minutes Tara breaks the silence. "Are you sure you're okay?"

I inhale and scratch my bare leg. It feels strange to have any part of my extremities exposed, let alone all the way up to my thigh, but most of the young women walking along the avenue are wearing short pants or skirts, with their legs showing.

I remember Hannah's words, "When in Rome . . . ," and I try to pull myself together. "I guess I'm just a little nervous."

"Well, that's understandable." She chuckles. "We're playing the number one team in the league today. I know nothing usually makes you nervous, but I'm glad to see that you're not superhuman after all." She awkwardly pats my arm, and I realize she's trying to help. She looks at her device. "You got dressed so fast, we have time before Coach wants us there. Let's take a walk and you can try to relax? The new owners of Belcourt Castle are retiling the slate roof. My mother asked me to take a look. If we walk fast, we can make it."

My heart brightens when I realize what she said. Belcourt still stands. I find myself nodding. I definitely want to see something familiar, even if it's Alva Belmont's mansion, where my aunt's nemesis holds court.

I follow her lead and we start walking. "Why do you care about the roof?" I ask.

She purses her lips and waves her hands a little, like she doesn't quite know what to do with them. "My mother wants me to start getting more familiar with the architecture at The Elms. She thought it might help me build up my portfolio if I could compare what the other properties are doing. All I've got so far are a couple of Spanish-style colonial buildings from my visit to my grandparents in Mexico last month."

She mistakes my silence for disapproval and inhales sharply. "I guess you're right. They're such different properties. I'm not sure the comparison makes sense."

"No, that's not what I meant." I shake my head. There were too many questions flying around my brain to form a coherent sentence. "You're from Mexico?" I'd never met anyone from there.

"Um. No, I'm from Rhode Island." She stares at me with an unreadable expression, like I've crossed a line. "But my family is Mexican."

"Please forgive me." Things are different in the twenty-first century, that's for sure. I've never known anyone from her culture—I've never really thought about why. I start again. "You're studying architecture? That's amazing. I've never really paid any attention to how the buildings are designed. They are just there. But someone has to think about it." I wonder who cares for the building exterior at The Elms back in my time. "I'm sorry, Tara. I think it's so . . . cool . . . that you like architecture." I wonder if I've used the term "cool" correctly. "Your mother likes it too?" I stare at her, hoping my apology is enough to change her expression.

"Well, she better!" She smirks. "She'd have a hard time as the director of buildings and grounds for The Elms if she didn't!" She purses her lips. "You know that, though. What is your problem today, Hannah?"

I slap my forehead. Not only have I offended her, I'm making Hannah look bad in the process. I need to pull myself together and not act so surprised by things that are different in this time. I try to think of something comforting to say so Tara doesn't suspect that something is wrong.

"I do apologize, Tara. I *am* teasing you. I meant no offense." I hope my apology is enough. I've been trained well to be polite. In my time people like to gossip; I pray that is still the case. It might help Hannah's investigation if I ask Tara some questions. "How much do you know about the theft of the Mary Cassatt portrait of Margaret Dunlap?"

"Only what you've told me. I'm not sure why you're so obsessed with that thing. Some hoity-toity heiress who used to live at The Elms," she says, swinging her arms.

I'm not exactly sure what "hoity-toity" means, but it doesn't sound nice.

"Please do not speak of her like that." The tears threaten to return, and I brush at my face. I hate the thought of history painting me as spoiled and useless. After all, I am not Colette.

She frowns and pokes my arm. "Why are you talking like that? Are you practicing for one of those reenactment events coming up in the fall?"

I think about Hannah's odd way of speaking, and I know I'm not doing a good job of mimicking her. "Yes." It seems like the easiest answer.

"Oh. Phew. You had me going. I totally thought you were losing it." For a moment she looks like she might turn around and run the other way, but after a brief pause she continues swinging her arms as we walk. We're headed down Bellevue Avenue, and I'm pleasantly surprised at how familiar the area feels. There are many new structures, but there are also a lot of houses that look the same. Or close to the same. It makes me feel less like crying. I take a steadying breath, trying to get control of my emotions.

"I get why you love history, Hannah. You know I do. And all those costume dramas. And the books. But seriously, you have to tone it down." She sounds genuinely concerned. "People will start to think you're weird," she adds, almost like an afterthought.

I find myself trying to put words into Hannah's mouth, though I have no idea how she would reply. I don't know Hannah well enough to know how her friends view her, but I know what it's like when people—specifically my cousin Colette—pick on me because I'd rather read than attend a social outing. "Everything that happens in the world today is a result of something that happened in the past. The whole world is based on what has come before."

She nods knowingly, like I've shared some sort of deep dark secret. "Like breaking the glass ceiling."

"What?"

"You know, like a woman can be CEO of a company or be an ambassador or a senator or run for president of the United States." She taps my arm. "If women hadn't protested over the years for equal rights, the world wouldn't have so many women in positions of leadership. And someday," she says, an expression of confidence on her face, "a woman will *be* the president of the United States."

I nod, having no idea if this theory is correct or not, but it's the same thing Hannah said this morning. "Maybe. Yes."

It's so confusing. Some things have changed for the worse—beautiful buildings being replaced by ugly structures. But many things are better—like women playing ball games and wearing trousers. And being able to vote. And running for president.

I think about the women I know. My own dear nanny at home in New York, Mrs. O'Neil, my cousin, my aunt. All the socialites from Newport. I've overheard some of them whispering about fighting for women's right to vote. When I get back to 1905, I must be sure to ask them what they would think about a woman running for president.

Chapter Seventeen

Hannah

I AM A CHAMPION LURKER.

It comes from all the shadowing I do of the docents' tours so that I can "fact-check." I mean, *someone* has to make sure all the accurate historical dates and data are being passed along to visitors. Okay, so maybe interrupting with my corrections usually ruins the lurking part, but I can be quiet when I really need to be.

Turns out, this is an invaluable skill when time traveling and trying extra-super-hard not to call attention to yourself.

At the moment I think I've probably gone one step past lurking to full-on stalking. I'm flattened against the wall in the coal tunnel, trying not to worry about how much trouble Maggie is definitely going to get into when someone catches sight of the back of this pale-blue dress. Coal dust, tunnels, and silk do not play nice together. (But I couldn't find anything more low-key in her closet, and even if I had, it would have been impossible to convince the lady's maid who insisted on helping me dress—which was extra weird, lemme tell you, even if it wasn't technically my body that the maid was seeing.)

Edward Berwind made his fortune in coal, so it's only logical that his mansion would have an entire underground tunnel—complete with railroad tracks— off its basement. It runs all the way to Parker Avenue, where a delivery truck can open a hatch in the street and dump its load of fuel down, down, down into a giant cart waiting below.

The cart travels along railroad tracks back to the house, ending in the furnace room, so all that coal can get dumped in. Kind of genius, really. When I was a kid, this was my go-to spot when Dad and I played hide-and-seek. The tunnel is brick and about half a mile long. It's (somewhat) lit by a string of dim lightbulbs in cages, but even with the lights on, the tunnel is pretty spookily dark.

And empty.

Meaning it's the very best place to corner Jonah alone.

I happen to know one of his jobs as kitchen boy would be getting the coal, so he has to be here eventually. Sooner would be especially awesome. It's like there's a tiny clock ticking alongside my heartbeat, counting down the hours until the ball. (It's only midmorning, so I have some time, but still.) I can only hope and pray that no one is stealing the portrait at this exact second, because that would just be the worst luck ever.

Maybe I need to be more "take charge" about things, to speed this up a bit. I creep a few steps toward the light at the end of the tunnel (ha—so philosophical!), and then press hard against the bricks when I hear an odd shuffling.

RAT?!

STRANGE PERSON?!

Which would be preferable right now?

A small cough lets me know it's most definitely a person (unless we're talking about an XXL rat . . . with a head cold), and I hold my breath tight in my lungs.

The cart begins traveling down the track, and I flatten even tighter against the wall by instinct, even though I know perfectly well there's plenty of room for it to pass by me. The person walking alongside it, though? Maybe not so much. At first all I can make out is a shadowy outline, but it's enough that I can tell it's someone close in size to me and wearing pants, which means definitely a boy. No pants for girls in 1905.

Please be Jonah, please be Jonah, please be Jonah, please be—

I screw up all my courage and whisper, "Jonah?"

The shadowy figure jumps about forty-seven feet and stumbles on his landing. "What in the dratted blazes!"

"Sorry," I say in my normal voice, rushing forward to help. I peer into the boy's face as I crouch next to him, and relax a little. It *is* Jonah.

Jonah does the exact opposite of relax when he sees it's me—er, Maggie. He springs up faster than my old cat Muffintop used to when she heard me shake a can of treats.

"Apologies, miss. I didn't . . . That is, I . . . ," he stammers. "Please forgive me for using such language in front of a lady. I never expected . . . No one is ever . . . Much less someone who's not a servant . . . and I—"

"Oh no, please. It's my fault. I'm sorry for scaring you like that," I say, hoping my smile looks reassuring and friendly and not more like, *Sound the alarm. There's a crazy person in the cellar.*

He squints at me in the weak light.

I exhale. Here goes nothing. "I was waiting here to talk to you. I didn't want anyone to spot me, but I guess I didn't think things through enough to realize I'd scare the pants off you."

His eyes blink extra fast at that expression, and he does a quick check of his waistband, to make sure it's in place. Oops! I have *got* to be better about the slang thing.

He recovers quickly, though. Enough to ask, "Waiting to talk to *me*? But . . . but . . . why *me*?"

Okay, so did I say "here goes nothing" before? Nope. Here *really* goes nothing. "I know this is going to sound strange, but I have undeniable proof that there's going to be an art heist at the ball tonight."

I kinda sorta skip the part where he's the one blamed for it by the history books.

"An art heist?" he repeats. His voice sounds a little dazed. He's probably in shock. It's bad enough to come across this girl who's basically his boss—and who he talked to for only the first time yesterday—in a coal tunnel under the house. In the dark. Unexpectedly. But then she goes and opens her mouth and starts talking about an art heist that hasn't even happened yet.

If I were him, I'd probably be checking to see if I was on some hidden-camera TV show.

Of course, there aren't hidden-camera shows in 1905. Or *any* TV shows. Or video cameras, for that matter.

So maybe it's not surprising that instead of looking around, he plops down on the brick floor and shakes his head a few times to clear it. I watch him closely to try to determine if he's in shock because someone (me!) is onto his devious plan to take the painting, or if he's merely extra surprised by the combo of finding his employer's niece in the coal tunnel and all the info I dropped on him.

After a couple of seconds he takes several breaths, then looks up. "How can I help you prevent this from happening?" he asks, his eyes much clearer and calmer now.

I mean, really. What kind of a criminal mastermind would have *that* immediate response? He's so not the one. I just know it. My gut has never steered me wrong before, and it's practically screaming at me that Jonah isn't the thief.

Even so, I'm going to stick to my original plan, which is to keep Jonah close while I rule him out. If I can do that while finding a way to keep my eyes on the portrait for anyone *else* who might try to take it, I'll be #winning.

I don't feel like I can tell Jonah about the whole *Freaky Friday* body-swapping, time-traveling thing just yet. The poor guy has had enough of a shock for one day, and I'm positive that hanging out with the niece of his employers is probably blowing his mind quite enough, thank you very much. So I'll just stick to the very basics here and hope they're enough to make him go along with my plan.

"Do you believe in psychics?" I ask him, sticking out my hand to help him stand up. He stares at my palm, eyes wide, before hopping to his feet on his own. I can tell I'm gonna have to get him over this whole "you have the power to fire me" thing sooner versus later. But for now I wait on his answer.

"Do you mean as in fortune-tellers?"

"Sure, close enough."

Jonah pauses for a second, like he thinks maybe I'm asking him a trick question and I'll run and tell Maggie's aunt if he fails my secret test. I smile to let him know that's sooo not what's going on here. He winces a little at my grin but then answers, "I—I guess so? Do you?"

"Pretty much." Technically I don't, but that's not important right now. "The thing is, one of the house parties I went to last week had a carnival theme, and there was a psychic who set up shop in this tent in the backyard."

People back then—I mean back *now*—are forever throwing ridiculously over-the-top parties. One couple had a giant papier-mâché watermelon wheeled in that opened up, and a *person* sprang out of it and gave all the attendees gold cases and watches as party favors. (Totally beats the make-your-own lip gloss kit I got at the last birthday party I went to, and I was pretty psyched with that, actually.) But anyway, it's entirely possible there was a carnival party. And if there wasn't, Jonah would never be in a position to know that.

Which is why he's nodding along right now.

I continue. "So this woman was super-convincing, even though her crystal ball was a little sketchy looking. She said that the portrait set to be unveiled tonight would be stolen before the ball began."

His mouth drops. "And you—you believe her?"

I nod like I'm a bobblehead, which seems to convince him. Or maybe it's just that he would never contradict his employer. Either way, he's definitely on my side. Yes!

"Do you think maybe you could help me?" I ask, biting my lip. It's not for show, either; I really am nervous about his answer. I don't know what my plan will be if he says no.

Jonah's nodding himself now, though, almost before I finish asking the question. "Of course, miss. I'd be honored."

"Oh, whoa. You don't have to do the whole 'miss' thing. Han— I mean, 'Maggie' is fine."

It's pretty dark in the tunnel, but I'm positive that this makes him blush. "Of course, miss," he answers. "Whatever you'd prefer."

Okay, so clearly I'm gonna have to work on getting him to relax around me, but for now I'm just grateful to have an ally. Turns out adventures are a thousand times less overwhelming when you have a plus-one along. And while the real Maggie is on my side in this mission, it kind of doesn't count when she's a hundred-some years away.

"Great!" I exhale a big sigh.

He clears his throat. "Er . . . did this psychic give you any further indications as to the nature of the theft?"

Man, people talk so old-timey in this century. It's one thing to read their letters from back then in the archives, but to hear the words spoken . . . I stifle my giggle, though, and give him a straight(ish) answer. "She didn't. All I know is that sometime in the next few hours the painting of me that's hanging hidden under a sheet in the drawing room is going to disappear forever, and I need to make sure that doesn't happen, or else . . . Well, let's just leave it as 'or else.' I could use a second brain on this one."

"Well, what if you just sat in the drawing room all day? No one would attempt to steal it out from under your nose, would they?"

He's probably right, and that was basically my plan, even though preventing the theft from happening by just plopping myself in one of the armchairs and reading a book sounds anticlimactic. And way too easy. I mean, could it really be that simple?

"That's what I was thinking too," I answer.

Pride flickers across his face, but he hides it quickly. "Well, miss, I'm happy I could be of service."

He begins to push the cart along the track, heading deeper into the tunnel.

"Wait!" I call to Jonah, whose shape has nearly been gobbled up by the shadows as he walks away from me. He pauses and turns.

It can't be that clean-cut. Whoever made this time-traveling thing happen, however this happened, there's no way I switched places in time to stop an art heist just by . . . sitting around. What if spotting me on the couch prevents the theft today but the culprit returns tomorrow to snag it? Or the next day? No. Not good enough for me. I have to actively catch whoever it is in the act and make sure justice is served.

"What if I don't want to just prevent it?" I begin, taking a few steps toward him. "What if I want to solve it?"

He tilts his head; I'm close enough now that I can see a flicker of something in his eyes before he forces his expression back to something way more neutral. Intrigue? Aha! Jonah has an adventurous streak. I totally relate. I can already tell we'd be good friends if I lived now. I mean, if I lived now as someone who was allowed to hang out with servants, that is. Sigh. It's glamorous here, but there's lots that these people have to learn about how to treat others like equals. Although, if I'm being honest, I guess the same could be said about my time too. We just aren't usually as obvious about it . . . which might be even worse.

Jonah is quiet for several long seconds where the only sound in the tunnel is some clanging from far off in the kitchen. Then he asks, "What if you pulled a bait and switch?"

Okay, this is more like it! I have a partner in crime. I mean, a partner in crime-*busting*. "I'm listening. . . ."

He starts to talk faster now, clearly getting into his role as chief crime-stopper. "You could swap out the painting and replace it with some other piece of art. With the sheet covering it, no one will know the difference.

You could hide behind the curtains and wait for the thief to arrive, and then apprehend him."

"You mean 'we'?"

"Pardon?" Again with his head-tilty thing.

"*We* can hide behind the curtain and *we* can apprehend the thief," I say.

He glances at the floor. "Oh . . . I . . . With all due respect, miss, my place is down here."

"Well, what time do you get off? I mean, they can't work you all day, can they? You're just a kid."

I know I'm really lucky to have the life I do and that there are kids in my time who live in poverty and probably *would* work full-time to help their family if our country didn't have child labor laws against it. But of the kids I know personally, if any of them do have a job, it's just occasional babysitting or something, and mostly to get money for in-app purchases instead of because they have to, like, put food on the table. I help out on tours all the time—much to Trent the Evil Docent's dismay—but it's not like it's a *job* job. If I have a soccer game or something else I want to do, it's no biggie to skip out on the tours.

But right this very minute, if I got into a horse and carriage and ventured out of this neighborhood, I could find kids working in factories, in terrible conditions.

Jonah probably figures if he gets fired from here, that's exactly where he'll end up. It makes me both sad for him and kind of ashamed that I get to live this carefree childhood that he never will.

I've followed along on our Servant Life Tour countless times, and I know how hard the staff worked back then . . . er, back *now*. Regular hours were seven in the morning to eleven at night, six days a week. But it could be even later on nights when there were special events, like tonight's ball. Would a kid have to work that long too?

"I . . . well, to be honest with you, today is technically my day off. Once I finish up from taking delivery of the coal, that is. And I'll be back to help during the ball tonight, of course. It's always all hands on deck for those, and there will be all sorts of vegetables to clean and prep for Chef for the midnight supper."

"So you have to work all kinds of hours on your day off too?" Wowza. That stinks.

He ducks his head. "I don't mind. I'm grateful for the employment. It's an honor to work in a home as fine as this; my mother is proud."

And I get that. It *is* a good job for a kid who's not well-off in this day and age. But you know what would be even better? School. And summer vacation. I mean, it's not like I loooove math tests or annotating assigned reading or any kind of homework ever, but those still beat nonstop chores all day long, for next to no money.

I shake my head. "Well, now I feel extra bad about asking this, but any chance you'd want to stick around this afternoon and help me? I mean, but, you don't have to. I know I'm technically, like, your boss or something, but please don't feel like you have to say yes, if you have plans. And, um, I could see that you get paid for the time if you do decide to stay." Mental note: make sure to tell Maggie so she can take care of that once we switch back.

I watch him closely, trying to be calm about it, but inside my brain is a constant chant of *please say yes, please say yes.*

"Do you mean . . . upstairs?" he asks, with a touch of wonder in his voice.

When I nod, he says, "All due respect, miss, but I've never even been up there."

He works in this house for, like, fourteen hours a day, six days a week, and he hasn't left the basement level?

"Never?!"

He shakes his head. "I enter and exit from the service entrance, which is also where I receive the food deliveries for putting away in the pantry. On occasion I will run an item to the butler's pantry on the ground floor, but it is attached to the servants' stairwell, so I've never set foot in any of the rooms where you live. I'd never have a purpose to do so."

I can tell that he's nervous at just the thought of it, and I try to reassure him. "Don't worry, it's not that different from down here. A little brighter, of course. Although, except for this tunnel, it's fairly cheerful down here, too. All the white tiles in the kitchen? And all the copper pots and the stove shining. It's nice."

Jonah ducks his head. "I'm flattered you noticed all that, miss. I spend most of every morning cleaning the stove and a good part of every afternoon polishing the pots. I've developed this paste of flour, salt, and vinegar that—" His hand flies to his mouth. "Beg pardon. Surely you don't have an interest in drudgery such as this."

I hold out my hand and add a finger to each point. "First of all, it's Maggie, remember? Second of all, I *do* want to hear. I find it fascinating. I've always, always wondered who you were." I stop abruptly because I almost just blew my cover. Jonah can't find out that his name is known to someone a hundred years in the future, and, for that matter, he can't know that *I'm* from that time. I rush to cover my mistake. "I mean, every summer I've visited my aunt here, I've been curious about what went on down here and who did it. Um. Anyway, so yeah, upstairs. I think you'll like it. Less coal dust. A few million dollars' worth of art and adornments. You know, about what you'd expect."

Jonah looks like he's not at all sure what to make of me, so I try another tactic. Maybe if I can get him to feel invested, then he'll be on board. "Any suggestions for somewhere we could hide the real painting during the bait and switch?" I ask, slipping the "we" in and hoping he doesn't argue with my including him before he's actually agreed to help.

To my relief his face lights up. "I've already been thinking about that!" he says, squeezing carefully by me and striding deeper into the tunnel. "Come look!"

It's even harder to see back here, where the light-bulbs are spaced farther apart, but my eyes have adjusted enough that I can make him out a few steps ahead of me. Which doesn't keep me from crashing right into his back when he stops suddenly.

"Oh! I'm so sorry!" he says, sounding horrified.

"No biggie."

"Pardon?"

Whoops. Slang alert. It just slipped out. "I'm fine, is what I meant."

He relaxes and presses his hand flat against the brick wall of the tunnel, motioning for me to do the same. "Feel around. Should be right here," he says.

"What should be?" I can't let on, but I've been in this tunnel a ridiculous number of times. When Dad's friend from college visits, his little boy is forever begging me to take him on a ghost tour of the house. (For the record, I've lived here for twelve years and counting and have encountered exactly zip, zero ghosts.) We always end up in basically this very spot near the end of the tunnel. So I've "been there, done that" when it comes to this space, and I am positive there's nothing to see or feel.

Except I'm wrong.

I catch my breath when my fingers touch a tiny, worn-smooth square of metal, and I gasp when they encounter a small jagged opening in the center of it.

"What is it?" I ask.

I can't really make out any details on Jonah's face, but his voice is super-smug when he says, "Keyhole."

Say what?

"There's a door perfectly camouflaged into the brick. The hinges are on the inside, so there's nothing to indicate that it's even here, aside from this minuscule key-hole. Amazing, isn't it?" he asks.

A door! How come I've never found it? I mean, a door in a brick tunnel doesn't ever go away, so it has to be there in my time. To be fair, it's still pretty dark in here even in the future, and I've never run my hand all along the bricks. I usually walk down the center of the railroad track, actually. But still. I'm totally shocked there's an inch of this house I don't know.

"You can get into it? What does it lead to?" I ask immediately.

Jonah's voice is smiley. "My secret break spot. Oh! I shouldn't have confessed that to you. Please don't tell your aunt or uncle! Or Chef or . . . anyone! I'd be fired immediately if they knew I was sneaking away from my duties."

I step closer, so that he can see me more clearly, then use two fingers to zip my mouth closed. I lock them with an imaginary key and toss it over my shoulder. By the weird look he's giving me, I'm gonna guess that particular kid-code for "my lips are sealed" hasn't been invented yet. Whoops. I try words instead.

"I would never do that. Your secret is safe with me. You can trust me completely."

His smile is shy. "Thank you, miss. Though, I do feel guilty relaxing when the others are so hard at work. I can assure you I don't do it for more than a few minutes each day."

"For what it's worth, I think you deserve all those breaks and then some. If it were up to me, I'd give you whole weeks or months off."

He ducks his head, either in thanks or in embarrassment. Either way, I can tell he'd rather change subjects ASAP, so I ask, "Is there a whole room back there?"

Jonah shrugs lightly. "It's more of a hollowed-out space behind the wall. It's not large, but there's enough room for someone my size to stretch out."

And more than enough to hide a painting.

I could hug him. "Jonah, this is GENIUS. You're, like, smarter than Einstein!"

"Who?"

Must. Remember. Time. Period. Albert Einstein's probably still in college or something right around now. "What I mean is, you're very, very smart and this is beyond perfect."

Jonah beams at me, and I pray it really will be beyond perfect.

"But how did you ever in a million years find this?" I

ask. "And where did you get the key to open it?"

Even in the deep shadows back here, I can see his smile dim. He sighs. "There was a man who worked on the construction of the house, and he was hired on to help maintain things after the opening. He . . . he was . . . very nice to me. He requested my help on many projects around here and even taught me some mathematics and a bit of carpentry; he said I could maybe be a builder's apprentice someday."

"Where is he now?" I ask, but I can tell from the little wobble in Jonah's voice that I'm not going to like the answer.

"He took ill," Jonah says simply. I can figure out the rest. People in 1905 only lived half as long as we do now, on average I mean.

"I'm sorry," I whisper.

"As am I." Then he shakes his shoulders, and his smile returns. "But I believe he would like to know this room is being used for such an important mission now."

I sure hope so. I even hope he's watching down on us now, because I'll take all the help we can get. This *has* to work.

Has to.

Chapter Eighteen

Maggie

TARA KEEPS CHATTERING ALL THE way to Belcourt Castle and halfway back again, and I don't say a word, mostly because I don't understand one thing she says. I'm still thinking about women fighting for equal rights. Women treated as equal to men. People from other cultures playing alongside one another. It's an amazing thought.

We pass old homes I remember, new ones I don't, and large buildings that don't seem to have an obvious purpose. Knowing that other summer cottages like The Breakers and Marble House and Rosecliff and Chateau-sur-Mer all still exist and are museums just like The Elms makes me feel slightly less ill than I've felt since this whole thing started.

"So, Alex told Cheyanne that he thought Brianna was cute. But then Cheyanne got super ticked off, 'cause you KNOW she always thought that Alex liked HER. Between you and me, he just likes to tease. It's a big mess! Bri isn't talking to Cheyanne or me! I mean, is she for real? And Alex expects me to smooth things over, just 'cause he's my cousin. I didn't even do anything!" She pauses to look at me. "You know?"

I can't begin to mimic her language, so I smile and nod my agreement. "Yes. Yes, I do know. How upsetting for you!"

Her language is so strange. I feel like I get more information from her tone than the actual words, though she is speaking English. It just comes out so fast. I believe she's telling me about a quarrel between two of her and Hannah's friends, but I can't be entirely certain.

She pulls out her device and glances at it. "We'd better start toward the field. We've only got a few minutes to get there. If we're late, Coach will have kittens." She makes a devious face. "By the way, Alex texted. He's going to be at the Tower later with Ethan. Wanna stop by?"

I hope my face does not betray my confusion. "Where?"

"The Tower, of course. As long as we don't hang too

long. I need to be home by three o'clock. But we should have time to make a quick stop." She rolls her eyes. This mannerism I recognize. It's the same one my aunt uses when she's exasperated with Colette over some indecent thing she's done.

"I know how much you've been dying to talk to Ethan after last week at the pier. Alex won't tell me outright, but he totally hinted that Ethan's got a new crush. I'm betting it's you." Tara tosses her head in a way that makes me think of Colette, and I understand. A hundred years later, and girls still make fools of themselves over boys. The thought of Colette reminds me that I'm supposed to be enjoying my time in the twenty-first century. She's the one thing from my own time that I do not miss at all.

Even though I feel like I'm getting to know Tara, my hands start to twitch. So far she hasn't really asked me too many questions, but pretending to play a game she's good at, and later having to speak to Hannah's beau? Things are bound to get much more difficult.

But saying no doesn't seem like an option. "Yes, of course. I am delighted."

"Seriously . . . you should probs put the kibosh on that old-timey talk." She shakes her head.

I try to remember Hannah's words from earlier. "I'm cool." I look at Tara, hopeful that I haven't made a huge mistake. She smiles and slips her arm through mine as we head toward Newport proper.

I can breathe. For the time being.

In the heat of the day in my own time, I would be expected to sit in the drawing room and sew. Or read, in my case. I hate—that is, strongly dislike (Aunt frowns on the term "hate")—sewing. In the afternoon my aunt makes us sit quietly to "digest" our lunch while she's out calling on neighbors. Aunt would rather I sew than read. Colette always threatens to tell when I swap my handwork for a book, but I've got enough on her to make sure she won't.

But now I am walking, as bold as brass, down the main street with only another girl my own age as chaperone. It feels like I'm breaking the law! It's absolutely invigorating. I inhale deeply and breathe in the sea air, which smells identical to how it is in my own time.

But I can't enjoy my newfound freedom. My brain keeps returning to the thought of this infernal game I'm supposed to be playing in a few short minutes. And Tara has a plan to meet some boys on the way home. I exhale. One thing at a time. I can think about only one thing at time.

All of a sudden, something looks very familiar. "The Casino!" I shout as we approach a crossroads with more modern buildings. Tara looks at me sidelong.

"The what?" She stops for a moment with her hands on her hips. She looks just like Mrs. O'Neil giving me the evil eye. "Please don't tell me you're going to make me call buildings by their old-fashioned names today." She chuckles as if this might be something Hannah makes her do regularly.

"Oh." I cringe. "No. What do you prefer it be called?"

"Well, I'm pretty sure Serena Williams would want you to call it by its normal name, the International Tennis Hall of Fame." She looks at me. "Like everyone else in Newport?"

This statement leaves me with so many questions. I stick to the most obvious. "Serena . . . ?"

"Williams, of course. She's the GOAT! You know, the greatest of all time? Jeez, Hannah. You're out of it today. Future Hall of Fame inductee? She was in town last week promoting her new clothing line; it's been all over the news." She's staring at me again like I'm a fool. "I know you're crushing on Ethan lately, but it's not like you to be so far under a rock. Especially when it comes to celebrity sightings in Newport."

"The International Tennis Hall of Fame." It feels like an appropriate name for the Casino. I wanted to see Bessie Moore play with Wylie Cameron Grant in the US mixed doubles championship at this exact spot last summer, but Aunt refused to let me attend. It was exhilarating to hear of a woman playing in such a high-stakes game, even if I'm not allowed to exert myself that much. "We could play lawn tennis later, maybe?"

She gives me that look again. "Lawn tennis? Um, sure. Maybe later. But right now we're playing soccer."

We turn right past the Casino and around another corner to where a large field opens up. The smell of cut grass envelops me. Girls of all shapes and sizes and skin color, dressed in uniforms like ours, run back and forth on the field, chasing one another, or a ball. I don't know which.

I blink at the chaos. I tell myself I shouldn't be surprised that so many of the girls look like they were born far away. They are probably like Tara: families from other places, but all from Rhode Island.

And they are all running. The girls are running. They look like they are exerting themselves a lot.

Sometimes Aunt allows us to walk on the grounds, if the day is cool enough. She always says the summer sun will damage my hair or my skin and I must preserve my good looks for my debut. Of course, running is forbidden. It will damage my insides, she says. I've never understood why it wouldn't damage a boy's insides. I realize there are a lot of questions I've not asked in my own time. About a lot of things.

As we get closer, my mouth falls open. These girls are perspiring. Some of them are soaked through their clothes. They look like they are having the times of their lives. I suddenly can't wait to run alongside them.

"C'mon. We don't have much time to warm up," Tara says. "That little detour took longer than I expected. Maybe Coach won't notice we're late." She pulls me toward her and drops her bag. She kicks off her shoes and pulls out a pair with the bumps on the bottom. "Well, are you going to get your cleats on or what?" She glances toward a woman striding in our direction. "You better hurry, Coach doesn't look happy that we're so late."

I flip off the shoes I hurriedly put on in Hannah's room, and slowly lace up the ones found in her bag. If I take long enough, maybe I can observe some of the game before I'm expected to play.

"Hannah!" Tara yells, almost like she's warning me.

A shadow looms over my shoulder. I leap up and hurry after Tara, who runs for the opposite side of the field with the other girls on the team. When we get there, one of the girls says, "Two lines. Dynamic warm-ups." I follow their lead, and before long I'm laughing with them all as we skip, hop, and kick our legs. No one seems to notice that I've never done this before. I can't believe it's so easy.

One of the girls gives a cry that sounds like "whoop," and soon everyone is yelling. I make a small sound that comes out like a quack, but when I try again, I find my voice and scream with the others. I've never had so much fun, and the game hasn't even started.

Tweeeeeet! A loud sound travels across the field. The girls freeze and look toward the sound, which comes from a woman wearing a striped shirt. "Game time!"

The smell of the grass; the wind blowing through my hair; all the girls running next to me, giddy with excitement . . . for a moment I have half a thought that I can do this.

The coach stands on the side of the field, next to the woman in the striped shirt. "Line it up."

Panting harder than I ever have in my life, I get in

line next to Tara. I have to bend over to catch my breath. The striped woman calls our names one at a time. Each of the girls steps out of line when her name is called and turns to show the big number on her back. Then she shows the bottom of her cleats and touches her sock. I can do this. It's going to be easier than I thought.

"Jordan?"

I smile confidently and stride out just like everyone else, like I know exactly what I'm doing. I turn. I show my cleat and tap my sock. I head back to the line.

"Hold it."

I freeze. No one else had to hold it. Coach stands with her hands on her hips. "Where are your shin guards?"

"My what?" I rack my brain, but I'm sure no one mentioned shin guards before just now. I look at Tara, but she seems to have abandoned me.

"Shin guards. Mandatory to play soccer."

"I . . ." I have no idea what she is talking about, but before I can say anything else, Tara runs over.

"Here they are. I forgot to give them back to you. I accidentally put them in my bag." She hands them to me, and with a raised eyebrow as if she realizes I have no idea what to do, she grabs them from me and stuffs one into each of my socks. She pats them hard and says, "Good to go." She gets up and pulls me into line. "What is wrong with you?" she mouths.

Coach shakes her head and gestures. "Bring it in, ladies." We make a tight circle. I sneak a glance around, but everyone's eyes are fixed on Coach. My stomach suddenly lurches.

"This is your game. You've been working hard and have improved so much this summer. Take a deep breath. Remember what we've been doing in practice. You're ready."

Her voice is steady, calm, inspiring. "We'll go with the regular starting lineup. Hands in. 'Team' on three." Coach puts her open palm into the middle of the circle, and all the girls put a hand in. I put mine on top. For a split second the feeling of doom evaporates and I feel something I've never felt before. Something like strength, like I'm part of something much bigger than myself. "One, two, three . . ."

"TEAM!" They shout in unison and throw their arms into the air.

Some of the girls run out onto the field, and the others go over toward the bench near the white line. Coach puts her hand on my shoulder before I have a chance to follow. "Hannah, where are your gloves?"

"Gloves?" I think about the silk pair Aunt Herminie gave me to wear to the ball. No one else is wearing anything like those.

When I don't move or say anything, Coach cocks her head. "Are you feeling okay?"

"Yes, yes, I'm fine."

"Well, go check your bag, then. Your gloves are probably in there."

I rummage around in Hannah's bag, and sure enough, I find a pair of large white gloves with a bright green stripe down the back of them.

"Gloves!" I call to Coach, and wave them in the air.

"Great," she says. "How about you put them on. We have a couple of minutes for a quick warm-up."

I feel warm enough already, but I sense that would be the wrong thing to say. I pull on the gloves. They're big but not too big; it's like they make my hands feel extra large. I like how white and clean they are.

Coach waits for me with a ball in front of the net. "Ready to make some saves? Here you go," she says, and tosses the ball at me. It hits off my stomach and down my legs and feet, before rolling back to Coach. "Sorry, I thought you were ready," she says, and tosses it again.

The same thing happens.

She stares at me, holding the ball under her arm. "Are you ready?"

"I think so."

"Well, how about trying out your new gloves?"

I'm supposed to catch the ball.

She tosses it to me again, and this time I reach my hands out and the ball hits off them. I look down to the other end of the field at the girl standing in the opposite net. She is catching every ball her coach throws.

"Do your gloves feel okay? You're a little off today."

I'm thinking she's just being kind, as this must be more than "a little off" for Hannah.

"Yes. They are quite comfortable. I'm sure I'm just nervous, ma'am."

"Ma'am?" She hesitates, then grins. "It's okay to be nervous, Hannah. Take a few deep breaths. You're an amazing goalkeeper. You've made some awesome saves in practice. Just play like you know how, and you'll do fine."

That's the problem, I want to say. I have no idea how to play.

"Your gloves are probably still a little slippery because they're new. Just spit on them and that will help."

"Did you say spit on my gloves?"

"Like you always do. Remember? It helps to grip the

ball." She demonstrates by spitting on her hands.

She watches me until I reluctantly spit on my gloves and rub my hands together.

Her patience with me is running thin, I can tell. "Okay, I'm going back to the bench. Maybe you just need a few minutes to regroup." She begins to walk away. "You've done this before. Just keep it simple!" She turns back and with a wink adds, "Make sure the ball stays out of the net." She gives me a big smile and a hearty thumbs-up.

A couple of girls shout and clap for me. "Go, Hannah!"

I give them a weak smile. I'm afraid Hannah will never forgive me if I ruin this game. My knees wobble. I think I may need to vomit. Coach, Tara, and the rest of the team are depending on me, and I don't know what I'm doing.

Coach said to take deep breaths. I take one and another and another. It helps. I look down the field at the other goalie and have an idea. I've been imitating someone else all day! I'll just do what she does. I can do this. I take a full breath and feel my heart return to a normal pace.

The whistle blows and the game begins.

The other goalie crouches a little, so I do the same.

She waves her hand now and then, so I do too. The ball is being kicked back and forth mostly in the middle of the field far away from me. It seems to go off the field a lot, which causes the woman with the whistle to blow and pause the game. *I can do this,* I keep saying to myself. All I have to do is watch. And mimic. It should be easy.

The girls from both teams seem to be fighting over the one ball, kicking at it. There are bags of extra balls next to the benches. I don't know why they don't just give one to everyone.

Across the field Tara gets the ball, and she runs fast toward the other goal and kicks the ball hard at the net. The other goalie jumps sideways with her arms all the way extended and catches the ball before she hits the ground.

I stare in disbelief. "Outstanding!" I shout, but when I start clapping, someone from my bench yells to me, "What are you doing? You don't clap for the other team!"

My heart pounds again as I realize there is no way I could ever dive and catch the ball like that girl. I couldn't even catch it standing still. Then, like a lightning bolt, understanding strikes. The goal of the game is to try to get the ball into the other team's net. They expect me to not let the other team kick the ball into our net. All at

once my hands feel cold and clammy. I can't stop a ball!
I can't jump! I can't catch!

Suddenly someone breaks free and runs full speed
at me.

"All you, Hannah!" a girl yells from the bench.
"You've got this!"

But I definitely don't "got this." My heart pounds
harder. My insides are all fluttery and jumbled. I'm trying to catch my breath. I'm having a hard time not pan-
icking. Maybe this is what my aunt has been worried
about—are my insides being damaged?

My teammates chase after the girl with the ball. But
she has a clear lead, and it's just her and me. My mind
goes blank as soon as I realize that she has kicked the
ball and it's headed like a pellet right at my face. At the
very last second I wince and withdraw, collapsing to
the ground.

"Goal!" announces the striped woman.

I breathe a sigh of relief. But my team has a different
reaction. The girls sitting on the bench yell at me. "Seriously, Hannah?"

"Why would you duck?"

"This is a big game!"

"Are you trying to make us lose?"

"What was that?" Coach's hands are in the air, and there's a look of complete dismay on her face.

How can they be mad at me? Didn't they see that that girl tried to kick the ball at my face? What kind of game is this anyway? I loved the running and warming up, but this kicking the ball at my head is barbaric.

It gets worse.

The other team scores again when the ball hits off the bar across the top of the net and then off my back and into the goal. I try not to cry, but it stings. It may leave a mark. The next goal comes when an opposing girl practically runs me over. I stick out my hands, but I never get close to touching the ball. The girl runs right past me like I'm invisible.

The next one is close. The ball strikes me in the chest and knocks the wind out of me, but I make the save. Unfortunately, it bounces out and someone kicks it back in.

With every goal the other team scores, my team gets madder and madder. Why would Hannah want to play this ridiculous position? Why wouldn't she want to run around? Having people kick a ball at me and run into me is not my idea of fun. And now everyone is cross. I bite my lip.

At a break in the game (they call it "halftime"), Coach says, "Jenny, you're going to play net for the second half."

Now I'm trying to hold back tears of joy. I'm finally going to get to sit and rest! But before I have a chance to celebrate, Coach turns to me. "Hannah, take off your gloves. I know you feel bad about the goals. So I'm going to have you start the second half as a forward. Give you a chance to make it up. You were hitting some awesome shots in practice last week. Go rip a few."

Rip a few? Tara must know what Coach means, but I can't ask her, because I'm quite certain she isn't speaking to me right now. I assume that "forward" has something to do with trying to score.

I just want to go sit on the bench and sip water like some of the other girls. Why do I have to get stuck being on the field?

When the whistle blows to start the second half, we put our hands in again. The energy in our "TEAM" call seems to have lost its vigor. I can't help but feel it's my fault. Perhaps I can make up for it playing at forward. The other team seemed to have an easy time scoring goals on us. Maybe it is our turn now.

I jog out with Tara, and she stands next to me and the ball at the middle of the field. The other team takes their places on their side. "We have the kickoff," she says.

I grin stupidly because I have no idea what else to do.

The whistle blows. Tara taps the ball and runs away. Other members of my team sprint in various directions, leaving the ball at my feet. I pause, watching. Not moving. The other team's players start coming at me. They want the ball. I have come to learn one thing about this game of soccer: the ball is like the treasure; everyone wants it. My team is yelling at me to move, to kick the ball.

And then I have the most brilliant idea. I reach down, scoop up the ball in my hands, and hold it over my head as high as I can.

"Here!" I yell, and toss it at Tara. Yes! I can't believe it. I've outwitted these girls at their own game. They are so stunned by my brilliance, no one has moved.

But instead of catching the ball and cheering my amazing move, Tara lets it drop to the ground. She looks bewildered, more than she has all day.

TWEEEEEEEEEEEEEEEET! The striped woman blows the whistle for a very long time. She seems angry.

"HAND BALL!" she shouts. "Direct, this way." She places the ball back down near the middle of the field and gives me an extremely odd look.

"What the what, Jordan!" someone from my team says, and elbows my ribs. "Are you wacked? Get with the program or get out of the game!" she shouts as she runs off.

My eyes sting.

"Hannah!" the coach yells. "Are you sick? What's going on with you? Hit the bench."

I take that to mean I'm out of the game. Finally.

Just watching the rest of the soccer game would have been glorious. Girls running, playing, being a part of something exciting. Exerting themselves, as Aunt would say. Perspiring, even. I would never have believed it if I hadn't experienced it. But I've ruined something for Hannah with my failure, and I can't shake that terrible feeling. I won't blame her if she hates me for it.

"Bad luck on the game, Han," Tara says as we walk away from the field among the crowd of girls. We have to dodge slow-moving automobiles as they stop to pick up players. "What was up with you out there? Are you getting enough sleep? Are you sick?"

"I . . . I don't know." I sigh. "You don't have to pretend. I was horrible. The whole team hates me."

She's not protesting, so I know I'm right. I think

about the game again. "I love running. But I didn't like being a target for the ball."

"Don't worry about it. We all have off days." Tara repositions her bag on her back and expertly changes the subject as we pass the Casino again. "So . . . are you still up for heading to the Tower to see my stupid cousin and Ethan?" She glances at me hopefully.

"Is your cousin really stupid?" I can't tell if she's serious. I certainly wouldn't call Colette stupid, though there are a lot of other words that describe my own cousin.

"Nah. You know he's my best friend—well, next to you." She flicks her finger against my arm, and winces. "He's just been really annoying since he started liking girls. It used to be great when we could all just kick a ball around, but now that he's trying to get me to give him all the inside scoop on my friends, not so much."

"Why are we going to meet them again?" After my failure at soccer, all I want is to go home and crawl under the covers, but I need to do something helpful. It's one thing for someone to be suspicious of Hannah's odd behavior. And another to lose a game. But I've watched Colette talk to boys, and I am confident I can do this.

"You really are clueless today, Han. Do I have to spell it out? I know you like Ethan. God knows why. Alex has been hinting that Ethan likes you." After shrugging her shoulders, she shakes her head and for the first time looks doubtful. "On second thought maybe you're really not up for it. Maybe it's not the right day." Her voice wavers as she stops and looks at me. "Want to wait for when you're feeling better?"

I made a fool of myself—Hannah—during the game, but maybe I can make it up to her. "No. No, of course I'm okay. I do want to see . . . Ethan."

Even though I'm too young to be courting, I've watched Colette flirt with all the boys in Newport this summer—this will be easy.

"Okay. Whatever you say. Just don't mess this up. You don't want Ethan to think you're cray-cray going into the school year." She whirls her finger in a circle around her ear. "Lay off the weird talk."

As we walk, I continue to be distracted by so many buildings and fast-moving automobiles and people, but as soon as we get near the park, things look familiar. A group of young people our age congregates on the granite next to a fence that surrounds the Tower—and I realize I know exactly where we are. The Touro Tower is the ancient remains of a windmill built centuries before my own time. It's in the same spot, even though you can usually see the harbor. The familiar appearance gives me a shot of confidence. This is still, after all, Newport.

We're only three blocks away from the ocean, and my feet are itching to see what changes have been made at the waterfront. But instead I must face a sea of unfamiliar faces.

The group appears to be having a meeting, but I cannot imagine what the topic could be. Most of them stare down at their tiny devices. I scan the group, wondering which one is Ethan—Hannah's beau. I glance at Tara for a clue.

"There you are," says a dark-eyed boy with brown hair, running at us. He punches Tara in the arm and then looks at me, shaking his head. "Hey, Hannah. Bad luck on the game."

"How . . . how do you know what happened?"

He holds up his device. "Cheyanne Snapchatted your best misses."

A girl with long black hair, held back by a headband, waves from a few feet away. I recognize her from the game. She was watching, pointing her device in my direction.

"Sorry." The boy shrugs. "Good news, though," he says, perking up. "You're going viral." He looks a little like the puppy that lives at Arleigh, like I should scratch behind his ears. I know without a doubt that this is Alex, Tara's cousin.

"I . . ." I can't even pretend. He's saying words that make no sense. "Viral . . . that's good?"

Tara laughs. "Duh, Hannah. Viral is the best!" She pauses. "Although, maybe not for those reasons."

"Nah. It's all good." Alex gestures to the five or six people loitering nearby. "You're da bomb, Han. So funny! Ethan here"—he gestures to a tall, blond boy walking toward us—"was just telling me how funny he thinks you are."

"In a good way, right, Alex?" Tara looks concerned. "You're not laughing *at* her. We've all had our bad days. I mean, you ran into the metal goalpost in the first five minutes of your first game and were out with a concussion for three weeks."

"But we don't talk about that, cuz." He scowls and waves Tara away. "Ethan!" he says, and raises his fist. The other boy bumps Alex's fist with his own. I'm not entirely sure, but I think this ritual is a gesture of manners—like a handshake—and a boost of confidence shoots through me. I understand manners.

Ethan has fair hair and pale skin, and when he smiles, I see two rows of metal attached to his teeth. His baggy shorts skim the top of his knees, and he wears a blue shirt with a pair of red socks and the number one on the front. I assume it must be his team shirt.

"Hi, Hannah," he says shyly. Alex rolls his eyes, but he takes Tara by the arm and leads her away so that Ethan and I stand alone, staring at each other. Except for his clothing, he looks a lot like one of the Vanderbilt cousins. Colette would approve, although I'm more partial to Alex's puppy-dog brown eyes.

The rest of the group chatters behind us, no doubt talking about the abysmal soccer game. A soft sea breeze blows across the otherwise hazy afternoon.

This is my chance to redeem myself. I take a breath and then hold out my hand to Ethan. I've seen Colette do this a dozen times. The boy is supposed to take the girl's hand and kiss it gently. It's a sign of good breeding.

"It is a pleasure to see you . . . again." I try not to stammer, but the words don't flow in the coquettish way Colette performs them.

"Um . . ." Instead of kissing my hand, he shakes it limply at the fingertips.

Applesauce. People don't kiss hands anymore? I'm ready to retreat back to The Elms and hide in Hannah's room for the duration of my time here. But the boy doesn't seem to be affected by my faux pas.

"Do you— I mean . . . would you like to . . . um . . . Do you wanna hang out some night?" He can't keep his feet still while he stammers out the question.

"At night?" I don't mean for my voice to come out so loud. And I can tell the boy is nervous. But that's no excuse for the most forward invitation I've ever heard. As if Hannah would go out with a boy after that pathetic excuse for a request! And at night? Aunt Herminie would forbid Colette to speak to the boy ever again.

Tara's head whips around from a few feet away, where she's talking to Alex.

"Well, yeah." His feet shuffle in the dry grass. "A bunch of us are going to see the new zombie flick down at the cineplex, and I know you like that scary stuff. And it only plays after nine." After the last word he picks up his head and stares me in the eye as though daring me. It is extremely forward of him.

I will not allow this boy, no matter how attractive, to sully Hannah's good name by offering an evening date. It would be extremely improper. She'd be lucky to ever get another invitation if she accepted such a suggestion. "Perhaps we could go for a stroll along the Cliff Walk.

Some *afternoon.*" I lower my eyelashes. "And Tara could serve as chaperone."

"Well, sure. That would be okay too." He looks over his shoulder at Alex with a confused look, as Tara sidles up next to me.

"Hannah, I think you've been out in the sun too long. You're starting to sound like the reenactors from the Antiquities Society again. Let's get you home." She pulls my arm.

"Oh. Of course. Ethan, my dear." I hold out my hand again, hoping he will behave properly this time. But of course he does not. I rack my brain for the most poetic verse I know. I come up with the perfect one. "'In vain have I struggled. It will not do. My feelings will not be repressed. You must allow me to tell you how ardently I admire and love you.'"

Even Colette would be proud!

Tara succeeds in pulling me away from the boys, who look like they've been struck dumb. "Over the top, Han," she whispers. "Way too far over the top."

As soon as we get around the corner, onto the cobblestone street of a bustling marketplace, she doubles over laughing. "Did you see his face? OMG, I can't believe you had the nerve, Hannah! What was that quote from?"

Seeing Tara laugh makes me smile. "Do you not know *Pride and Prejudice*?"

"Oh, sure. I knew it sounded familiar, from when you made me read it last summer. Why didn't you tell me you were going to do that?" She's taking gasping breaths as she tries to stop laughing. I'm not sure why she's so amused.

"Was it not 'over the top,' then?"

"Of course it was over the top. But if you ask me, Ethan Grimes is a bit too high and mighty for his own good. He's cute; just ask *him*." She rolls her eyes. "And I hated to say something because I thought you had a thing for him. But taking him down like that is exactly what that boy needs."

I'm suddenly afraid I've done something that Hannah will regret even more than failing at soccer.

Chapter Nineteen

Hannah

DUST TICKLES.

I mean, for something so minuscule that it usually floats through the air undetected, when it gets into your nostrils and you can't sneeze because you're hiding behind heavy drapes in the drawing room, waiting to foil an art thief, it's a surprisingly *enormous* issue.

I scrunch my nose in a hundred different directions to fight off the sneezing fit, which works, but which also makes Jonah nearly laugh out loud as he watches me from behind the window's other curtain. I widen my eyes at him in warning. Jeez, who would have thought being quiet would be this much of a problem, especially for a self-proclaimed master lurker like me?

Except it turns out there's a pretty big difference between lurking—which usually involves (mostly harmless) eavesdropping on a conversation or (mostly harmless) spying on some kind of activity—and waiting. Which is how I've been wasting my one precious day in the past. And now I'm supposed to be meeting Maggie in less than two hours to switch back, and I have nothing at all to show for my time here.

I wish I could at least chat with Jonah to pass the time. I find his life fascinating, and he's really sweet and nice. But of course that would require something other than complete silence, so I've had to amuse myself with making faces at him to try to get him to smile. He's extra good at his poker face, but I've gotten him to at least crack one a couple of times. The rest of the time, I catch him darting his eyes everywhere, like he's trying to memorize every detail of the crazy-extravagant drawing room. He's totally fascinated by the elaborate painted mural of the god of the north wind that covers most of the ceiling.

But other than that it's been a whole lot of . . .

Just. Waiting.

Boring, mind-numbing, nothing-to-do-or-listen-to waiting.

Well, not *nothing* to listen to. The house is full of people scrambling about to prepare for tonight's ball. But none of them are venturing into the drawing room, and none of them are cheerfully calling to each other or kidding around the way our staff at home does when we're decorating the mansion for the holidays or prepping for a wedding on the grounds. This household is all quiet efficiency. Would it kill them to crack a joke here and there?

I startle when Jonah's foot stretches across the distance between our hiding spots and nudges mine. I raise *What the heck?* eyes to his, only to find him looking all freaked out. He jerks his head to the side twice, and I finally catch on.

There's someone out there!

We've had exactly three false alarms in the several hours we've been hiding back here. (Yes, hours. If my sneezing doesn't give us away, my rumbling stomach might.) The first was a maid doing a quick straightening up of furniture and a run over the wooden surfaces with a feather duster. (I felt like whispering, "It's the *curtains* you should really think about dusting!") The second was a different maid, watering Mrs. Berwind's potted ficus. And the third was a footman passing through on his way to the conservatory. Other than that the room has been as quiet as my middle school on a snow day.

But this is not a false alarm, and it's not the butler looking for the jar of silver polish. It's a man creeping up to the sideboard, where the landscape filling in for the real portrait is propped behind a white sheet.

OMG, ART HEIST IN PROGRESS!

My yawning boredom disappears in a split second because there is a man putting grabby hands on the painting, only two feet to my left!

It's really, actually happening!

I don't recognize him, but I know he's not a servant, because he isn't in uniform. He's wearing a white button-down shirt, but it's loose, and the sleeves are rolled up and there are streaks of red on his arms, almost like—

Like blood! Is he a *murderous* art thief?! No one said anything about that being a possibility, and I would like my money back, please. I didn't sign up for this!

I'm scared to turn my head to look at Jonah next to me, because what if that makes a sound? Just knowing that he's here with me is comforting, at least. (Although, I would actually prefer if it were maybe more like thirty-seven Jonahs, who were all wearing shirts with the letters *FBI* stamped across their backs.)

The man has his fingers on the edges of the painting, still wrapped in the sheet. Is he gonna just walk out with it? I mean, that's basically what Jonah and I did earlier, and we didn't encounter a soul, so I guess it's as good a plan as any, but is it really this easy to steal precious masterpieces?

Jonah's foot nudges mine again, and this time I chance turning my head toward him. His eyes stare pointedly at the camera on the windowsill next to me. Oh! Right! I'm supposed to be getting photographic evidence.

I found this Brownie camera in Maggie's room when I was killing time there this morning, and although it takes pictures more slowly than a website loads in the Wi-Fi dead zone of my bedroom, if I act carefully, I should be able to catch this dude in the act. I wonder if this is Maggie's prized possession or if it was the one thing she begged for at Christmas, like me with my iPhone. Or maybe she's got twenty of these, one for every house she visits. As much as I always felt like Maggie and I would have so, so many things in common if we ever met up, being mega-rich isn't one of them.

Wow, I get rambly when I'm nervous. My thoughts are skittering all over the place, just like the pulse in my wrist. *Focus, Hannah! Get the picture!*

I ease the camera out between the opening in the curtains and try my best to hold it steady in shaky hands. I practiced snapping a shot of Jonah earlier (he blushed like crazy, as if it were the first time anyone took his picture or something), but I only took the one because I can't tell how much film is left in the camera. I already know it doesn't take pictures anywhere nearly as fast as my phone does. But I have to work with what I've got and cross fingers that a fuzzy picture combined with Jonah's and my witness statements is enough to do the job.

The man slides the painting off the sideboard. He struggles to get his hands around both sides of the giant frame and staggers backward a little under the weight of it. One step, then two. I hear the tiniest cough from Jonah, urging me on.

CLICK!

I take the shot. The noise from the flash bounces off the walls and echoes against the high ceilings, and the man freezes.

I lower the camera.

The man swivels and stares dead into my eyes.

I can't swallow or breathe.

Jonah steps out from behind his curtain, and the guy's gaze switches to him. Jonah squares his shoulders and returns the gaze, hard. (Go, Jonah! Go, Jonah!) After a second the man swallows thickly and turns back to me. He sets the painting, still wrapped in its sheet, on the ground at his feet and smiles brightly. Too brightly to be believable.

"*Je l'avais tout simplement amené à Mademoiselle Cassatt pour une retouche de dernière minute,*" he says.

"Say what, now? Try English, buddy," I order.

His forehead wrinkles. "*Je ne comprends pas.* You spoke French so perfectly during the sitting."

Okay, so:

Of course Maggie speaks flawless French. I'll bet her tutor has been drilling it into her since she was in diapers.

Are diapers a thing in 1905?

Focus, Hannah!

Sitting. He said "sitting." Is he—

"Who *are* you? Are you involved with the portrait somehow?" I ask.

His eyes squinch up. "*Mais oui.* We have been working

together for weeks now. How is it that you do not recognize me? I am Mademoiselle Cassatt's apprentice."

I dart a glance at the red streaks on his arms. Not blood. Paint. Um, *phew*! I exchange a quick look of relief with Jonah, then turn back to Mr. Frenchy Pants.

"Of course you are. I knew that. But—but why are you stealing a painting of hers, then?"

"Stealing? *Non!* I'm bringing it to Mademoiselle for a last-minute touch-up. Stealing! Ha! You have quite the imagination, young miss." He barks out a laugh that sounds faker than fake.

I'm not buying it. And the "young miss" thing is so . . . demeaning. I always assumed Maggie would get mad respect for being an heiress, but I guess, even here, money doesn't trump age. Kids never get any credit from adults for having actual, functioning brains in our heads.

I sneak a peek at Jonah. When I catch his eye, I raise my eyebrows to silently ask him what he thinks of this guy's flimsy excuse. He shrugs, but I can see a whole lotta doubt on his face. I'm guessing he doesn't feel like he can speak up, seeing as he has neither age nor money on his side.

But the thing is, it's not like we can prove anything.

My gut says this guy is lying, but that plus a nickel . . . leaves me with a nickel.

The man can tell I'm hesitating. He takes advantage of my indecision and picks the painting back up. "*Au revoir*. I must deliver this to Mademoiselle Cassatt."

He hoists the frame higher in his arms and peeks around its side to see his way to the door.

Uh-oh. Not only have I not stopped a heist, but now there's going to be deep trouble when Mary Cassatt whisks off that sheet and discovers that the portrait she worked on for months is not there. We were careful, but what if someone saw me and Jonah sneaking around this afternoon and puts two and two together? Maggie will kill me if I ruin her life in a matter of one afternoon!

I'm just standing with my mouth open, watching the empty doorway that Mr. Apprentice Guy disappeared through, when Jonah puts his hand on my sleeve. "Excuse me, miss?"

I snap, "Maggie! Call me Maggie." When he fumbles back a step, I realize what a jerk I'm being to literally the only person who's been nice to me in this entire century. It's not *Jonah's* fault I'm a total fail at foiling art heists.

"Oh my gosh, I'm so sorry," I say. "I didn't mean to say it like that. It's just that it feels weird to have you call me something so . . . so . . . formal. I mean, we're both kids, so . . ."

He looks confused. "What does our age have to do with anything?"

I know what he's getting at. We're the same age, but he and Maggie are not of the same social station, and that matters a lot here. A lot a lot. He's probably been trained since the day he started not to address the occupants of the house unless spoken to first. Most likely he's been told to even avoid eye contact with me. For him to have agreed to help me today wasn't just nice of him. It was taking a big risk with his job. And here I repay him by being totally rude. *Nice one, Hannah.*

"I really am sorry. Please. I know it might not feel natural to say, but it would mean a lot if you could call me Maggie instead of 'miss.' If you could, well, maybe think of me as"—I give him a small, hopeful smile before continuing—"a friend?"

His eyes grow wide at that, and I offer, "I know that's not really normal for two people like us, but . . ."

I trail off, and it's a second before he answers. "But it would be nice. To have a friend, I mean. I don't have much free time to spend with the others my age in my neighborhood. Most of them work too, and our days off rarely match. Of course, I'm friendly with all the kitchen staff, but they're so much older and it's not the same thing."

Once again my heart hurts for him. What kind of a childhood is that? I can't help asking, "Doesn't that bother you?"

He shrugs. "It's simply life as I know it."

My throat aches. He doesn't even sound upset, so much as . . . resigned. I spend so much time back home surrounded by the glamorous side of the Gilded Age and daydreaming about the outrageous parties and the elaborate dresses and the ridiculous wealth, but it wasn't golden for everyone. Not even for *most* people. Definitely not for Jonah, and hearing it in person really drives it home in a different way than just reading about it.

The thing is, he's right. This *is* life as he knows it, and it won't change for him either. He may work his way up to chef someday, but otherwise this is probably how his whole future will look. Working here or somewhere just like it. People like Jonah didn't have the luxury of big dreams. Which is also true of lots of people—even kids—in my time too, and that sucks just as much.

But actually, even some people with *all* the luxury didn't have the freedom to dream big. Like Maggie. Sure, she's as pampered as can be and will never want for anything material, but she's a girl, which means she'll never get to decide for herself what she wants to be when she grows up. She already knows she'll be a wife and maybe a mother (who only sees her kids an hour a day, because that's the custom), and a society woman who spends time visiting only with other people from her same class.

The reality is, if I actually did live here, chances are next to zero that I'd be able to be friends with Jonah. Even if he weren't a servant, he's still a boy, which means we wouldn't be allowed to hang without a chaperone. (But the servant thing would kill everything first.)

Of course, I *don't* live here. I won't even be here in a couple of hours. Maybe it's not fair of me to offer Jonah friendship.

My shoulders slump. I've made a mess of things. What was all this for, if it wasn't to solve the mystery of the stolen painting? I should have just gone exploring Gilded Age Newport, instead of lurking for eons in a dark coal tunnel and hiding out for even more hours behind a dusty curtain and involving someone who was minding his own business. Great. Just great.

And all for nothing.

If anything, I made things worse. As soon as Mary

Cassatt finds the dummy painting, the whole house will be in an uproar over the missing one, and I'll have to expose Jonah's secret break spot to show them where the real painting is hidden, and that's going to take some major explaining, and what if Jonah gets fired for helping me and he can't help his family put food on their table and they—

"Maggie?"

Jonah's voice snaps me out of my spiraling thoughts, and it takes me a second to realize he's used my (well, Maggie's) first name.

"Hey, you called me—" But I break off when I see his face and how urgent his expression is. "What is it?"

"I just thought of something. Is the paint an artist uses very different from other paint?" he asks.

"Different how?"

"Is it oil-based?"

"Not always. There are watercolors and acrylics and others, but yes, the portrait was done with oils. Why?"

Jonah fidgets with his hands and glances away. "I'm just a kitchen boy, so I don't know anything about fancy things like portraits . . ."

"But?" I urge him on.

He takes a deep breath and locks eyes with me.

"But last winter I helped paint some shelves in the wine cellar, and we used an oil-based mixture. It took three solid days before the shelves dried enough to replace the bottles. Do you think—that is to say, would it be likely that the artist would truly chance a touch-up only hours before the unveiling? I wondered if perhaps the paint would still be—"

"Wet!" I interrupt. "Jonah! You're right. She would never, ever do that." Just like that, my bad mood evaporates and my head is back in the game. "They'd put the sheet back on to hide it until the big reveal, and the paint would definitely stick to that and it would be a giant mess! Mary Cassatt wouldn't chance that. Meaning, that guy was lying through his teeth! I *knew* he was. You really *are* a genius. I don't care if you don't know who he is yet—I'm calling you Einstein from here on out. We have to find that man and confront him again. Let's go!"

I take two steps toward the hallway, but Jonah doesn't follow.

"C'mon. We have to hurry if we want to catch him!" I urge. "I know he doesn't have the real painting, but I still want to bust his smug old liar-liar-pants-on-fire face."

Jonah is frozen in place. "I cannot be caught out there," he says, eyes wide. "Not on this floor of the house.

Not on my day off. There wouldn't be a plausible explanation I could give for any of it." He looks genuinely scared, and my heart hurts for him.

"I'll take full blame," I promise. "I'll say you were helping me. That I ordered you to do it. They can't get mad at you if you were following orders from a lady of the house, right?"

Jonah shakes his head slowly. "It wouldn't be honorable of me to allow you to lie on my behalf."

It wouldn't be honorable? Boys in my century could learn a bunch from this kid. I kind of like this guy at school, Ethan, but I can tell you right now he'd never worry about something like honor.

"Well, then I do order you. There. Now it's not a lie," I say, but he doesn't look any more convinced. I puff my bangs out of my eyes and force my voice to stay soft. "How about this, then? How about we just don't get caught?"

I barely know the guy, but I'm already onto his tell. It's that tiny twinkle in his eyes when he thinks about having an adventure. I watch him closely, and grin. "So you're in?"

He keeps me in suspense for a second, but then he nods sharply. "I suppose it would be even less honorable to allow you to go after him on your own. Let's find this cad."

I'm gonna have to give him a pass on that "allow" thing because he's living in this century. And also because, even though I fully believe girls are just as capable as boys, if I'm being totally honest, I definitely would feel better about confronting the "cad" with a backup at my side. But I'm so taking the lead on things, just to prove a point.

Jonah sticks close behind me as I peek out into the wide marble hallway that connects all the rooms on this level. Empty. I figure we've wasted at least two or three minutes talking since Apprentice Dude disappeared with the painting. He could be anywhere by now.

"Which way?" I whisper.

Jonah thinks for a beat and then whispers back, "He has a head start on us, but he also has that big painting to wrestle with, so he's not moving fast. He thinks he has the real portrait, so he'll be looking to make a quick getaway, but he still has to keep up his cover story until he gets off the grounds, in case he runs into anyone else."

I nod along, and he continues, "The artist is staying in the guesthouse closest to the stables; I heard Mr. Birch instruct one of the footmen where to deliver a telegram that came for her last week. So my guess is that her assistant will keep to the path toward her cottage until he hits an opening in the estate wall that will let him out into the street. I know just where that is; it's not far from the servants' entrance."

I turn to gape at him. "Okay, forget Einstein. Your new nickname is Sherlock. Have you read any of those?"

He ducks his head and murmurs, "No. I—I don't read very well."

Drat, Hannah. You should have anticipated that. Now you've embarrassed him, when it's so not his fault that he doesn't go to school. I keep my voice light. "Well, he's a brilliant detective, but I think you might be his match. We have a thief to catch. Ready?" I swing the camera around to my back, peek into the hallway again to make sure the coast is still clear, and then signal for Jonah to follow me. I do my best Catwoman impression as we dart from doorway to stairwell, then slip out the front door. We edge along the exterior wall until we turn the corner.

"There!" Jonah says, pointing to a skinny man wobbling under the weight of a sheeted painting, far in the distance at the edge of the estate grounds.

"Run for it!" I shout, taking off down the path. Jonah

follows, and if he thinks it's weird that a girl is keeping pace with him, despite all the layers of fluffy stuff underneath my dress and a camera slapping against me, he doesn't say a word. He just huffs and puffs alongside me, pumping his arms as hard as I am.

Apprentice Dude doesn't even sense us coming. All it takes is one teensy nudge by me from behind, and he goes toppling over, getting all tangled in the sheet that comes loose as he drops the frame.

"You!" he gasps. He struggles into sitting position, then spots the exposed painting on the ground. The one that is NOT of Margaret Dunlap. "The portrait!"

His eyes dart back and forth among Jonah, me, and the canvas. Finally he sputters, "I—I don't understand."

"That's right, you don't, buddy," I say, jabbing my finger into his face. It's two against one, I'm exhilarated from my run, and he's all twisted up in a sheet; the combination makes me extra brave. "But we do. Mademoiselle Cassatt's not doing any touch-ups hours before an unveiling. That would be crazy. So you lied. Because you were trying to steal the painting. Just admit it."

He ignores my order and asks, "But where is the portrait?"

Jonah snorts.

I roll my eyes. "Wow, you really don't get it. You're toast. You never had the real painting, and you never will. Deal with it."

The man puts his face in his hands and hangs his head. "I was so close."

"Yeah, you were soooo close to stealing a worthless landscape," I say. "Gold star for you."

The man shakes his head, still covered by his hands. "The portrait's not much more valuable. It wasn't about that."

Interesting. Now I'm intrigued. "What, then?"

"I didn't want it unveiled," he says through his fingers. "I didn't want anyone to see it."

I exchange a look with Jonah, but it seems Sherlock hasn't pieced things together yet either, because he looks just as puzzled as I am.

"But you told me you were there for the sittings," I say. "And you're Mary Cassatt's apprentice. Wouldn't that make you feel proud of it? Wouldn't you want the whole world to see what she created?"

He drops his hands and looks at me, and his eyes have this weird hard look in them. "I knew that if no one had the chance to see this portrait, Mademoiselle Cassatt's bright light would begin to dim, and attention would move on to the painting world's rightful artistic virtuosos, such as myself. Everyone knows men are the ones who should be honored and acknowledged for our creative genius. She doesn't deserve glory. Not—not a weak-minded *female*!"

He spits the last word out of his mouth like it's a watermelon seed.

I drop my jaw. "Seriously, dude?"

Both Jonah and Frenchy stare at me.

"Dude? What is this 'dude' word? *Je ne comprends pas.*"

I just laugh softly. "Listen, I've got news for you. Your boss is . . . She's . . . well, let me put it this way. In a hundred years her paintings are gonna hang in museums all around the world, and schoolkids are gonna do reports on her. Who are *you*?"

"Augustus Renaldo," he answers, tilting his head in confusion.

I pretend to think hard for a second. "Yeah . . . nope. Not a single person in the future will have your name on their lips. The only way your memory is going to be preserved for all time is in the picture this camera contains. The one proving you're a spineless, gutless, sneaky *nobody*. Oh, and by the way, in case it isn't totally clear"—I drop my voice to a whisper and lean down so he can hear me—"this here weak-minded *female* just B-U-S-T-E-D BUSTED you."

There's dead silence when I stop speaking, and then Jonah quietly claps. "That was amazing."

I flash him a giant smile. "Thanks."

We both turn to face Augustus-You-Bustus, who's studying the grass.

"What were you planning to do with the painting?" I ask.

"Nothing! That is to say, I planned to destroy it the first opportunity I got."

Wow. Just wow. The guy's ignorant *and* heartless. I can't even.

"What will you do with me?" he asks.

My intention all along was to see justice done and turn the thief in, and he definitely deserves to rot in jail. But then I realize what will happen if I run yelling for the Berwinds right now. Gossip about the attempted theft will be all over Newport in an hour and cause chaos for the ball. The drawing room—aka the scene of the crime—will fill with cops and there won't be any chance for Maggie and me to switch places. That's so not fair to her. She deserves to be back for her own ball. Maybe it's enough just to know that the painting is safe and sound.

I narrow my eyes. "You're really extra lucky that I don't have time today to turn you over to the authorities, like you deserve. But if I'm gonna let you get away with this, I do have terms."

"Terms?" he asks, sounding scared.

Good. He should sound scared.

I raise my finger, as if to poke him. "You're going to leave. ASAP. Pronto. Don't say a word to anyone, do not pass Go, do not collect two hundred dollars. And don't try to figure out what that means. Just leave. And never, ever, EVER come back or try to contact Mademoiselle Cassatt, or anyone in my family, or even anyone remotely related to any of the families I might know in passing. You should probably just switch to painting houses, in fact. Or fences. Or porta-potties, whenever those become a thing. Do you get me?"

He nods so fast, I'm afraid his head might pop off his neck. Wow. This is actually kind of FUN! I feel like a superhero. Jonah looks like he's trying not to laugh, but in a supportive way, not a mean way.

"How do I know you won't use that picture you took against me the minute I leave here?" he asks.

I sigh, because he's seriously pushing his luck. I hold the camera out in front of me and flick open the door that contains the roll of film. It unspools toward the ground, ruined. "Satisfied?"

Jonah gives me a look that can only be interpreted as, *Why did you DO that?* but I just shrug. "I have my reasons," I whisper.

He nods, and we both watch in satisfaction as Augustus-You-Bustus gets up and slinks out the opening in the wall, onto the street.

I turn and high-five Jonah, who seems a little unsure of how to do it but plays along. Jeez, is the high five not even a thing yet? There sure are some major inventions coming in the twentieth century!

"What do we do now?" Jonah asks.

"We have to put the portrait back on the wall, so it's all ready for tonight."

Jonah shifts from one foot to the other. "I owe you an apology. I did not put full faith in the words of a fortune-teller, but I'm a true believer now. She said there would be an art heist, and there *was* an art heist! Or an attempted one, at least."

I blink. If Jonah's mind is blown by that, imagine if he knew the rest of the story—like the fact that I hail from the future.

A future I'm about to zoom back to. I should be

crazy-excited about solving the art heist (and hello, vindication—I knew Jonah was innocent!), and part of me is. I'm so curious to see what it will be like to go home and have the original portrait hanging there and no one talking about the art heist, because it never even happened. It's going to be so weird. At least it's one less thing Trent can mess up on his tours.

But as great as all that is, I can't help being bummed that so much of my short time here was spent hiding and waiting, when there's all this history to explore. I never even glimpsed Mr. Berwind! And I wanted more time to hang with Jonah where we could just chat.

I know I shouldn't be greedy, but I really wish this weren't all ending so quickly.

Chapter Twenty

Maggie

AFTER CHANGING OUT OF MY DIRTY uniform into a pair of very soft pink trousers and a blouse I found in Hannah's closet, and then taking a short nap, I feel much better. I still cannot believe the softness of these clothes. I flip through a couple of the books on her desk and ponder how to smuggle them back to my own time. After skimming the books on her shelf, I pull out one whose title I recognize. It's a brightly colored version of *The Wonderful Wizard of Oz*, and it strikes me that there are things in this time that are similar to my own. It makes me feel hopeful that not everything fades away for something newer or shinier.

Just before seven o'clock I hover near the reproduction

portrait. I've looked at it from all angles, close, far, left, right. It is not a bad facsimile. The dress is all wrong, but the artist got the lighting mostly right. I remember how many days I had to sit still in order for Mademoiselle Cassatt to capture my likeness. If I could do it again, I would ask her more questions about her life, even if that horrible Monsieur Renaldo pulled faces at me behind her back. It's a shame all her work was for nothing, since the original was never unveiled. I hope whatever we're doing here fixes that wrong, and Mademoiselle gets the credit she deserves. I feel like she is one person from my own time who would appreciate the advances made by women in this century.

And now, more than a century later, a photograph can be taken that looks as clear as real life. I must admit that there's something about painted portraits I like better. The texture and the brushstrokes breathe a life that's different from the two-dimensional photographs that adorn the shelves across the room.

"Hannah, dear?"

"Yes, ma'am?"

An elderly lady standing in the opening to the ballroom looks from me to the portrait and back to me again. She startled me, but I try not to let it show.

"I know I've been here for only a short time, but please call me Florence. You seem to be quite preoccupied with Miss Margaret this afternoon." She steps closer and looks up at the portrait again. "Is there something new you're seeing?" Her expression is curious, and though I've never seen her before, she makes me feel safe.

I take a deep breath, knowing I need to suppress all my recent thoughts, even though I want nothing more than to confide in this woman for some strange reason. "Did you ever wonder if the artist who re-created the portrait got it wrong?"

"Actually, yes, I have." She winks as she gestures for me to come closer. "The rumors are that the dress was originally green." She stares serenely up into my face hanging on the wall.

"Wha—?" I try to close my mouth, but I approach her side and gaze up. She's right about the dress, but at that moment something flickers in the mirror under the portrait. Clearly this woman must not be permitted to see Hannah and me talk.

"Did you hear that?" I ask, turning toward the front of the house.

"Oh goodness!" she says, taking a step toward the ballroom. "I'm sure it's the bride's mother stopping down to make sure the flowers have arrived. She's a big donor, so it's all hands on deck tonight. Elaine, the wedding planner, wanted to be here when the woman arrived, but the last time I saw Elaine, she was busy trying to make sure the caterer's truck could fit under the arboretum. I'll go run interference. I suggest you keep out of the way tonight."

"There's a wedding here tonight?" I feel a thrill of excitement, thinking about what a wedding in the twenty-first century will look like, and then a jolt of reality. How am I going to switch back with Hannah when preparations for a bustling party are happening behind me?

"You could probably stay in here and watch; the wedding will be intimate and confined to the ballroom, not this room." She pauses halfway to the doorway and looks at me, as if she's about to say something else.

I nod, hoping she leaves quickly, but not wanting to be rude. "Thank you."

I am a bit nervous to tell Hannah what a mess I've made of her life. Although, I've been thinking about it all afternoon, and I am fairly certain I could get better at running and kicking, if given the chance. I need to figure out how to sneak in some running when I'm not being watched at home. My heart jumps a little at the thought of creeping around behind my aunt's back. Avoiding my father when I'm back in New York will be easier, even though there won't be anywhere to run in the city. Perhaps at least I can modify my skirts somehow and run up and down the stairs. I imagine other girls in my time being interested, and for a brief moment I construct a fantasy in which I form a ladies' running club when I get back to school. I must admit that it will be nice to get home to a place where things make sense, even if I do plan on finding ways to resist some of society rules; now that I've been here, I can see how silly they are. It makes so much more sense for women to be able to do the same things men can do.

I sigh in anticipation, knowing it is a sound that would be admonished by my aunt as self-indulgent and childish—but then I giggle recklessly at the thought of her dismay at my planned rule-breaking. I take a deep breath to try to get control of my emotions. Any moment now Hannah expects me to appear, ready to return to 1905. As Florence slides the pocket door shut, I turn to the mirror and climb slowly onto the sideboard, thankful the tourists are all gone.

I push the portrait frame aside. The mirror shimmers, and Hannah's (or rather, my) face appears in the glass.

A large painting is propped next to her on the sideboard. "Hey, Mags. There's no time to catch you up on what's been going on here, but guess what? We caught the thief! It's wasn't Jonah. He's totes innocent! It was really this dude named Augustus Renaldo."

"What? That horrible man? Now that you mention it, though, he likely should have been on my list of suspects." I think about the way he's been glaring at me during all our portrait sittings. I clear my throat. "Before you continue, Hannah, I must confess something."

"Uh-oh." Her face falls. "What'd you do? Don't tell me I'm grounded for life!"

"I—I don't think so," I stammer, though I don't know what "grounded" means.

She turns at a noise behind her and then faces me again. "Confess later. It's getting busy around here, so if you want to attend this ball, now's your chance. Unless you'd rather stay me a little longer?" Her voice sounds hopeful, but I shake my head.

"No, I'm ready to return."

She nods slowly. "Yeah, I get it." Then she gives me a big smile. "Don't worry about me, Mags. I can totally fix whatever you messed up. I'm glad we got to do this." She glances behind her again. "Are you ready?"

I nod my agreement. "It will not be easy going back to wearing stiff petticoats. Should I hold on to something?" There are no handrails, but I steady myself against the wall.

"Wouldn't hurt. Here goes nothing." She lifts her arm and places her fingers on the edge of the age spot. The mirrored glass shimmers. It looks as though someone dropped a pebble into still water. I reach out to touch the same spot, and press my fingers to hers.

And . . .

Nothing happens.

My panicked expression must match Hannah's. I remove my fingers and press anew, so hard that I half expect them to pass straight through the glass.

Nothing.

Hannah's eyes—well, mine actually, only Hannah's controlling them, of course—are as wide as saucers. "It's not working!" she says.

I am quiet, my mind racing. Am I truly stuck here? What is happening?

Hannah removes her hand and jerks it through her hair. "Think, think, think," she murmurs.

"Pardon?"

She glances up as if she'd forgotten I was here. "Sorry.

I talk to myself when I'm trying to work something out. I was so positive that our swap had to do with the stolen portrait. I mean, it has to. It's waaaaaay too coincidental that I would land here on this exact weekend. But I stopped it from happening, so . . . mission accomplished, right? All that's left to do is hang it back up and wait for the big reveal."

"Perhaps that's it!" I cry.

"Huh?"

I press my palm against the mirror. "Perhaps it's not fait accompli until the portrait is hanging in its rightful place again."

"Fate what?" she asks.

"It's French for, how did you phrase it . . . 'mission accomplished.'"

Hannah nods. "Well, that's worth a try. Hang on. Gimme a sec, 'cause this frame is heavier than fifty algebra textbooks."

She struggles to lift the painting beside her but manages to get her arms around it. The back of it comes closer to the me in the mirror, and then—

Something crashes behind me, and I turn, expecting to see Florence or Hannah's father enter and scold me for being perched on the furniture.

What greets my eyes is completely unexpected, and I blink, trying to absorb what I'm seeing. It's not Hannah's father or anyone else I've met in the twenty-first century. It's not Aunt or one of the servants from 1905, either.

Another crash catches my attention, and I look down to the floor. A small boy with wheels on his shoes whizzes past the sideboard I'm perched upon. He doesn't see me, so I quickly scramble off the edge and hide behind a large potted plant near the window.

The room has somehow transformed. The antique furnishings have disappeared. A giant divan with plush cushions takes up most of the middle of the room. An enormous TeeVee hangs on the opposite wall. Even the sideboard I was perched on is different. It's made out of some sort of metal. The only thing the same about the room is the painting that covers the ceiling, the mural of the god of the north wind being driven out by spring.

What in heaven's name is happening? I pray Hannah is still at the mirror. As soon as the boy glides out of the room into the foyer, I leap back onto the sideboard and push the painting aside again.

Hannah is peering into the mirror around the side of her frame, with a tortured look on her face. "OMG, Mags, there you are. I was so freaked that you'd disappeared! What's the deal there?"

"I . . . I don't know, but I suspect that you've changed the future by hanging that portrait. The house appears to be a private residence, no longer a museum."

"Noooooooo! Then where's my dad?" Hannah gulps, and she quickly removes the painting from its hangers. She stares hard past me as though she's trying to see through me to what's happening in the room behind me.

The mirror shimmers again, and this time when I look around, the room has gone back to the way it looked before—antiques and the sounds of the wedding preparations from the next room.

I breathe a sigh of relief. "It worked. All is as it was before."

"Okay, then. We caught the thief, but hanging the portrait back where it belongs makes the future go all wonky *and* clearly doesn't switch us back. I don't get it." Hannah takes a gulp of air. "What are we supposed to do now? If the goal wasn't to solve the crime, what is it?"

I have no answer.

Chapter Twenty-One

Hannah

THINK, HANNAH, THINK.

My skin prickles everywhere, like I'm hugging a porcupine, and my throat is so dry, it's as if I gargled cotton balls. Yes, we got back to the normal time line by taking down the portrait, but what if the only way to keep things like they should be is to . . . not switch back?

I can't believe I'm even having that thought.

Up until now this whole experience has been mind-blowing and weird and cool and intriguing. I wanted even more of it. But now? What if I really am stuck in 1905 . . . forever?

What if Maggie and I have actually done something

to the whole space-time continuum? What happened to everyone I know in that alternate-reality version of the future, where The Elms wasn't a museum? Was Dad trapped somewhere else in time? I refuse to believe, even if he was, like, king of the world in that time line, that he was happier without me. And I definitely was born in that time line too, because I didn't shimmer away to dust particles when I hung the painting. What if what we've done isn't fixable? Would I be willing to live out the rest of my days here in this century, to keep everyone I love in the future they're supposed to be having? Sure, Dad would be raising Maggie-me instead of real-me, but he wouldn't know that. And, I mean, I always wished so hard that I could see this place in its glory . . . but not for forever!

WHY IS THIS HAPPENING?

A few hours ago I was having so much fun playing detective with Jonah, aside from the boring waiting-around part. We solved a real-life art heist, for crying out loud.

But now?

Now I'm scared. Legit scared.

And I don't like it one bit. Okay, so, Slender Man is super-creepy and that *Doctor Who* episode with the weeping angel statues mega-freaks me out, and I'm dying to see that new zombie movie that just got released, but this is a different kind of fear. Those are hide-under-the-covers, tiptoes-up-your-spine, but secretly-kinda-love-the-adrenaline fears.

This is a cold, raw, brick-size-battery-leaking-acid-in-my-belly fear.

I feel light-headed, and it's not because my dress is laced too tight. It's because my whole *life* is feeling very *un*laced.

No. No, no, no. I can't fall apart. Or give up. That is not the Hannah Jordan way. The Hannah Jordan way is to choose a new plan of attack.

It's what I do on the soccer field when the opposing team's defender intentionally jabs her elbow into my side as we fight for possession.

It's what I did last summer when Trent threatened to get the Antiquities Society to say I couldn't swim in the fountain after the museum closed for the day, and I retaliated by putting on Dad's Halloween werewolf mask and hiding out in the Narnia wardrobe in the Satinwood Room until he appeared. (Let's just say he was very invested in keeping his reaction just between us.)

And it's what I need to do now.

I square my shoulders and suck in a deep breath that almost makes its way into the super-deep part of my lungs. Then I face Maggie.

"I'm good. Just needed a sec. Okay, so now we gotta figure our way outta this mess. Do you have any ideas?"

Maggie shakes her head slowly, and I drop my chin. "Me neither."

I raise my eyes when I hear her whisper. "What?" I ask. "I didn't catch that."

"I'm scared," she repeats. I can only nod, because the lump in my throat is growing by the second, much as I try to push it down through sheer will. She puts her fingertips to the mirror, and I match mine to hers. Even though I know it won't switch us back through time, it's comforting to connect with a friend at a moment like this. I wish she were here in person, so I could actually feel her touch. So I'd have a friend to turn to, instead of being stuck a hundred years in the past, entirely on my own.

Except . . . I'm not *entirely* alone. Jonah's been the very best kind of friend. The kind who helps first and asks questions later. And he's smart. Supersmart. Maybe three heads are better than two.

"Maggie, I think—I think maybe we should tell Jonah

the whole story. We don't have any bright ideas, and I just have this feeling about him. Like maybe he will."

It's so weird to watch my own face in the mirror as all kinds of expressions pass over it. But in the end, she nods. "If you feel you can trust him, I suppose it couldn't hurt at this point."

She barely gets the words out before I'm off the sideboard and racing for the kitchen, my dress flapping.

I try to make myself invisible as I sneak past and head straight for the coal tunnel. When I left Jonah after we brought the real painting back to the drawing room, he confided in me that he was planning to catch a nap in his secret spot, before reporting to work to help during the ball. I hate waking him up, but if this doesn't qualify as an emergency, I don't know what would.

I rap on the door, and step back when he opens it.

"Maggie?" He squints at me in the shadows, and I can hear the sleep in his voice.

"Can you come with me again?" I ask, gasping for breath.

He nods quickly, stepping into the tunnel. I'm head lookout as we (yet again) sneak back up to the drawing room. I breathe a sigh of relief when I spot Maggie patiently waiting in the mirror.

Jonah's reaction is . . . not quite a sigh of relief. He nearly jumps out of his shoes, and I grab his arm to steady him.

"Okay, so I know this is going to sound loony tunes," I say.

"Completely insane," Maggie adds, and Jonah jumps again.

"Who's she?" He chokes out the words, not taking his eyes off the mirror.

"She's me," I reply.

"And I'm her," Maggie adds.

Jonah sinks to the floor. I plop down beside him. I'm pretty sure I hear Maggie catch a breath at how unlady-like I am about it, but she keeps quiet.

"So it's like this . . . ," I begin. With a little help from Maggie, I bring him up to speed on the last twenty-four hours.

He shakes his head a lot. A lot a lot. I even catch him pinching his own arm to try to wake himself up. But when Maggie demonstrates my iPhone for him in the mirror, I can see him start to come around to the fact that—as crazy as it sounds—we might be telling the truth. "I—I don't even know what to say, what to think. I did puzzle at your manner of speaking," he says, looking at me in wonder, "but I told myself it was only that I didn't spend any time among the upper class."

I can't help a tiny giggle. "Nope. It's a futuristic thing. We all talk like this."

"I'm sorry if I'm struggling to wrap my brain around this. I *am* trying," he says.

I snort, which seems to surprise him. Not sure if it's because I'm not taking his apology seriously or if girls in 1905 just never snort. Or maybe both. "Like that's something to be sorry about? If some weirdo popped up in my basement and started going on about psychics and body swaps, I'd have called 911 faster than you can say, 'Hey, Siri, dial 911.'"

"I—I don't—"

"It's a phone number for the cops. You know. The po-po? The fuzz? Five-oh?"

Jonah just gives me a look and shakes his head. "The future must be a very odd place indeed."

"Oh, you have NO idea. We have Kardashians, my friend."

I don't have a chance to explain (probably best, since how could you ever explain them?), because Maggie speaks from behind me.

"It is odder than you could ever imagine."

I jump a little. I was so distracted, I kind of forgot she was still here(ish).

"Maybe, but I'm pretty eager to get back there," I say as I stand up and begin pacing the room, like my grandpa Fred does when we play chess and I have him almost cornered. He claims pacing helps him see "the big picture" and all the possible outcomes. Considering that I've beaten Grandpa Fred at chess exactly once (and even that was on a technicality), I'm thinking that pacing might work. Plus, I'm desperate to try anything at this point. "Call me crazy, but in my gut I still feel like the answer to switching back has to do with the painting. It's the only thing that makes sense with the timing, and the fact that taking it down from the mirror made us swap in the first place, and hanging it back up made the time line shift," I say.

I was mostly speaking this out loud to puzzle through it on my own, but from behind me Maggie pops up with the same follow-up question I was about to ask myself.

"But then why didn't it work when we hung the painting back in its rightful place?"

I turn to face her, my eyes big and sad. "I don't know. And how can we restore the painting to where it belongs without creating a ripple effect in the events of history?"

Jonah is quiet, leaning against an upholstered chair in the center of the room, his eyes all faraway-like. He even rubs his chin the way people on TV do when they want everyone watching to know they're thinking deep thoughts.

After a second he says, "What if you didn't have to?"

"Didn't have to what?" I ask.

He lifts his head and looks back and forth from Maggie to me.

"What if the painting could still hang in its rightful place at the conclusion of all this, but you could put it there without disturbing this time line?"

"How would we accomplish that?" Maggie asks, but my own brain is whirring.

I blurt out, "By hanging it there in the future! Jonah, I'm picking up what you're putting down! I'll say it again: you're brilliant, Einstein!"

He blushes and ducks his head. "Hardly. I have barely any schooling."

I wave him off. "Pfft. Whatevs. You have street smarts. In lots of ways that's even better."

"Might someone kindly explain what it is we're speaking of?" Maggie asks. "The two of you appear to be on the same page, but I'm afraid I have no idea at all what you're going on about. Whatever do you mean by 'hanging it there in the future'?"

I share an excited smile with Jonah, then turn to Maggie. "The only way we can be sure we're not affecting anything that happened between now—I mean, then—I mean, now for me—ugh. Sorry. This space-time continuum stuff is mega-confusing."

Maggie is squinting at me. I'm sure what I'm saying is harder to decipher than those Instagram posts that are nothing but a zillion hashtags strung together. I take a deep breath and try again.

"The future rippled because if the painting was never stolen, that fact changes the way things unfold from that moment forward. A hundred tiny things could happen differently all because Augustus-You-Bustus never took off with the portrait, and that's how we end up with a totally different time line, one where The Elms is some little kid's house instead of a museum. We changed the past, and in doing so we changed the future."

I pause to take a deep breath and make sure Maggie is still with me here. She's nodding, so I race on. "What I'm trying to say is that we have to make sure everything happens exactly the way it already does in the history books. Anything that's recorded there has to stay exactly that way. *But* we can still return the painting to the wall and set things right. You'll just have to do it in modern time. No one has written the future into any history books yet, so there's nothing to disturb. And then we get to switch back to our own times. Easy peasy lemon squeezy."

Jonah laughs. "I like that expression."

"Heck yeah, ya do," I reply.

His eyebrows come together above his nose, but then he smiles and shakes his head.

I shrug and smile back.

For her part, Maggie still looks a little confused. "But if you have the painting *there*, how am I meant to hang it *here*?"

I'm ready for that question. The answer has been bouncing around in my head ever since I caught on to what Jonah was saying. "We leave it for you to find. Somewhere where it will be safe for the next hundred-plus years. Somewhere, say, in a tunnel under the house, for example."

Jonah grins and waves the key to the tiny hidden room. "Exactly what I was thinking."

I know it's the perfect hiding spot. Clearly no one in my time has any clue that place even exists. At least I'm pretty sure they don't. Dad definitely would have mentioned it to me. It's exactly the kind of thing he'd geek out over.

The painting will be safe there.

All we have to do is hide it in the tunnel room and then hide the key to the door somewhere where Maggie can find it in the future. She'll pretend she stumbled across the hidden room, discover the painting, and alert the proper authorities. Then we'll swap back right in time for me to be the one basking in the fame and glory of finding The Elms' precious missing masterpiece. I wonder if the Smithsonian will want to interview me. Or maybe even the *Today* show! Either way, I will finally, *finally* get the respect I deserve from the docents and everyone else who thought I was just a bratty kid getting in their way. It's going to feel amazing! Honestly, this scenario is even better than just swapping back and having the painting hanging there because it was never stolen. My heart trips in excitement!

"Okay, Maggie. Hang tight. Jonah and I are going to sneak the portrait to its hiding spot and lock it up. Then we'll figure out where to hide the key so you can find it in the future."

I step closer to Jonah and gasp when I take a good look

at the key in his hand! I didn't get to see it clearly when we were in the dark tunnel, but in the bright drawing room it's clear that it's not just any key but an old-timey skeleton one that—

No. It can't be.

"Can I see that for a sec?" I ask.

Jonah nods and passes it to me. I cradle it carefully in my hand, step to the sideboard, and climb up. Maggie's eyes go wide when I hold the key so she can see it.

"It looks just like . . ."

She doesn't even have to finish, because I'm already nodding hard. "I know."

We both blink as I carefully set the key flat against the mirror age spot that Maggie and I were both touching when we swapped places. It lines up perfectly.

The key and the age spot are an exact match.

For a second I think maybe *that's* going to be the thing that switches us back, but nothing happens. Even still. It's all the sign I need. We're totally on the right track now!

Jonah and I are supersleuths as we institute Operation Hide Maggie's Portrait. Fortunately, with all the preparations for the dinner party that comes before the ball, everyone is too wrapped up in their own work in

the ballroom and the dining room to pay us any attention. We wait for the coast to be clear, then duck down
the servants' stairs and straight into the furnace area.

In less than ten minutes we're back in the drawing
room, smiling at Maggie.

"This is the best plan ever. I have a very good feeling
about this," I say. I walk her through exactly how to find
the door in the tunnel, then add, "Okay, now to find the
ideal hiding place for the key."

I look around the room carefully, noting pieces that
aren't part of the museum in my time, and ruling out
obvious spots that would never sit undisturbed for an
entire century.

"What about one of the sconces?" Maggie asks.

"No good. They're reproductions. The originals
were sold at auction when Julia—"

I break off. I don't know how much Maggie wants
to know about her future. Maybe she's been reading
the signs around the museum or taking the tours. But
maybe she hasn't. If it were me, I would definitely NOT
want to know what's coming for me and everyone
around me, and if she's the same, I don't want to be the
one to tell her the house gets sold when her other aunt,
Julia, dies in the early 1960s. A bunch of stuff inside

went to auction before the Antiquities Society stepped in and saved the mansion from demolition.

Luckily, Maggie doesn't question why I just clammed up on her, and Jonah saves the day by distracting us when he flips a corner of the elaborate Oriental rug on the floor and gestures to the sewn-on label.

"What if we slid it in between the stitches attaching this tag? No one would ever think to look here. Is this rug still there in your time?"

"It is, but I'll bet the vacuum would catch on the bump the key would make."

"Vacuum?" Jonah asks.

"Never mind. Oh! This chair!" I point to a Louis XV armchair off to the side of the rug. It's 100 percent still there in my time and is too perfect a match to be a reproduction. Plus, the arms are padded underneath the upholstery, so if we can slip the key into the padding, there won't be any telltale lump to hint that anything's inside. It's the perfect hiding spot. "Be right back. I'm gonna grab a letter opener off Mr. Berwind's desk upstairs."

That takes me less than thirty seconds, and in another two I've made the tiniest of tears along a seam in the chair and buried the key inside.

Our timing is spot-on, because I'm just saying, "Mags,

do you want to—" when voices in the hallway make me slam my lips shut.

Someone's coming!

"And then I believe we should rearrange some of the seating in the drawing room. I don't want the petals laid until just before arrivals, so they don't begin curling at the edges, and I expressly do not want anyone near the portrait, of course, so please do . . ."

It's Mrs. Berwind giving instructions to one of the staff.

I shoot a desperate glance at Maggie. Jonah is standing every bit as still as one of the statues of cherubs in the conservatory next to us. His eyes are sheer panic.

Thinking fast, I hiss, "Maggie, your aunt is coming and they're talking about ball prep for this room! It's going to be too crazy in here to get privacy now. I'm so, so sorry but we *have* to push to tomorrow for the switch. Seven a.m. your time? This is all on you now, anyway. You know what to do?"

She nods, and I turn before even making sure her image fades. I grab a vase of fresh flowers and tip it over so that the water inside splashes across the marble floor. Three steps later, I'm next to Jonah.

Mrs. Berwind enters the room with the butler, and

both stop in their tracks when they see us. Maggie's aunt's hand flies to her neck. "Margaret! Whatever is going on in here?"

"Hello, Auntie." Yikes, I hope I got that right. Colette used this term when she was talking about Mrs. Berwind before, but if I'm misremembering, I'll totally blow my cover.

She doesn't react, so I must be okay. Her eyebrows arch, though, and I realize she's still staring at me, waiting for an explanation.

"I, um, well, I accidentally spilled some water, and everyone up here was so busy running around trying to get ready for tonight, so I slipped downstairs and grabbed this boy from the kitchen to help clean it up. I didn't know what else to do!"

Please buy it, please buy it, please buy it. I don't care if I get in trouble (I'm guessing Maggie will forgive me), but the last thing I want to do is cause problems for Jonah.

Mrs. Berwind's head cocks to the side. "Oh, honestly, Maggie. That clumsiness of yours is going to be the death of us both. What does it say about a young lady of your position?"

I wrinkle my nose and whisper what I hope is a super-legit-sounding "Sorry."

"And do keep your facial expressions mild, darling. You don't want your features freezing in any of those ghastly faces you make. I've been told on quite good authority that that is a genuine possibility. What a terrible tragedy that would be, come your debutante year."

"Yes, ma'am," I whisper, hiding my grin. Probably not the time to tell her how wrong she is about the whole face-freezing thing. Because, yeah . . . *science.*

"At any rate, thank you for your assistance," she says, turning to Jonah.

Beside me, Jonah nods but doesn't speak. I can almost feel him shaking with fear.

"Mr. Birch, can you please see to it that this is taken care of? Boy, you may return to your duties downstairs, and we are grateful for your help."

Jonah scoots out the door before I can even get a good-bye in, and Mrs. Berwind turns back to me. "Now, Maggie. Shouldn't you be dressing for the evening, young lady?"

My jaw drops open. I didn't even think about that. I'm 99.9 percent sure we've solved the mystery of switching back, but if I'm not meeting up with Maggie until the morning . . .

"Margaret?" Mrs. Berwind prods when I don't answer her right away.

"Oh. Yes, ma'am. Dressing. Evening."

Annnnnnd, I guess I know what this means.

I'm going to a ball.

Lemme try that again.

I'M GOING TO A BALL!

Chapter Twenty-Two

Maggie

MY EMOTIONS ARE A JUMBLED MESS when I realize I will miss the ball in my honor. I admit I was nervous about being the focus of attention, but I *was* looking forward to it. I think about how Aunt Herminie will be so disappointed, but then I remember that to everyone else in the world, I *will* be there. There's an odd sense of rebellion in my stomach at that thought. Even if no one knows, I'm doing something against the rules.

There will be other balls. And perhaps I'll have time to read some of those books in Hannah's room. I don't have time for too much adventure, however. I have to retrieve a key that opens a mysterious room in the lower reaches of the house.

"Hey, you. Doing some last-minute dusting?" Hannah's father chuckles, catching me off guard as I'm climbing off the sideboard. He is dressed in a tuxedo, with a name badge clipped to the lapel, no doubt ready to work the evening's festivities. "Have you started packing yet?"

"No, sir." I look up and catch his eye. I have to forcefully make myself not glance at the upholstered chair in the corner, wondering if the key has been hidden under my nose the whole time.

He blinks once before he smiles. "I can tell something's going on with you right now, and I can't pretend to know what it is, honey. But you know you can talk to me if you need to." His expression tells me he's considering that statement. "Don't you?" He pauses again. "You really do need to think about packing, though, my dear Miss Hannah. Our flight is"—he checks his watch—"T minus fifty-six hours. Since you always wait till the last minute, why don't you start early this time while I'm busy with this wedding?"

I don't want to think about flying to the other side of

the country. If he makes me leave the mansion, I may never get back to where I really belong. Not to mention my abject terror at the thought of what it means to actually fly.

The tickle of a tear threatens, and I hurriedly wipe it away before he notices. I envy Hannah. She seems to be handling this time travel so well, and all I've succeeded in doing is making her father and Tara suspicious, forcing Hannah to lose her game, and frightening her beau. I briefly wonder what would have happened if Colette had traveled through time. Would she have gracefully slipped into the twenty-first century? Am I the only one who could mess things up so badly? And now I'm not even sure if I'll ever get back to my own time.

I must start searching for the key, but before that I've got time for a question that's been on my mind. Hannah's father turns to walk out of the room, and I find myself speaking. "Excuse me, Father? I mean, Dad?"

"Yes, Hannah." He sounds exasperated.

"Do you think people are much different now from how they were a hundred years ago?" I fold and unfold my hands. Finally, I clasp them behind me to stop fidgeting.

He looks thoughtful as he gazes out of the floor-to-ceiling glass door that faces the lawn.

"You know, I don't guess they are. Not really. I mean, we talk differently. We have different clothes and tools and even food. Technology, of course." He scratches his head. "But down deep? I'd guess that emotions and love and fear are mostly the same."

I stare at his face and let out a sigh of relief. My own father would have scoffed and left, with the question still hanging in the air. Would this man believe me if I told him I'm not really Hannah?

"I like that answer," I say.

"Why do you ask?" He crosses his arms across his chest.

"No reason. It's just something I think about." The idea of people essentially being the same under all their exterior appearances is comforting. It makes me feel as though things aren't really all that different.

I don't want to stay here forever, but knowing that human nature hasn't changed makes me feel less frightened about being trapped here for a little while.

"Kiddo, you never cease to amaze me." He stares at me like he's seeing me for the first time, then shakes his head as though he's changed his mind about something. "Go pack, Bug."

As soon as Hannah's father leaves the room, I scurry

to the chair and ever so gently run my fingers along the armrest. Hannah no doubt stitched up the seam, since it's no longer torn. I'm impressed that it's in such good condition after a hundred years. It's a shame I have to damage it. I pick at a loose thread along the braided cord sewn onto the fabric, and trying not to make a big tear, I slip my finger into the opening. No key.

"Well, you silly goose, you didn't really think you'd find it on your first try, did you?" I say quietly to myself. It must be in the other arm, and I cringe, knowing I've got to make another rip in the fabric.

No key.

Closing my eyes, I take a deep breath. I check the legs of the chair, to make sure it's the right one. But maybe it's not the only one. Maybe there's a match somewhere else in the house.

I run through the ballroom, around the tables that have been set for the wedding, to the dining room. I search the entire house looking for another chair that matches the one in the drawing room.

No chair.

No key.

I need help.

I've already asked a strange question of Hannah's

father, so I'm reluctant to ask him anything else right now. I'm at a complete loss for what to do. Standing in the middle of the foyer, I try not to cry as servants hustle around me, setting up for the wedding. I feel invisible. Suddenly the silver-haired tour guide from this morning walks past. He must know something about the folklore of the house. Even so, I remember our interaction in the Rose Room and brace myself for an angry response.

"Excuse me, sir?"

He stops and stares at me. "Did you just call me 'sir'?"

"You know a lot about this house, right?" I try to keep my voice from shaking.

He narrows his eyes at me. "Are you making fun of me, young lady?" He huffs. "I don't have time for silly questions."

"No, please," I say, wringing my hands. "Do you know anything about a key? Some story about a skeleton key being found in this house?"

He scowls and starts to walk away. "I know everything about this house. If there were a tale about a mysterious key, I would know it."

"But I heard . . ." I jog after him. "Are you sure?"

"Hannah Jordan. You purport to know more about this house than any docent." He wags his finger at me, and it makes me take a step back. "I'm sure I'm not going to waste my time playing the fool for something that is untrue. There is no story about a mysterious key." And he strides down the hall toward the servants' staircase.

"Is there another chair that matches the one in the drawing room?" I shout as he disappears out of sight, but he doesn't answer.

What now?

As much as I'd love to curl up on Hannah's bed and wait for someone else to fix this problem, I've got to try to find that key. There's no one else who *can* do this. It's all on me . . . for the first time in my life. Hannah's and my futures depend on it. I'm scared to death at the thought of messing this up for both of us. But instead of falling apart, I push my shoulders back and start up to the second floor, thinking maybe I missed seeing the chair the first time. As I climb the stairs, I spot the older woman from earlier. She knew the correct color of my dress in the portrait. Maybe she can help.

"Excuse me, Mrs.—" I almost curtsy, but I stop myself. "I'm sorry, I don't remember your name."

"It's okay. I haven't been volunteering here very long. I'm not surprised you don't." She smiles and holds out her hand. "Florence Ensminger-Burn. Just 'Florence' is fine."

With a sigh of relief, I say, "Can you help me with something? Or are you in a rush?"

"I was just going to get a bite to eat and then head home, now that everything is sorted out with the bride's mother. What sort of help do you need?"

My shoulders relax. "Do you know anything about a key that might have something to do with the mystery of the house?"

She looks thoughtful and then shakes her head. "I don't know anything about a key. But I do know a lot about the house—you might call it an obsession. Tell me more about what you're trying to find."

I can't help but smile. "It might have something to do with the upholstered chair in the drawing room."

A large woman pushes a cart with a wedding cake past us, and I'm momentarily distracted by the spectacle. I didn't expect something so elaborate, based on my observations of this time so far.

When I look back at Florence, she's laughing. "Oh, Hannah, you're too funny."

At the sight of my stricken face, she stops. "I'm sorry, dear. I thought you were joking. I thought for sure you knew the details about the furniture. Trent has been telling me how much you've studied the house."

As another member of the staff pushes a cart laden with table service past us, Florence takes hold of my arm. "Walk with me. Let's get out of the way of the traffic." She pulls me into the corner and guides me into the chair behind the ticket desk. "I didn't mean to laugh at you. When Julia Berwind died in the 1960s—Mr. Berwind's last surviving sibling—none of the other relatives could afford the upkeep of the house. Most of the furniture and paintings were sold at auction. It was only due to the Antiquities Society that the house wasn't bulldozed. It was quite an accomplishment by the society to save it."

I can't help but gawk. Seriously? Colette's mother inherits The Elms? I can't help but wonder why it's not me or Colette, or one of the other cousins. Part of me wants to know if Florence knows what happens to us. To me. I take a deep breath and close my eyes for just a second. At the very least, I know The Elms survives. It's probably not wise for me to know too much about what happens to my family. I shake my head to stop my thoughts from racing out of control. All that's important is finding that key, so that I can get home. So that

Hannah can get home. I try to remain calm.

"Some of the furniture is original, but not all of it?" I look past her to the ballroom, where elaborate floral arrangements are being placed on the tables.

She nods. "Most of it is original, actually. The Antiquities Society was able to buy back a lot of the original furniture over the years."

"The chair in the drawing room is original, right? The upholstered one?" I wonder if somehow I misunderstood which chair it was. But I know Hannah and I were talking about the same thing.

"A few items in the house are replicas. That piece is a spectacular reproduction. The Antiquities Society was able to commission an exact fabric match. Even the best of experts have trouble telling the difference." Florence smiles at me, as though the story is finished.

"I can't believe I didn't notice that." I feel almost as if I've betrayed my aunt and uncle.

Florence beams at me. "I know you're a history buff, my dear, but there's no reason why you would have known that. It's extremely hard to tell."

The key isn't in the house. What am I going to do? I close my eyes to control the panicky feeling in my stomach and tell myself it's fine. We'll be able to fix this.

I'll just meet Hannah in the mirror in the morning and advise her to hide it somewhere else, as soon as I find out from Florence which items of furniture are original.

Perfectly fine. No reason at all to panic.

Chapter Twenty-Three

Hannah

CINDERELLA. MIA IN *THE PRINCESS DIARIES.*
Giselle in *Enchanted*.

And now me.

Ball attendees, all of us. (And here's hoping mine doesn't end in disaster like two out of those three did. Unless you count a "stolen" painting as a disaster, because I can pretty much guarantee mine's ending with that one.)

But I'm optimistic anyway. I know the painting's not actually lost forever, and I'm feeling confident in the fix we came up with, which means that, for the first time since I landed here, I can actually let myself just relax and soak it all in.

And oh my WOW is there a lot to soak in. I mean, I grew up riding my scooter past the floor-to-ceiling shelves of china dishes in the butler's pantry, and hiding in the vault that houses the silverware (emphasis on "silver"), but I've never seen the real stuff all laid out on the table the way it is tonight. We'd never dare use it for any of the events we hold at the museum.

We have an art restoration expert from Venice coming to brighten up the mural in the dining room, but I can't imagine she'll ever be able to get it to shine like it is tonight. Shining like it's brand new. Because it is. This place come to life is better than I imagined any of the zillion-and-one times I've dreamed about it.

I could probably squeak four years of college tuition out of what the Berwinds dropped on this one shindig. While I was upstairs dressing, the entire downstairs was transformed by about forty billion rose petals that form an actual carpet over the floors. The ballroom is also covered in flowers—all varieties of roses bunched in big clusters, climbing the walls. There's even a rose-covered arbor set up in the doorway between the ballroom and the drawing room. Wow. This crew did a LOT in just a couple of hours. Although, obviously, people were busy assembling this somewhere else ahead of time. Maybe for months.

Tonight's ball is also a costume one, and the theme is Venetian. For whatever reason, high-society peeps super-love dressing up. They're like the grandparents of cosplay, I guess. I giggle at that thought. But honestly, the *dresses*. OMG.

Some of them are so wide, with hoops and petticoats underneath them, that the women have to walk sideways to get through the openings between the dining room and the ballroom. It's crazypants.

And the jewels. Dripping. Positively dripping. This one lady has a pearl necklace that reaches all the way down almost to her ankles, and at the bottom is this egg-size, canary-yellow diamond that practically scrapes the floor. Whenever she moves, she has to kick it out in front of her. Like, she's just kicking this massive diamond the same way I dribble my soccer ball down the field. If I weren't so busy gaping, I'd totally be laughing.

Of course, as grown-up as thirteen was back in Maggie's day, it's still not old enough to fully participate. Maggie won't get to actually attend any balls as a real guest until she makes her society debut. So while most of the women here will toss out their ball gowns (that probably cost as much as brand-new cars in my time) after they wear them once tonight, I'm in the same taffeta dress Maggie has on in the painting. The same one I "arrived" here in yesterday. Someone on the staff has cleaned and pressed it since then, but it still feels familiar . . . comforting.

That doesn't mean I didn't have to endure hours of mad-crazy preparations that involved a team of three. There was no way I could turn away Maggie's lady's maids without looking suspicious, but lemme just say, it is super-weird to be dressed by someone else. I don't really remember my mom much, because she died when I was only three, but I'm sure she must have tugged me into clothes. Since then? Uh, yeah. No.

Too bad corsets don't cinch themselves. (I did draw the line at the maids' bathing me, though.)

The one time I was really grateful to have someone else handling things was when it came to my hair. Curly hair is all the fashion, and let's just say that curling irons are pretty, um, primitive in 1905. They don't plug in; instead they're heated in the fireplace. I'm pretty sure Maggie would not be thrilled to come back to a head full of singed hair, so I let the maids have their way there.

I would have loved to wear makeup to the ball, since Dad puts his foot down on that at home, but no one suggested it. And it's not like anyone would have seen makeup on me anyway, since the party's theme means I have a real straight-from-Italy silk Venetian mask to hold up to my face. It makes me feel like more of a spy than I already am. I can hide behind this thing and people-watch all night.

Or at least for as long as I'm allowed to stay up and take part. It's okay for me to be here for some of the stuff—and I'm even kind of a guest of honor because of the portrait unveiling—but I probably won't be doing any actual dancing.

Still.

It's the best theater around, and these people aren't even acting.

"Darling, I do wish you wouldn't, just this once," a woman gliding by me in a rose-colored dress is saying to the man next to her.

"But I love it so. At a party of this sort—" He breaks off and taps a waiter on the shoulder. "I'm in need of a hard-boiled egg and a cold glass of milk."

The waiter's mouth falls open, but I guess he's well-trained, because he snaps it shut and smiles. "Certainly, sir. I'll see to it straightaway."

The woman drops her mask for a second, and I

know exactly who she is! She's Elizabeth Drexel Lehr. In my time a life-size portrait of her hangs in the ballroom, and postcards of it are sold in all the mansions. Which means the guy with her is her husband, Harry. They lived—*live*—across the street from The Elms, but their house wasn't as lucky as ours when it came to avoiding the wrecking ball. Now the weirdo request makes sense; he was meant to be a total jokester. I'll bet he thinks it's hilarious to make the staff scramble to fill his order. Me: not so much. Maybe because I know at least one person in the kitchen, working his butt off to make tonight a success, and now he—or somebody else down there—is going to have to interrupt the carefully choreographed meal prep to make a stupid hard-boiled egg. All so this guy can get his laugh.

That's just mean, if you ask me.

I don't wait around to see how long it takes Harry Lehr to get his milk and egg. Instead I slip into the conservatory and try to blend in next to a giant urn, so that I can observe and eavesdrop. Everything I've read about this time is so right on. These people are crazy-rich and crazy-obsessed with the weirdest stuff. Two women stand with their backs to me and give solid burns about the headpieces of at least four other women walking by. I know these families donate whole chunks of their fortunes to build orphanages and libraries and schools, so they can't be totally horrible, but they'd be shoo-ins for a *Real Housewives of Newport* reality show. Yikes.

The ones I'm really hoping to catch a glimpse of are Henry Jacobs and his wife. They have my favorite story of all. Mr. Jacobs had a brain tumor that left him convinced he was the Prince of Wales, and instead of checking him into a hospital, his wife just . . . went along with it. Like, she spent half his fortune hiring actors to play gentlemen-in-waiting in his court and ambassadors from other countries, and she brought in experts from London to make sure Mr. Jacobs got exact matches to everything worn by the real Prince of Wales so he could live out his days happily in his delusion. That's love, people.

Sadly, I don't see any guy dressed like a prince. Or no, really, it's more like *all* the guys are dressed like princes, but none are calling themselves actual royalty.

It's so strange to me that this is their everyday life. And this is not even that special an occasion, since they probably all have another ball to go to next week and about a billion musicales and sailing parties in between. I can't even imagine doing stuff like this all the time. It's amazing for tonight, but every night? I live for my flannel pj's and Netflix binges too much to give them up for nonstop red-carpet living.

Of course, that thought jerks me right back to reality. Because what if this *is* my future? But no. No, no, nope. I promised myself I wasn't going to stress tonight. The key is in the chair, the painting is in the tunnel, and we're going to set everything right first thing in the morning.

I exhale a deep breath. Or at least as deep a breath as I can manage. Corsets are torture devices. Maybe it's a good thing I won't be dancing tonight.

"There you are, my sweet. Why, you're practically one with the drapery. No wonder I've had to look every-where for you." Maggie's aunt looks so beautiful with tiny diamonds tucked here and there all over her fancy hairdo. The mask she's holding in her left hand has even more jewels catching the light from the chandelier above us. I can't believe I'm hanging out with *the* Herminie Berwind, whom I've spent my whole life hearing about.

"Are you ready for the big unveiling, darling?" she asks. When I nod, she smiles. "Now, don't be nervous. I know you don't love being in the spotlight, but everyone will be too busy looking at the portrait to stare at you."

I definitely don't say, "Or not."

But it's true. No one will be busy looking at the portrait, because you can't look at a painting that isn't there. This night is not going to go at all the way Mrs. Berwind thinks it is, and I feel bad for her. Maggie clearly adores her, and she's been nothing but nice to me, even if I'm still a little annoyed with the way she called Jonah "boy" without bothering to ask his name. It's too bad her name is about to be forever linked in the history books to the mysteriously missing Mary Cassatt portrait.

Mrs. Berwind takes me by the arm and pulls me gently into the drawing room and over to the sideboard, where that very Mary Cassatt is waiting, with a smile on her face.

When we reach her, she says, "*Bonsoir, ma cherie.* Are you ready to reveal the efforts of all these past months to everyone else?"

I feel terrible all over again, knowing how upset she's about to be, and the role I played in that. I wish so hard that I could just lean over and say, "No sweat, Mare. Your portrait is safe and sound in the kitchen boy's napping spot."

But I can't, obviously.

Because she'll want to rescue it, and that can't happen.

Not until Maggie does it in the future.

Instead I smile and nod. "I cannot wait." Not technically a lie.

The orchestra set up in the ballroom stops playing,
and I get my first glimpse of Mr. Berwind when he steps
next to us and clinks a spoon on a wineglass. He's larger
than life, just like I always imagined him. Masked guests
begin drifting in from the adjoining rooms, and in a matter of a minute there's a huge crowd. Colette is right in
front, and she shoots daggers at me—probably because
I'm on display with the Berwinds and she's blended into
the crowd. But whatever. I don't have time for her right
now. I keep my own mask fixed to my eyes and hope it
hides the panic I'm suddenly feeling. How is this going to
go down? How will everyone react when that curtain on
the wall drops and there's only a landscape of Newport
Harbor hanging there?

I don't have to wait long. Mr. Berwind clears his
throat and then talks in a deep, booming voice that
reaches the high ceilings.

"Thank you, honored guests, for joining us tonight
and sharing this special evening with us. As you may
be aware, we have our beloved niece Margaret Dunlap
spending time with us this summer, as she does each

year, and we're particularly happy to have her pres-
ent now as we invite you to witness the unveiling of
a quite impressive portrait of Margaret completed by
our esteemed guest, Mademoiselle Mary Cassatt. We
are humbled that she accepted our commission of this
painting. And now, without further ado . . ."

He lifts his arm, and I gasp along with everyone else
as two men roll down from velvet ribbons attached to
the ceiling directly above us. When did someone hang
those ribbons? Is that what all the hammering was earlier
when I was getting dressed? But how did those men get
up there? It's like Cirque du Soleil time! They flip and
twirl above us and then begin swinging in a giant back-
and-forth motion that brings them closer and closer to
the painting with each swing.

Each time the men's outstretched hands nearly reach
the curtain covering the portrait, the audience holds their
breath, wondering what they'll finally see. And each time
the men's fingertips brush the fabric, I hold my breath
too, knowing what they won't.

Finally it happens. The men swing close enough to
grab the fabric, and with their next arc back the curtain
whooshes from the wall.

Basically everyone exhales at once, and then it's

totally quiet for about three heartbeats, and *then* the entire room fills up with confused talking. Everyone is yammering over everyone else. I hear a whole lot of "I thought it was supposed to be a portrait of the girl?" and "But that's a painting of the harbor!"

Mr. Berwind is bug-eyed, and Mary Cassatt is clutching the sideboard like she needs it to hold her up.

Mrs. Berwind faints straight to the floor, her glass of red wine tumbling out of her hand and splashing everywhere.

Yep. Just exactly as shocking as I thought it might be.

Someone calls out, "We should send for the authorities!" followed by "And the doctor!" and "Yes, I can offer my carriage."

Mr. Berwind bends over his wife, fanning her face with his handkerchief, and after a few seconds he gets her awake and into a seated position. Phew. I was pretty sure the shock didn't kill her or anything, because that would have definitely been all over the history books, but still. It's a relief to see her upright.

I'm not exactly sure what I should be doing, so I just hang back out of the way as much as I can, and pretend to be too shocked for words. Once the carriages have taken off to grab the police and the doctor, things start to calm down a little and guests begin to shuffle around, like they aren't quite sure if they should go back to partying or leave or what. Definitely no one *wants* to go, because this is the best gossip in town, and I'm positive everyone is thrilled that they'll be able to say they were here to witness it. But they all have perfect manners, too, so I can tell it's a real dilemma for them. The whole crowd seems psyched when, at some signal from Mr. Berwind, the butler dude tells everyone they should adjourn to the ballroom and promises that fresh trays of champagne are on their way up from the kitchen.

In a matter of minutes the drawing room empties out, and the butler pulls all the doors into the room closed, sealing us off completely.

"Well done, Birch. We mustn't disturb the crime scene any more than it already has been," says Mr. Berwind, looking up from where's he's still bent over, fanning his wife.

Something about the words "crime scene" sends a bitter taste straight into my mouth.

Oh. My. Gosh.

I'm such an idiot.

How could I have let myself ignore the totally obvious?

If we play out the heist the way the history books have it recorded, that means the sweet, helpful, funny, smart kid working his butt off in the kitchen right now is about to have his entire life ruined. Because JONAH IS GOING TO BE CHARGED WITH STEALING THE PAINTING.

Chapter Twenty-Four

Maggie

I ROLL OVER AND THEN CURL AROUND Hannah's stuffed bear, trying to squeeze out a few more minutes of sleep. But with the light streaming in through the high windows, I know it's time to rise for the day. Her device chirps, and Tara's face lights up the screen. I take a chance and press the square that says "talk."

"Hello? Hannah? It's Tara."

Father installed a telephone at our New York City apartment, but it is three feet tall and affixed to a wall. You have to speak into a cone to be heard on the other end of the line. I love that I can hear my aunt's voice when she is at home in Philadelphia and we're not at the summer cottage together. This century has somehow condensed that technology into this handheld device.

"Hello, Tara," I yell at the device. "How. Are. You?"

"Do you have a bad connection? Why are you yelling?" Now Tara is yelling. "You weren't answering my texts, so I thought I'd call instead." The stilted timbre of her voice makes me wonder if she's still angry from yesterday. What she says next comes as a surprise.

"I'm sorry for what I said about Ethan. You're not mad, are you? Sorry it's so early. I've been up all night worried that you're mad."

Sweet Tara thinks I'm angry with her! "Tara!" I yell at the device, hoping she can hear me. "Of course I'm not mad. Friends are more important than boys."

I hear her sigh on the other end of the line. "Are you feeling better today? Do you want to come over later and watch a movie?"

"I have to be honest. I am not feeling well. I don't think I can spend time with you today, but perhaps tomorrow when I'm myself again. I'm not mad." I make a mental note to tell Hannah how sweet Tara has been. "I'm sorry, but I have to go now."

This technology isn't so hard to manage. Between my talk with Hannah's dad last night and the way I handled that telephone call, I'm beginning to feel slightly more confident in my ability to survive in the future, but thankfully we are going to fix this today. I might even be home by lunchtime.

I start to run downstairs—but then, with a pause to make sure no one is watching, I sling my leg over the railing and slide down a stretch of banister. It is as exhilarating as I've always imagined! At the bottom I dust off my trousers and then jog the rest of the way through the ballroom, into the drawing room, and scamper onto the sideboard. The clock reads just after seven o'clock—I'm a minute late. Hannah is already in the mirror, waiting. I'm sure my face is flushed, but perhaps she won't notice, given what I have to tell her.

"Good morning," I say, breathless. "There's a slight problem. You must move the key. The chair here . . ." I gesture to the room behind me. "It is a replica. The original was sold in the 1960s. Perhaps in Uncle E. J.'s wardrobe or Aunt's desk. They are both original furnishings, as confirmed by Mrs. Ensminger-Burn."

But before I finish my thought, my eyes drift over Hannah's shoulder.

My heart plummets. "Where's the chair?"

Hannah turns around, and I see Jonah behind her.

When she faces me again, she's gone pale. "I . . . I'm not sure. They took a bunch of the furniture out to make room for everyone at the unveiling. But no . . . It was here when the ball started. The police—they were taking things for evidence, and what if—"

Jonah dashes out of the room. I turn my attention back to Hannah. The color still hasn't returned to her face, so I try to console her. "I'm sure it has just been moved to another room. It often takes some time to return everything to its proper place after a ball." I do not tell her that it's far more likely the staff would have restored everything to where it belonged after the party, even though it would have been the crack of dawn after a full work day and night when they did.

Jonah returns two minutes later. He takes a deep breath. "The chair has been sent out for cleaning! Someone spilled red wine on it last night."

"Mrs. Berwind!" Hannah exclaims. "Her drink tumbled to the floor when she fainted. This is a disaster!" She closes her eyes and leans against the glass. I wish I could say something comforting, but I can only put my hand on the mirrored reflection. Her words are hard to make out. "Omigod, omigod, omigod."

Jonah's expression morphs several times. "Miss . . . I

mean, Mag— I mean, Hannah?" He's clearly struggling with how to help—and it occurs to me that he shouldn't even be out of the kitchen, let alone in the middle of the drawing room. "I'm sorry. I was hoping to steal away long enough to say good-bye in person, and I really wish I could stay and help now, but Chef is going to notice I'm gone if I don't get straight back. I can't afford to get caught."

Hannah's face pales, as though a ghost skidded through the room.

I'm not sure what that's about, but I don't stop to puzzle it out. We don't have time to delay. "Jonah, you should go!" I channel my father's most take-charge voice. "Listen to me, Hannah. You've got to find out where that chair is going. Find it and get the key back if you can—move it to my uncle's armoire. In the meantime I'll do my best to break into the tunnel room."

Hannah finally looks up at me with hope in her eyes. "Yeah. Maybe you can get into the room without the key. Go try that now. And then meet back here this afternoon at my five o'clock, after the last tour goes through on your end."

"By the way, we don't have much time. Your father is planning a two-week trip to California. We—that is to say you—depart in two days." I jump down before she can react. I'm afraid my own fear will show if I look at her too long. If I'm to retrieve that painting before Hannah's father tries to make me leave on vacation with him, I have to find a way to open that door.

The house is quiet, and most of the evidence from the wedding is gone. The front doors will open for visitors soon. I creep down the back servant stairs to the kitchen. It's the first time I've been down here in the future, and it's as silent as a crypt. I'm used to the main floor being quiet, but here on the lower level it should be bustling with servants preparing the morning meal at this time of day. A red light mounted in the corner of the hall blinks. I know now that it's a device designed to alert Hannah's dad to intruders, so I'm not worried.

I creep through the butler's pantry and past the kitchen, briefly pausing at the framed posters under glass on the wall. I still have a hard time believing my very existence is now condensed into historical anecdotes about how things were done in the early days of the house. I resist the urge to stop and read.

Hannah and Jonah gave me very specific directions on how to find the location where the painting is hidden, and I know exactly where the coal enters the house.

Uncle E. J. brought me down here once to show me the train track coming into the basement. The deeper I get in the house, the more my teeth chatter. It's damp and cool, but I'm also afraid I won't be able to find the painting. I pull open the door that leads into the boiler room, and then I descend a set of metal stairs. As I walk between the brick wall of the tunnel and the tracks, I peer into the cart resting on the rails; bits of artificial coal line the inside, obviously to show guests what the lifeblood of this house used to be. The only light comes from a series of bulbs hanging from the ceiling.

Aunt would faint dead away if she could see me down here! But this is important.

I feel along the wall. Hannah said there was a door, but I can't see very far down the tunnel, so I have no idea how long I need to walk. When I reach the end, there's just a brick wall. No door. I think I must have missed it, so I retrace my steps. It must be here! But it takes four trips up and back in the tunnel before I'm able to feel an indent. Even with my forefinger on the keyhole, I can barely make out the door about two feet off the dirt floor, flush with the brick wall. There is so little light down here, it's almost impossible to see. There's no handle. I can't find any hinges. There's nothing to grip, but I try inserting a fingernail into the tiny crack. Hannah's nails are disgusting nubs, but even with my longer ones, I wouldn't be able to make the door budge. At all.

I'm relieved to think there is a chance that it has not been opened in more than one hundred years, but on the other hand, I have no idea how to get inside.

I rummage in my pockets, hoping something I brought with me to pick the lock will work. There weren't many sharp objects in Hannah's room, but I found a pencil, a tiny jeweler's screwdriver (I'm amazed, but apparently Hannah makes jewelry—she has a whole box of beads and wire), and a piece of metal bent into a spiral.

Nothing works.

There is no way to get into that room without the key. Or dynamite, which doesn't seem plausible. The only person I can think to ask for help again is Florence.

She's my only hope to try to track down that chair and key, if Hannah can't do it in 1905.

Chapter Twenty-Five

Hannah

TURNS OUT, IT'S NOT HARD TO FIND the chair. Well, sort of. It's not hard to find out where the chair *is*, if you know who to ask . . . which Jonah did. (He was able to slip a note—well, part note, part drawing, since he doesn't read or write all that well—into the sugar bowl of the tea service that was sent up from the kitchen for me. Don't get me started on how completely terrible I feel over getting Jonah involved in this mess, especially now that he's going to get blamed for a crime he didn't commit. It really doesn't ease my guilt that he still keeps risking his job to help me.) The problem is that the chair is nowhere near where we are. Specifically, it's on the

6:02 a.m. train to New York City, where it will get some sort of special remove-red-wine-from-imported-silk dry-cleaning process.

I can only hope the focus of their attention is going to be the stain itself and not on the whole chair. I know I tucked the key deep into the padding of the arm and Jonah stitched the rip neatly, so a surface cleaning shouldn't reveal its hiding spot, but still.

Here's praying it won't matter either way because in the meantime Maggie will have broken into the tunnel room and found the painting and all will be set to normal in both our time periods.

But at the moment I'm having a super-tough time clinging to that hope. I know how hard that room is to break into.

Because Jonah and I are currently trying to do it too. Luckily, his job involves lots of time in the coal tunnel, so as long as I'm not caught with him, he won't arouse any suspicion by being here. At least we have that going for us.

If Maggie can't get in but we can, the endgame is the same. We can find a new hiding place for the painting, she can find it there in the future, and all will be perfection.

If we can get in.

We've already tried a slew of other keys I was able to sneak out of Mr. Berwind's desk drawer, but no go on any of them. Nada.

"Maybe a hairpin?" I suggest. Even if Maggie can't wear her hair all the way up, she has a ton of these, probably to keep the sides pulled from her face. So luckily I have one handy. The only good thing about big skirts is that they come with big pockets.

"Who builds a door with hinges on the inside?" I ask, but Jonah just grunts. He's crouched eye-level with the lock, concentrating really hard on trying to pick it with the bent pin.

I answer my own question. "I guess someone who doesn't want the door to be discovered, huh? Was your, um, friend who gave you the key the one who installed it? Or do you think it was the architect's inside joke? Or maybe Mr. Berwind ordered it? It's really kind of genius."

"He did say Mr. Berwind didn't know about it. I'm fairly certain only he did. Too bad he made it impossible to break in," Jonah says, falling back onto his butt. "I don't see any way to retrieve the painting without the key itself. Besides, we'll have to clear out of here. It's almost time for the coal delivery, and this tunnel will get busy for a bit. I'll have to help with that, but perhaps we can continue to share ideas for possible solutions via notes in your lunch service."

But what possible solutions? As much as I've been dying to see things outside this house, I can't just leave Newport and race to New York City to track down a chair. For one thing, how would I get there? It's not like I can order an Uber or hop an Amtrak. Yes, Maggie lives there most of the year, but she can't just take off for home on a whim. A girl my age in this time would need a proper chaperone, gobs of luggage, *believable reasons for going*.

I have none of those things.

And forget sneaking there. As Maggie, I'd have zero chance of blending. Society women—even girls—attract attention. While I know a ton about this time period, I really wouldn't have the first clue how to get around on my own outside the walls of The Elms; I'm barely treading water inside them.

But all this worry is masking what's really making me feel like all Mr. Berwind's keys are in the bottom of my stomach, as opposed to in my pockets.

Jonah.

If we DO find a way to get to the painting and hide it somewhere Maggie can find it in the future and set things right for her and me, Jonah's life is still ruined.

And I have to tell him that he's the one who has to take the fall. I don't know exactly when he's accused, but he is. Only, how do I tell him that? I lay awake for hours and hours last night trying to come up with a plan to clear Jonah's name, but there's no possible way. We can't change what's already written in the history books. Clearing him would strand Maggie and me and alter the time line of history.

And yes, it's true that we already changed things slightly by ensuring that Augustus-You-Bustus didn't end up with the painting. But I'm desperately clinging to the hopes that in the time line where he did steal it, he followed through on his plan to destroy the painting right away to keep Mary Cassatt from getting credit for it, and then he resumed his regular life as a struggling artist, so therefore the course of his own future didn't alter based on whether he nabbed it or not. At the very least his name was never recorded in the history books, so I think we're okay there.

But Jonah's name is all over history's pages.

It totally stinks, but in order to get back to the right time line, so we can swap places and history can unfold the way it is supposed to, Jonah's gonna have to take the fall. And I'm gonna have to convince him to do it.

Jonah, who has been nothing but kind and eager to help, and who's been a true friend to me in a place where I had none.

I steal a glance at him as I trail him out of the tunnel. He smiles at me, and it's so sweet and friendly that my gut twists even harder. This guy didn't even know me before yesterday, and he has totally risked his job a billion times since to help me. He believed everything I told him when literally no other sane person would have, and his ideas and support have been the only things holding me together through all this. I don't know if I would have had the courage to confront Augustus-You-Bustus either time if Jonah hadn't been beside me as backup. I mean, I never would have known where to hide the painting if he weren't here.

And now I have to take a knife and stab him in the back.

Which sucks big-time.

Jonah holds up a hand to stop me just before we step out of the tunnel, and I crash into his arm. He puts a finger to his lips and jerks his head at the opening. Someone's there!

Once again Jonah saves the day. Couldn't he be a

jerk or something, so it wouldn't feel so terrible to tell him he's about to spend his life on the run? We ease deeper into the shadows.

"Goodness, it's distasteful," the voice is saying. Colette! What's *she* doing down here?

I hold my breath and strain my ears so hard, they hurt.

"I can finish taking your statement upstairs, miss. I can search for the kitchen boy on my own and return once I have what I need from him."

Oh God, it's happening already. I thought I had more time! Next to me Jonah gasps. I nudge him with my foot and whisper the quietest "Shh!" imaginable.

Colette must be talking to a police officer, since he said that thing about taking a statement.

"Of course it's true. My niece would have no occasion to lie, sir."

Mrs. Berwind is down here too? This is getting worse and worse.

"Beg pardon, ma'am. I certainly didn't mean to suggest otherwise. So, you were saying, you were on the staircase and saw . . ."

Oh no! What if Colette spotted me talking to Maggie in the mirror? How would I ever explain that one to the Berwinds?

"I saw a boy around my age, maybe even younger, dressed like a servant. I'd never seen him before, and I know all the upstairs staff. I mean, maybe not by name, but . . . Well, at least I recognize all their faces. He wasn't one of them."

Gee, aren't you just so wonderful, Colette? Couldn't be bothered to learn the names of the people who wait on you hand and foot. But that's okay, because you could pick them out of a lineup. Ugh.

The cop talks next. "So you didn't recognize this person?"

"I did not. Though, when I described him to Aunt, her lady's maid was in the room, and she said it sounded like I was talking about this Jonah person. She said he'd have absolutely no reason to be upstairs. None at all."

Colette sounds positively giddy as she continues. "Since I was just turning the corner on the staircase, I saw him but he never saw me. He poked his head into the hallway and looked around to make sure no one was watching. Then he darted out and dashed away. Clearly he was doing reconnaissance and planning his escape route. There's no other possible reason why he'd be in the drawing room when his place is down here. Well, that's it, then! I've solved the crime, haven't

I? I suppose the newspapers will want my interview. Auntie, I may need a new dress for the photographs."

At least it's Colette who made the accusation. It's already so easy to hate her, so I won't have to tarnish my good feelings about anyone I grew up admiring, like the Berwinds themselves.

But then it slowly sinks in.

I might not be the one placing him under suspicion, but *I'm* responsible for Jonah being charged in the first place. The newspaper articles from the time of the theft said only that a reliable eyewitness account from a member of the household put him at the scene of the crime and that his disappearance from Newport led investigators to believe he was guilty. But he never would have *been* at the scene of the crime yesterday if not for me! So it has always been my fault. My stomach churns, and I'm afraid I could throw up right here and now. I can still admire the Berwinds, but I just might despise myself.

"Just a moment," Mrs. Berwind says, jerking me back to attention. "Mr. Birch, was this the same boy who was helping Margaret with the water spill yesterday? Might that have been what he was doing in the drawing room? We did encounter him there ourselves, after all."

Beside me Jonah exhales slowly at the exact time that I tense.

No. No, no, no, no.

"Indeed it was, madam," the butler answers. "Shall we find your niece and clear this confusion up?"

"Let's be on with it, then." Mrs. Berwind leaves, and there is a rustling of skirts outside the tunnel.

"I have to get to my room!" I whisper as soon as the noises fade. "No—wait! You have to come too and hide there! We can't let them find you."

"Who cares if they find me? You'll be upstairs telling everyone I was in the drawing room helping you yesterday. On the other hand, discovering me in your room would create an entirely different sort of confusion."

I exhale, grab his hand, and pull him from the tunnel with me. "Jonah, I need you to not ask any questions right now. I'll hide you in my bedroom closet, but we have to hurry up the back staircase before they make it up the front one. So I need you to run."

To his credit he picks up the pace even as he says, "But—"

I look over my shoulder as I take the stairs two at a time. "Jonah, please. *Trust me.*"

I try not to let the lead weight that hits my stomach slow me down as I utter those words.

The fact that Mrs. Berwind is the perfect society woman means that she moves serenely and deliberately along the first-floor hallway to the central staircase and then up it. It's close, but we have just enough time for me and Jonah to reach my room using the servants' stairs, and I slam him inside my closet before there's a knock on my door.

I try to slow my gulps for air, which is not exactly easy after booking up two flights of stairs. "Coming," I manage.

Taking another deep breath, I answer. "Oh. Hello."

Here's hoping they buy my innocent act.

"Margaret," Mrs. Berwind says, following me deeper into the room and gesturing for Colette and Mr. Birch to join her. The officer lingers in the doorway, looking about as uncomfortable as I feel. "This gentleman has some questions for you regarding the boy who was helping you with that water spill in the drawing room yesterday."

"Oh. Okay. I mean, um, certainly." If ever there were a time to remember to speak like Maggie, it's now. *No slang, Hannah. You can do this.*

The policeman clears his throat and says, "Now, you

fetched this Jonah person to clean the water?"

Even though the door to my closet is shut tight, it feels like Jonah's eyes are pinned to me. I know that he's in there one thousand percent expecting me to eliminate him as a suspect and move the investigation along to someone else.

And I want to so badly, it hurts.

But.

If I do that and they clear his name, the time line shifts. The whole future changes. What does that mean for everyone I love? Jonah and I are becoming friends and he's great, but we're talking about people I love with all my heart. Like my dad.

As much as I want to help Jonah, I just can't take the risk.

I take maybe my deepest breath ever and face the policeman. "Well, I wouldn't use the word 'fetch.' After all, he was right outside the door. Almost lingering, to be honest. Which I found odd, but he was there to help with the spill, so I guess I didn't really think about it too much." I pause, making sure I have everyone's full attention. Then I add, "Only . . ."

They lean in. I squeeze my eyes shut for the quickest of seconds and say a brief prayer for forgiveness.

"Only what?" Mrs. Berwind asks.

"Well, I didn't think anything of it at the time, but he did keep glancing at the sheet covering the portrait, and . . . I'm just now remembering this! He asked me if I was excited about the unveiling, and when I said yes, he said, 'It's such a lot of money to just hang on a wall,' which was a very odd thing to say. I replied I didn't know anything about its value, and he just said, 'A custom portrait like that . . . it must be worth a lot.'"

Colette sucks in a breath. I can't be sure, but I swear I hear the softest thud from inside the closet, almost like Jonah slumped against the wall. The lead in my stomach moves all the way to my feet. I've never felt so horrible in my entire life. But I have to keep going. I *have* to do this.

"I just attributed it to him being from a different class, and I thought perhaps it's not rude to mention money where he's from, so I let the whole topic drop. But then . . ."

This time it's the officer who says, "Go on."

This is it. I go in for the kill. "Well, a bit later I decided I wanted to thank Jonah for his help, since my aunt and Mr. Birch here interrupted us before I'd had the chance, so I asked Mrs. O'Neil if she might point me to where I could find him, and she said . . . she said . . ."

"What?" Mr. Birch urges, before remembering his place and clearing his throat. "Pardon me."

I shrug. "She said yesterday was his day off, and once he'd taken delivery of the coal in the morning, there would be no reason at all for him to be in the house prior to reporting in the evening to assist with the midnight supper that accompanied the ball."

The police officer snaps his notepad shut. "I'd say we have what we need, Miss Dunlap. Thank you."

"Let's remember who first cast suspicion on this Jonah person," Colette says, pushing past me to follow the officer into the hallway. Mrs. Berwind and the butler follow. "I'll still speak to the press. Auntie, I *can* get a new dress, right?"

I close the door on them and sink onto my bed. Not only is the chair containing the key hopelessly far away, and the room containing the painting helplessly locked, but I'm dreading the moment when my closet door will creak open and I'll have to stare at those two betrayed eyes.

Chapter Twenty-Six

Maggie

IN THE FOYER I'VE JUST ABOUT WORN a trench in the marble floor. I've gone over it a thousand times. If I am to find the key, I have to determine who bought that chair at the auction. I'm not sure what time Florence arrives, but I hope it's soon—and that she knows how to help. I plunk onto the step inside the front door to wait.

"Hannah. You're not supposed to be here." It's the unhelpful silver-haired man from yesterday. "Guests will start arriving in a half hour, and I can't have you sitting here, looking like a bump on a log."

I bow my head. "Of course. I was waiting for Florence. Do you know when she arrives this morning?"

He frowns. "You should not be bothering Mrs. Ensminger-Burn. I have no idea if she's planning to be on the property today. And even if she is, she does not have time for your antics."

"What?" I stand and almost trip up the few steps into the foyer. "I need to talk to her. She's the only one who can help me."

"I do not care one iota about what you need. Your father is supposed to be keeping you out from under my feet. I suggest you make yourself scarce." He taps his foot and points toward the servants' staircase until I start to move.

I'm tempted to retreat to my tree, but I turn back. Maybe he can answer a question before he banishes me. "The chair in the drawing room. The one with the floral pattern. Do you know how I can find out who purchased the original?"

Aunt would suggest that his scowl might freeze in place if he continues to make that face at me. "No. Maybe you should Google it."

What does *that* mean?

I close my eyes as he strides away, leaving me feeling like a fish out of water. Or a girl out of time. I imagine a normal morning in my own life. The carriages passing the front of the house. Aunt getting ready to have a bite to eat in the breakfast room before she heads out to make social calls to the neighboring cottages. The morning after a ball, the rest of the house would be sleeping in, but the kitchen staff would have meals ready for anyone who decided they needed food. Colette would be being Colette somewhere. But I also remember the freedoms I don't have in my own time, and it gives me pause.

"Hannah. Are you okay?"

When I open my eyes, Florence is standing in front of me. Her white hair is perfectly coiffed, and her suit is yellow today. I'm still wearing the pink cotton pants and the shirt I've had on since yesterday. Aunt would be so disappointed in how sloppy I have become, but these pants are so comfortable that I don't know how I'm going to go back to corsets and stockings.

I can't help but throw my arms around her. "Oh, Florence. I'm so glad you're here. Mr. . . . ah . . . Mr. Trent said he didn't think you were in today. I wasn't sure what to do."

"It's okay." She awkwardly pats my back, but she returns the embrace. It makes me feel better. Stronger. "Trent doesn't know my schedule, dear. What did you need?"

I take a breath, trying to reclaim my composure. "Do you know if there is a record of who purchased the furniture at auction in the 1960s?" I don't mean to be abrupt as I say it, but we don't have much time left. I'm sure that the moment I see Hannah's father today, he's going to ask me about packing.

She tilts her head to the side, as if she's thinking. "Of course. The Antiquities Society has meticulous records going back decades. There were a few files damaged by a water main break in the seventies, but I think those were only personnel files, not auction records. Why would you need to know about that?"

For a moment I think about telling her the whole story—after all, once he got over the shock, Jonah reacted so positively when he found out about our swap—but I worry that she'll think I'm crazy and be unwilling to help. "I'm curious about who purchased it. I heard a rumor about something hidden in the fabric, and I thought it would be interesting to find out if it really existed."

She chews on her lower lip for several long minutes. "I haven't ever heard that rumor, but it doesn't mean it isn't true. Who did you hear it from?"

I am not prepared for this question. "A guest on a

tour yesterday mentioned it." I try to keep the question mark out of my voice.

She looks skeptical, but she nods. "I've gathered from talking to Trent that your, er, *enthusiasm* for The Elms doesn't always go over so well with the docents, but I happen to think there are far worse things a young lady your age could be doing with her time. And . . . well, let's just say I share your passion for this particular house." She gives me a warm smile. "Besides, history buffs like us are always up for a little treasure hunting, aren't we? I've gone down a rabbit hole once or twice before because of a long shot."

"Well . . ." I breathe a sigh of relief. "I mean, thank you. Trent said . . . but I just wanted to be sure. . . . Don't you have responsibilities?"

She nods. "I'm afraid I do. I have a number of people I need to speak to this morning at The Elms. I won't be able to slip away until"—she looks at her watch—"eleven thirty."

I'm sure my face shows my disappointment, but what other choice do I have? "Who do you need to speak to?"

"Don't worry about that. Just come back and find me then." She smiles and pats my hand. "Have you ever been to the archives at the Historical Society? It's one of my favorite places. I know the librarian there, and I'm sure he'll help us."

We walk away in separate directions just as Trent opens the enormous front doors and the first of the day's guests enter. Many of them hold devices or tiny cameras. I still can't believe that this house in which I've spent so much time is on display for all the world to visit.

I have an hour and a half to wait. I spend part of that time in the tiny gift shop near the kitchen. I'm amazed that they sell replicas of my lucky locket. On a long shot I ask the clerk if she's ever heard of a mystery involving a key. (She hasn't.) I run across the grounds to the weeping beech and back to the house four times. (I feel sure I'm getting faster.) When I get tired of that, I wander through a few of the rooms, reading the notes on the walls about the history of the house (taking care to skip over anything about what happens to the inhabitants).

Finally it's time.

Her automobile is on the side of the house where all the visitors park. It's yellow, but that's not the only thing that is unusual. "Your . . . car . . . looks different from the others."

"This, my dear"—she gestures proudly at the

machine—"is a 1953 Packard Caribbean. I'm particularly partial to the whitewall tires."

She opens the door for me, and I slide into the interior. It's made of a soft caramel-colored leather. "Did you say 1953?" It's still fifty years after my own time, but as far as I can tell, the car is a time traveler like me. "I like it," I say when she nods. "My uncle has a 1905 Buick," I say, without even thinking about it.

"Does he?" Florence gasps. "I would dearly love to see that. Is that your father's brother?"

It's too late to correct my mistake, and I have no idea if Hannah's father has a brother, so I just nod, hoping the lie won't get Hannah into trouble.

The ride is so smooth and quiet, it feels like we are riding on a piece of furniture. Riding in Uncle's automobile is bumpy and rough, although that might have a good deal to do with the quality of the roads in my time, not the car. I'm tempted to ask her to drive around a bit, but then I remember our looming deadline. I'm supposed to be back in the mirror at six o'clock to compare notes with Hannah.

"I appreciate your waiting so patiently for me, Hannah. I've been collecting some impressions on the house from some of the staff. I was able to speak to several of them this morning," Florence says casually as she eases the vehicle onto Bellevue Avenue. There are so many automobiles on the road—it seems like everyone must have one. In my time they are still a relatively new invention. She drives much more slowly than everyone else, so it's not much different from riding in Uncle's new car. Several times, someone honks and she waves good-naturedly.

"Are you a newspaper reporter?" I can't think of any other reason she would have for collecting impressions of the house from the staff.

She laughs. "Oh, nothing like that." But she doesn't elaborate, and we ride the rest of the way in awkward silence. Thankfully, the trip takes only a few minutes. We stop near the Tower, where we met Alex and Ethan yesterday. When we arrive, Florence leads me up the front steps. It's not a building I'm familiar with, but it feels like something that has been here a long time.

"Excuse me," Florence says to a clerk sitting behind a large desk. "I need to see Jeffrey."

A young man dressed neatly in a suit and tie emerges from a door behind the desk. "Mrs. E.-B.! It's always so nice to see you!" He pumps her hand enthusiastically. "To what do we owe the pleasure this morning?"

It is so obvious that this man is trying to win favor with Florence. I have no idea of his motives, but I've seen countless people fawn in the same manner over my father and my uncle when they are trying to impress them.

Florence nods patiently. "We need to see the archives of The Elms' auction in 1961."

"Well." Jeffrey clears his throat. "Of course." He leads us into a small room with a large table. He flips open an object the size of a thin book that looks something like Hannah's device, only bigger.

"So," he says, looking up and cracking his knuckles. "What do you need to know and how can I help?"

"Dear." Florence puts her hand on Jeffrey's shoulder. "We're working on a top secret project. Would you indulge an old woman who has been affiliated with this facility since you were in diapers? We just need a few minutes of privacy."

Jeffrey can't contain his disappointment. "But, Mrs. Ensminger-Burn . . ." He pauses, clearly hoping she'll change her mind. "I thought I could help you with the computer. . . ." His voice trails off.

"I'm perfectly capable of managing the technology, my dear," she says, patting him on the arm.

He sighs and stands up, as though his indulgence in

her request is exhausting. He pauses again, clearly hoping, and then with another big sigh, he quietly leaves.

Florence sits down in front of his device, gesturing for me to follow. "They digitized the records years ago. We can access decades of data archives through this."

"What else can that tell you? Information about the Berwind family?" I try to keep the quiver out of my voice.

"Yes. These archives have everything on Newport going back to the mid-1800s." Florence beams like Colette does when she has beaten me at something.

I take a deep breath. I am not here to find out about my life or the lives of my family. And I'm not even sure I would want to know how things turn out. "Right. As you know, I'm curious to find out who purchased the original of the Louis XV–style armchair reproduction in the drawing room at The Elms."

She touches the buttons on the device, and I realize it's the modern equivalent of a typewriter. I don't know how it works, but with just a few strokes to the keys, she looks up with a smile. "Ada and John Stillwater purchased that chair."

"That is astonishing." I can't keep the amazement out of my voice. "All that information is in that little device?"

She gives me a bemused look. "Well, of course not, dear. It's in the Net. Or the Web. Or the cloud. Or whatever they call it these days—it's hard for us old folks to keep up. Not like you youngsters, who were born knowing how to text those emoticon thingies."

I don't have time to ponder the mysteries of twenty-first-century technology. I'm just glad it works so quickly.

My palms are starting to perspire, and I move closer to Florence, peering at the screen. "How do we contact them?"

She cocks her head to one side. "Shouldn't be too hard." A few more swipes on the keys, and she says, "Oh no."

"What?"

"It looks like they moved in 1986." She lowers her glasses and stares at the screen.

It can't be. All this technology, and it's a dead end? How will I get back to 1905?

She makes a few more keystrokes. "Wait. Here's something."

"A Stillwater relative who contributes to the Newport Antiquities Annual Fund lives in Chicago." She smiles. "Do you want to know if they still have the chair?" She pulls out her device, and before I reply, she's entering numbers.

"Drat," she says, and holds up her telephone for me to hear a stiff voice on the other end of the line.

"This number is no longer in service. Please hang up and try your call again."

"Hello! Can you tell us—"

Florence hits the button with the word "end" before I finish asking my question. "It's a recording," she says. "It appears we haven't updated our records."

It takes three more tries with different numbers before someone answers.

"Hello? Mrs. Jones? Would you happen to be related to Ada and John Stillwater?" Florence asks, and then pauses. "Florence Ensminger-Burn from the Newport Antiquities Society. Your parents purchased a chair at auction in Newport, Rhode Island, in the sixties." She looks at me while the person on the other end talks. "No, nothing like that. We are just curious about the provenance of the chair." She grimaces. "Can I put you on speakerphone?"

She presses a button, and the laughter of a woman is amplified. "I love that chair. I'm not interested in selling it."

"Mrs. Jones," I say, remembering not to yell, and trying to keep my voice even, like Florence does. "My name is . . ." I pause so as not to stumble over her name.

"Hannah Jordan. My father is the caretaker for The Elms, and we don't want to buy the chair." It surprises me how easy it has become to pretend to be Hannah. "I'm looking for a key that might have been hidden in the armrest of that chair."

Florence raises her eyebrows at me, but Mrs. Jones gasps from the other end of the connection.

"How did you know? My brother found that key when he ripped the upholstery on the chair," Mrs. Jones whispers. "We never told anyone. We were kids playing hide-and-seek. He'd been forbidden to even touch that chair. It fell over, and the key slipped out of the upholstery on the arm."

I let out a breath. "You found it? Do you—"

She continues over me, speaking as though she's reliving a dream. "He was seven and I was nine. We thought it was magic, this big old skeleton key with a gold filigreed handle. When Todd picked it up off the floor, it was as though time stopped for just a moment." She takes a breath and goes on. "That sounds silly, doesn't it. Anyway, for years it sat on his desk, but when he was in high school, he strung it on a chain and wore it around his neck."

I glance at Florence. Even though she doesn't know

how important this is, she still reaches up and squeezes my hand. I whisper toward the phone, "Does he still have it?"

There's a sadness in Mrs. Jones's voice as she answers. "My brother died last year. But that key always brought him good luck. He wore it under his uniform when he shipped out to Vietnam in '71. He had it on when he was injured in battle. He always said it was the reason he met Genevieve in the hospital while he waited to get sent home." She sighs, and I can almost hear her wipe away a tear.

Florence clears her throat. "We are so sorry for your loss. Thank you, Mrs. Jones, for sharing your story."

"Wait!" I don't mean to shout, but I'm afraid one of them is going to break the connection. "Does someone in your family still have it?"

"It's funny that you're asking about that key. After Todd died last year and my nephew moved Genevieve into the nursing home, he gave the key back to me. We never really knew where it came from. I always had an idea that it must have been hidden in that chair for a reason."

"It was," I whisper. "And I have reason to believe that it could be the key to solving the mystery of the

Margaret Dunlap portrait heist." But as I'm saying this, I realize that if the key is with Mrs. Jones in Chicago, it will take weeks to get here. My heart starts beating as if I'm running again. I have to go with Hannah's father to California.

How can I ever do that?

"The heist, my dear?" Florence whispers, her eyes crinkling in confusion. "Are you sure?"

"Oh my goodness!" Mrs. Jones practically shouts from the other end of the line. "Really? I'm holding it in my hand right now," she says. "But I . . . I'd hate to part with it. It means so much to me."

We are so close. I can't keep the tears from forming, and I brush my face, hoping Florence doesn't notice. "I don't need to keep the key, Mrs. Jones. I just need to open something with it."

Florence inhales sharply and then looks at me with a sparkle in her eye. "Mrs. Jones. If I could guarantee that we'd return the key to you, would you be willing to let us borrow it? The Antiquities Society will cover overnight shipping, and I will personally ensure that you get it back."

Overnight?

"This all sounds so mysterious," Mrs. Jones says.

"And I do love a good mystery. If you will guarantee that I'll get it back, I don't mind loaning it to you for a while. I guess it does feel like it belongs at The Elms. I'm running out to do a few errands; I'll ship the key to you this afternoon. You'll see what I mean about it feeling magical."

I can't believe our luck. I've found the key. "We can really get it overnight?"

Now *that's* magical.

As I feared, the moment we are back in the automobile and even before she starts the engine, Florence turns and looks at me, eyes shining with excitement. "Tell me more about this key."

I bite my tongue. More than ever before, I want to tell her about the mirror and the portrait and about how I'm not really Hannah Jordan. But I can't. "Would it be okay if I told you the whole story tomorrow? I don't know for sure that anything will come of this key, but it's something I'd like to do for myself, if that's all right? I promise I'll tell you everything later, though."

"How do you know it has something to do with the heist?" she asks. I can tell she is trying to piece the puzzle together, but I just squeeze her hand. Even in the warm air, it's cool to the touch. "Where did you hear about the key again?" There's a familiarity about her that tugs at my heart, and I *want* to tell her. But I can't find a way to say the words "time travel" out loud.

"I need to be sure I'm right before I involve you more than necessary." I squeeze her hand again. "You know I appreciate your help."

She nods and starts the car. "I respect your request for secrecy, though I don't really understand it." Her tone is clipped and professional. Not at all the conspiratorial tone she had just a few minutes ago. "I've been obsessed with that portrait and the heist since I was a little girl. I've always wondered what the true story is."

We ride in silence for the rest of the drive to The Elms. I've hurt her feelings, and I feel terrible. But I simply cannot reveal the secret. If Hannah wants to, she can decide to tell Florence more after we swap back to our rightful places.

I think about how anxious I am to get home, but there are parts of the twenty-first century that are beginning to grow on me. I shall certainly miss the freedoms I have had here. I glance over at Florence driving. Tomorrow it will be back to being shadowed by a nanny and sewing with Colette and a total ban on running.

Except maybe it doesn't have to be.

Yesterday Tara said if women hadn't protested over the years, the world wouldn't have been ready for a woman to run for president. Generations of women must have taken lots of baby steps to earn these freedoms. Generations that include me. Maybe there's something I can do to help things along. I've heard Mrs. Belmont whispering to Aunt Herminie about trying to involve society ladies in a movement to help women get the vote; maybe I can join them! From there, anything's possible!

It's so very obvious to me why Hannah went back in time—she needed to prevent the heist. But I've been pondering my purpose for traveling forward. I thought it was only to clear the way for Hannah. But now I wonder. Maybe I needed to see things here to have a vision for what could be for me. My time here has been so short, but it has opened my eyes to something much longer in duration—a purpose for my whole life. My life doesn't have to be a whirlwind of meaningless balls and dinner parties; I can contribute something important. Something that will have a lasting effect.

I think I finally understand why all this is happening. I need to stop bemoaning the things I'm not "supposed" to do, according to my aunt and my father (and society at large), and start doing the things that make me happy, like running and reading as much as I want. Maybe even playing lawn tennis until I perspire and sliding down a banister once in a while. I bet there are a lot of girls my age and older who would love to get a chance to do something outside the so-called rules.

I'm suddenly beyond eager to get home and begin planning right away! I'll find out from Mrs. Belmont how to get involved. It's not going to be easy. Many people—including women—won't think that these changes are appropriate.

And no matter how outraged Aunt Herminie might be, I'm going to find a way to continue running! I will never tire of the wind in my hair and the feeling of freedom I get when I run.

My brain is whirring with the possibilities. "Did you ever play a sport when you were younger?" I blurt as Florence eases the car between the white lines painted on the surface of the driveway. It's suddenly important to me to find out more about her before I leave.

Florence looks at me in surprise, startled for a moment out of her hurt feelings. "I confess that's the last thing I expected you to want to discuss right now." She chuckles. "I'm more of an artist than an athlete. But my grandmother was a long-distance runner before it was acceptable for women to really be active in sports. She has always been an inspiration to me." There's a wistful tone to her voice, and I wonder if she's missing her family in the same way I'm missing mine.

We get out of the car and start up the path toward The Elms' front entrance, and I try to think of something to say. "Thank you for all your help."

"Oh, Hannah. You're welcome. I'm sorry about the way I acted when we got into the car. I respect that you would want to do your best to confirm a rumor before sharing it. I know you'll tell me more after the key comes from Mrs. Jones tomorrow." She squeezes my shoulder. "I need to confess something to you," she says. "I arrived the other day as a result of a complaint from Trent. About you."

I gasped. "What?"

"Now, don't worry." She waves her arms like she's swatting a fly. "The Antiquities Society knows that he is inclined to exaggerate. Actually . . ." She pauses. "He's a bit of a blowhard, if you ask me. But we still needed to investigate the . . . how did he put it? 'The bratty, know-it-all girl who interrupts my tours.'" She laughs. "*My* confession is that I never expected you to be a kindred soul with such a passion for history." She pulls me into a tight hug. "Promise me you'll never lose that passion."

I relax into her embrace; even though I can't tell her who I really am, I feel like she understands. As I pull away, I notice for the first time the edge of something silver peeking out from under her jacket.

"My lucky locket," she says, noticing my gaze and pulling it out for me to see. "It's an heirloom." She opens it to reveal a small picture of a child. "And this is my granddaughter."

My heart pounds for no obvious reason as I look at the locket. For a moment I wonder if it IS my locket, but then I remember I've left it at home. "I have one that looks very much like that, but the chain is shorter."

"The ones at the gift shop are best sellers." She tucks the necklace back into her blouse.

"Mine used to be for luck as well," I say, "but I don't need it for that anymore. Good friends are a better talisman."

Florence nods. "Good friends are a gift. That is for sure."

Suddenly I can't wait to tell Hannah everything.

Chapter Twenty-Seven

Hannah

MY DAD WOULD BIRTH KITTENS IF HE knew I had a boy in my bedroom closet.

Don't worry, Dad. This one refuses to open the door.

As soon as the coast was clear, I tried to get in to talk to Jonah, but he must have been holding the doorknob, because it refused to budge. And when I attempted to speak to him through it, he cut me off at "Jonah—"

"Please, Hannah. I can't talk right now." It sounded like he was speaking through tears.

I didn't know what to do, so I did . . . nothing.

Only, now it has been at least an hour, maybe more, and I've done my own share of crying, waiting for him to open the door. It doesn't seem like that's ever going to happen. It's perfectly quiet in there; in fact, there's been no noise on the floor at all since Mrs. Berwind poked her head in right after my big "confession." She started to fuss over me, but then Mr. Berwind showed up and hustled her out. I overheard him say she should leave me alone to rest because my "delicate female constitution can't handle all this drama, poor thing."

If I hadn't been so upset about Jonah, that would have made me scream.

Um, hello. Delicate females, my foot. Let me start a list for you of women who handle(d) the drama just fine, thank you very much:

Abby Wambach

Rey from Star Wars (fictional, but still)

Rosa Parks

Marie Curie

Susan B. Anthony

Malala Yousafzai

Wonder Woman (also fictional, but STILL)

I could go on for about ten years, but . . .

It's not what's important right now.

I slide off the bed and crawl over to the closet door again. I tap lightly. "Jonah?"

He doesn't answer.

I take a breath like I'm about to swim the entire Olympic hundred-meter dash underwater. Is that a thing? Well, whatever. I'd rather be doing that anyway. I'd rather be doing just about anything else in the world.

"Jonah, please?" It's all I can get out.

Nothing. But just when I'm about to give up and crawl back to my bed, the doorknob turns.

Jonah peers at me from the darkness of my closet, like a trapped animal. Which he kind of is. His eyes are the saddest thing I've ever seen, and he doesn't do anything more than stare at me, but the *Why?* is written all over his face.

I slide my earring from my lobe and drop it, so that I have a ready excuse for what I'm doing on the floor if anyone should barge in. *Breathe, Hannah.* "I know you don't understand—or maybe you do—but I know it sucks, and I just . . . *Do* you understand?"

He doesn't answer, just stares off into some nothing-ness over my shoulder.

"Okay," I say, taking another deep inhale. "The thing is, well . . ."

"I'm in the history books, aren't I? As the one blamed for the crime?" Jonah asks when I literally can't make myself say the next words. "You can't change it because it's already written." His voice is flat and dull, like he has already accepted his fate.

I nod because my throat closes up too much for me to speak. He really is so smart.

"You used me this whole time." He doesn't even sound angry, just sad. Betrayed.

"NO!" I nearly scream it, and I have to clamp a hand over my mouth. I don't want anyone coming in to check on me. "No," I repeat, more quietly but just as urgently. "I mean, I knew that history blamed you, but I always had my doubts and lots of people vouched for how nice you were and how you would never have done something like that. To be perfectly honest, when I first approached you in the tunnel, it was partly to rule you out as a suspect but also . . . well, partly to keep an eye on you in case you were the thief." I hang my head.

"I'm sorry," I whisper, before adding, "but you have to believe me. I swear I thought that Maggie and I could switch back whenever we wanted. We didn't know any of that stuff about the alternate time line until *after* you and I had stopped the heist. You know that! You were there!"

He raises his eyes to mine finally, and something

glimmers in there. Like maybe he remembers. Like maybe he believes me.

"But then you didn't say anything once you *did* realize," he says. "All last night. This morning in the tunnel. You were perfectly fine letting me continue to help you."

I take this with only a small wince. He's not wrong. "Things didn't click into place for me until the ball. What it would mean for you, I mean. And this morning I—I was trying to work up the courage to tell you when . . . when . . . well, you know. When we were interrupted."

He nods but doesn't say anything. I'm desperate to ask him if he understands how I never wanted any of this to happen, how all I wanted was to spend some time in the Gilded Age and then everything with the art heist stuff just started snowballing and . . .

I wish I'd never come here. I wish I were safe in my own room, curled up in my bed with my stuffed bear, Windy. I'm so homesick, it hurts.

But it's not about making *me* feel better. It's about Jonah.

He's quiet for a long time, and then he says, "What do the history books say? Do I go to jail for life?" He sounds totally resigned. I shake my head so hard and fast, it practically swivels off my neck. "NO! No, you don't! I promise. You—you escape Newport. You're never caught! It's like this huge century-old mystery or whatever. But I swear, you don't go to jail for it. At least, not in my time line."

Now it's his turn to exhale. About a hundred times. When he can speak again, he asks, "Never caught, huh? I'm a notorious fugitive?" There's a hint of something in his voice that kind of matches that adventure-y eye twinkle tell of his, and my heart leaps with hope.

"Um . . . I guess so?" I mean, the history books don't make him out to be Billy the Kid or anything. Mostly they just say he was never heard from again, and neither was any news of the painting, but if he wants to think of himself that way, I'm sure not gonna be the one to stop him.

"How?" he asks.

"Huh?"

"How can I possibly escape? Between my mother's and my jobs, we barely put food on the table. How would we ever afford to run away? Where would we go? How will we get new jobs without papers and a letter of recommendation from the Berwinds? I can't—I can't picture it."

"I know. We'll figure it out, I promise. This is all my

fault, and I swear I'm not going to abandon you. We'll figure it out!"

"You said that twice," he murmurs, sounding doubtful again.

"I know. I really mean it, that's why."

"Sure."

"You don't believe me?" I ask.

"I believe that *you* believe it. But you're from a different time. Everything is different for someone like you."

"Someone like me? What? It's not like *I'm* rich, like Maggie is," I say. "I *work* at The Elms in the future, just like you do here."

Only, that's not really true. Yes, I work at The Elms, or at least my dad does. But it's a hundred kinds of different. I have . . . options. I have education. And we're not rich, true, but we can afford things like vacations and new school clothes and soccer registration fees, and my dad is forever telling me I can be anything I can dream of, and I believe him.

Has anyone ever told Jonah that? Would he have any reason to believe them? Jonah definitely has serious street smarts, based on all his ideas for hiding the painting, but it's not the same. He's not a slave or anything, but he might as well be, for all the chances he has of changing things for himself in any real way. Without money and school, he's basically looking at an entire life doing exactly what he's doing at this age.

Jonah slumps farther into the closet, and my heart drops into my gut.

"I'll, um—I'll give you some privacy while I think of ways to do this escape. You probably want to, like, digest all this, I'm guessing," I say.

I leave the door cracked a bit, so at least he has a sliver of light, but he'll be safely hidden from anyone coming in. Then I cross the room and plop onto the lounging chaise. I wish these were still a thing in my time; it's like an extra-fancy version of a reclining beach chair. It's also the perfect place for a sulk.

My head hurts and my stomach cramps. It feels like every body part is encased in armor and like moving would be the hardest thing ever. Maybe I really am getting sick. Not from the drama but from how overwhelming everything feels.

I have no idea how to get to the painting. I have no idea how to help Jonah while still keeping everything okay in the future. I have no idea about any of it. And I miss home. I miss my dad and Tara and my phone and Windy and my whole entire *life*. I would give anything—

anything—to be back there now, with no worries bigger than how to get Ethan to ask me to hang out, which I couldn't really care less about right now.

I wish, I wish, I wish.

I have to wake Jonah after my lunch is delivered by one of the maids on a silver platter. I give him all of it. I don't think I could eat anyway.

I just want to go home.

"I'm really sorry about this whole entire mess," I tell him.

"Don't be. It isn't your fault."

"Um, actually, yeah, it's *exactly* my fault."

He smiles slightly. "I was trying to make you feel better. But truthfully, I didn't have to help you when you asked."

"Wrong again. What were you going to do? Say no to the niece of your boss?" I ask.

"You're very hard to cheer up, you know."

And that just makes my stomach twist even harder. Why should Jonah be trying to cheer me up when it should be the other way around?

"I really am super-sorry," I say again.

"I know."

But that's not good enough. I didn't give up last season when we were down by four goals in the second half of the division finals, did I? NO WAY! I'm not a give-up kind of girl. I've been mopey all morning, but what I should have been doing was figuring out a plan. The Louis XV armchair is gone, so there's no way Maggie can get the key in the future. It's up to me.

I begin pacing the room. I whisper, so no one (cough, Colette, cough) who might stick their ear to the door will hear talking inside, but I'm loud enough that Jonah can hear me.

"Okay, we need a plan of action to get you out of here and maybe get me home. Enough hiding and waiting. Here's what I'm thinking: I can't get to New York without attracting all kinds of attention, and you need to escape Newport, so it's only logical that we need to sneak you on a train to the city. Once you're there, you find the shop that has the chair and pretend to be Mrs. Berwind's errand boy, sent to check on their progress."

The more I get going, the more the plan just falls into place in my head. Like my brain was working behind the scenes the whole time I was sulking.

I race on. "I can disconnect the phone and intercept any telegrams, so there's no way the chair cleaners can contact the house to confirm. They'll definitely let you see the chair. Then you just have to pretend to inspect it and get close enough to sneak the key out. Okay, so maybe that's not as easy as it sounds, but I have total faith in you. I've seen how fast you think on your feet, Einstein."

Jonah blushes at that. But then his eyes drop. "My mother? I can't just—"

"I'll take care of that. Once everyone's in bed tonight, we'll sneak you out so you can get word to your mom. Can you reach her without anyone noticing?"

Jonah nods.

"Do you think . . . um, do you think she'll flip out?"

"If that means what I imagine it does, then yes, prob-ably. But the alternative is her son in jail for a crime he didn't commit. I think given that choice, she'll go along with whatever plan we come up with. I'll make it up to her, I swear it."

I duck my head. "I know you will. You're a really good guy. And I'm really, really sorry. Again."

Jonah nods quietly.

I blow out a breath. "Okay, so then you'll sneak back here and I'll let you in. You can sleep in the closet tonight."

Even in the shadows, I can see Jonah's cheeks turn

red. "I—I believe I would be more comfortable in the tunnel."

I shrug. "Whatever. If you really don't think anyone will go down there."

I resume my pacing, but this time I'm grabbing little items here and there and tossing them onto my bed. A silver brush. A hand mirror with a mother-of-pearl handle. I take off the locket Maggie had on when I swapped into her body and add it to the pile, but then I reconsider and instead add a hairpin that looks like it might have a real jewel in the center. If she was wearing the necklace, it might mean something to her. I'm hoping she won't mind sacrificing these other things to the cause.

"I'm guessing that selling off even one of these will bring in enough money to get you around New York and back here, once you have the key. Then it's just a matter of planning how to meet up so you don't have to risk coming back to the house, and then figuring out a plan for you and your mom to skip town permanently, but that will come to me."

I pause to finally take a breath. "I really think this could work!"

Then I realize what I've just asked of Jonah. "Oh

man. I'm doing it again. Forget New York and helping me with the key; obviously, escaping with your mom is the only thing we should be worrying about right now. I'll figure out the key another way. I'm sorry. Aaaah-gain."

Jonah looks a little dazed, but after a long minute I see the tiniest hint of a smile. "Except, I've always dreamed about seeing New York City. And my mother would never set foot in all that hustle and bustle."

I bite my lip. "Soooo? You're saying . . ."

"It's risky, but I think it could work. I'm in."

"You are the nicest person in any time period ever. Seriously."

We smile at each other, and then I rush on. "Okay, so my guess is the police will be expecting you to travel under the cover of night, meaning we have to outsmart them. You should take a train tomorrow afternoon, and if you can go to the next town over to board, even better."

"You seem to know a lot about these matters."

"I've watched only about a zillion-and-a-half caper movies."

He tilts his head in confusion, but I zoom on. "Let's work on how to sneak you out tonight. In a few hours I'll meet back up with Maggie in the mirror like we planned and ask her if this stuff is okay to take. Which, obviously, she'd better say yes to. Maybe she even knows where we can get our hands on a little cash so you can get a train ticket with that. It will be way easier to pawn all this other stuff once you get to New York."

For the first time all day, the knot in my stomach loosens.

We have a plan. Forward momentum. Too much drama for a girl's delicate constitution?

Pfft.

Not *this* girl.

The afternoon feels like it takes about forty-seven years to pass, but finally it's time for my mirror chat with Maggie. Wait until she hears our perfect plan. I leave Jonah safely hidden in my closet—daydreaming about the new life he seemed to latch on to pretty quickly once he allowed himself to imagine the possibilities—and head downstairs.

As soon as I'm on the sideboard, I take the trinkets from Maggie's room out of my skirt pockets and line them carefully on the mantel, so she can approve them as soon as she appears. They have to be worth more than enough to get Jonah to New York City and then off on a new adventure somewhere. Probably enough to get him to the moon and back, actually.

The mirror shimmers.

Before Maggie can even open her mouth, I speak. "Mags, we have the best plan ever to get to the key in New York. Wait until you—"

But Maggie's grin is even bigger. "You don't need to."

"You broke into the room! Wow, I give you so many props, because we tried and—"

She interrupts me. "No, I wasn't successful with that. But I did manage to locate the key. And it will be in my hands in a matter of . . . One moment, please."

She looks down at MY phone in her hand and punches a few buttons like she's a pro at it or something. "According to this tracking app Florence installed for me, delivery is scheduled for between one and four p.m. tomorrow."

My jaw drops. "You . . . What . . . It . . . How?"

This is even better than I ever dreamed! Everything is falling into place!

Chapter Twenty-Eight

Maggie

AT PRECISELY ONE O'CLOCK I STAND in the servants' entrance outside the gift shop. I still can't believe all the books written about the heyday of the summer cottages in Newport and the reproductions of art and artifacts. There is a whole stack of postcards featuring my portrait. I feel like scooping them all together and burning them. Who would possibly want me on a postcard? I wonder what they'll do with these when the original portrait is unveiled.

It was Florence's idea to have Mrs. Jones mail the package to Hannah's attention. I still can't believe it's possible to get a package from Illinois to Rhode Island overnight, but in the three days I've been here, I've seen stranger things. I just hope I don't have to wait three more hours for the delivery.

I half expected Florence to meet me here, though I'm glad she didn't. She's been such a big help, but I'm afraid that if I talk to her any more, she'll suspect that Hannah is crazy.

A brown truck pulls into the drive and stops in front of me. I consider taking a step or two backward, but before I can act, a young man wearing all brown, from his shoes and socks to his short pants and shirt, jumps down out of the truck with a package. "You're waiting patiently this afternoon. Is there a new Harry Potter book out or something?" He grins as he hands me a device and something that looks like a pen. "Sign, please."

With a flourish I sign Hannah's name, and then, hands shaking, I grab the package. Forgetting all polite manners, I turn and walk straight through the door and back toward the coal tunnel. In my mind the ghosts of servants rush past me as I pass the kitchen and descend the metal stairs to the boiler room, then walk past the coal wagon and into the tunnel still lit by sporadically placed bulbs hung from a cord attached to the ceiling.

As I walk, I rip the envelope open and dump the key into my hand. It has delicate gold filigree and is heavier than I imagined. Mrs. Jones was right. There is something magical about it. I'm holding the key to my past. Just as it was yesterday—and for the last hundred years—the door is sealed tight. Suddenly I'm afraid. What if the key doesn't work? I close my eyes and imagine my aunt and uncle, and my father, and yes, even Colette. They aren't perfect, but I do miss them.

I miss the comfort of my books, I miss the horses and carriages that carry ladies down Bellevue Avenue to their social events, I miss the sounds and smells of my Elms. At the end of the summer I'll return to the brownstone in New York City with Father, where I'll get back to my studies. I can't wait to shock Mr. Walsh, the headmaster of my school, with questions about rights for women.

I shake my head, sweeping my thoughts aside, and fit the key into the lock. It goes in smoothly, but it takes both my hands to make it move. At first it seems like I've turned it the wrong way, but then the chamber clicks into place. Using the key as a knob, I throw my whole body against the door until it opens. I'm not sure what I expected, an illuminated room with a ray of sun pointed at the portrait?

Instead I'm looking into a pitch-black void.

For a moment I consider my options. I could go

upstairs and find help. Either Florence or Hannah's dad could probably find a candlestick or a torch or a lantern somewhere. I try to use the ambient light from Hannah's device, but it's no good, it's not bright enough. I could climb into the void and feel around until I find the portrait. But the thought of bugs or rodents or something else lurking in the crypt stops me cold.

The tunnel is dank, dim, and dusty. I haven't come all this way to fail. I shiver, but then I see it. Just down the tunnel there's a bulb hanging low. With my arm outstretched I can touch the ceiling anyway, so it takes only a couple of attempts to pull the wire attached to the bulb a little lower. If I angle it just right, it gives me enough light to see into the chamber.

Nothing. What if it's not here?

But then I angle the light a bit to the right, and I spot it. Against the wall in the corner is a tarp covering an object suspiciously shaped like a portrait. Gritting my teeth and ignoring the thought of rodents, I crawl gingerly into the room and gently pull off the tarp.

And looking back at me . . . is myself. But not in a mirror this time. The century-old portrait that hasn't seen the light of day in more than a hundred years is in shockingly good shape, considering it's been kept in this disgusting space for so long.

The only thing left is to haul it upstairs without being seen, and then wait for the tourists to leave for the afternoon, so that Hannah and I can swap back to our rightful places.

All I can think is, *Cool.*

Chapter Twenty-Nine

Hannah

THERE'S NOTHING LEFT TO DO HERE, and I know it. I'm also desperate to be home. So why am I swallowing around a giant lump in my throat?

It's okay to leave. More than okay.

Most important, *Jonah* is more than okay. He snuck off before the sun came up this morning, after about a zillion hugs from me. True, at first he was slightly disappointed that he didn't need to go to New York City. But wow did that go away fast when he told me about his decision to go all Wild, Wild West. He'll take a new name, of course. Bye-bye, Jonah Rankin; hello, Jeremiah Duncan. It turns out Jonah/Jeremiah has always had an obsession with cowboys. He wants a whole ranch, with a big farmhouse for his mom and a zillion horses for him, a totally different future from what he thought he'd have, but one with way more possibilities for adventure. Doesn't everyone deserve that? And, as it happens, just the one ruby in the middle of Maggie's hairpin can actually make that happen. Thankfully, Maggie was more than eager to donate it and all the other items to such a good cause. She doesn't even think anyone will notice she doesn't have those things anymore. (Ah, to be filthy, stinking rich.)

I love happy endings.

And now it's time for mine.

Then why is it feeling so bittersweet? Crazy key drama aside, I always wished I could see The Elms in its prime, and not only did I get to see it, I got to live it. When I land home, I'll be playing the hero for a while because I'll be credited with finding the missing painting.

So why is my stomach doing backflips, and not in the good way?

"You ready for this?" Maggie asks quietly.

"Yes, no, yes," I answer.

She rolls her eyes. "You're weird, Hannah Jordan." Then she smiles. "And thank God for that. I can't imagine spending days trapped in some boring, stuffy person's body."

I smile too.

Yup. This is why my stomach is doing a world-class tumbling routine. Because it knows that as soon as Maggie pops that portrait of herself onto the wall, I won't get to talk to her ever again. Or at least it *thinks* so. Neither of us are even acknowledging that this theory of ours might not work.

It will. I can feel it.

"I'm gonna miss you like whoa," I say.

"Back atcha."

I giggle. "Where'd you learn that one?"

"I ascertained how to work the television remote last night. I've not been to sleep yet!"

My giggle becomes a full-on laugh. She's adorable. "I wish we had gotten more time to just chat, ya know? Like, when we didn't have to worry about solving art heists."

She grins. "Or finding keys missing for decades? Or figuring out how to explain away knowledge of their existence?"

"Exactly. I think we nailed that, by the way. One last mission for when you get back, huh?"

"I've got it covered. Though, returning to your original comment," she says, "I feel as if I probably know you better than anyone else in the world, after spending three days in your body."

"Ewww. There were some weirder parts to that that I'd rather not acknowledge, if you don't mind. No offense." I shrug, and smile.

"None taken." She chews on her bottom lip before saying, "Hannah? I've been working up the courage to tell you about some, er, incidences that took place during my time here. I'm afraid I may have—quite inadvertently and with only the best intentions, of course—taken some missteps in a few areas, and I—"

I cut her off. "Stop! I don't care. Unless you got a tattoo on my butt or something, I'm sure you didn't cause any permanent damage. Besides, everyone will be so caught up in the portrait discovery that I'm sure they'll forget all about anything weird I did or said or whatever. I don't want to spend our last minutes together on apologies."

She looks so relieved that I reconsider for a second. Just exactly what did she do? But I shake it off and continue. "This is gonna sound super-cray, so just go with it, okay?"

She nods, her nose wrinkling. I should totally skip

that move in the future; it makes my face look all kinds of messed up.

"Okay, so," I say, "when I was a kid and, um, maybe possibly right up until this week, I used to talk to your picture all the time. Like we were friends or something. And I always thought . . . I always thought we totally would be, if we lived at the same time."

"Oh, I'm quite sure of it!" Maggie says, and I smile.

"Me too. More than ever. But the thing is, I don't think I'm going to be able to anymore. I'll know it's not really you in there. It won't feel the same."

"I understand. But perhaps you can try anyway. You *do* have a spare copy of the painting now. Perhaps there's a place for it on your bedroom wall, next to the oversize picture of your friends with the instruments."

I burst out laughing again. "Those aren't my friends, you nut. That's a poster of the Five Heartbeats. Rock stars? Boy band?"

"Boy band?"

She looks completely confused, and I laugh harder. "You know what? Never mind."

She shrugs. "You also have your dad to talk to. And Florence is quite lovely. Of course, you have Tara. I'd love to have a Tara in my time."

I flash her a cheesy fake-innocent smile. "What? Are you saying you don't consider Colette your BFF for life?"

Maggie's eye roll is even bigger this time. "I don't know what 'BFF' means, but don't even utter her name!"

"I know, seriously. Wish I could help you there, but yeah. She's super-ugh. So . . . what will you be doing? You know, if I want to imagine you. And please don't say anything about debutante balls or husband-shopping."

Maggie shudders. "Hardly." Her face gets this thoughtful, faraway expression on it. "I have bigger plans than that. Now that I know everything it's possible for women to do and be in your time, I'm going to be the loudest voice there is to help the progress along in mine. After all, someone has to lay the groundwork. I know that a couple of the women in Aunt's circle are already discussing this issue, and I plan to join their ranks and expand their vision of what's possible for us."

I laugh. "So, like, rock the vote and all that?"

I swear, Maggie's eyes practically twinkle. "For starters. And only for starters."

"Awesome. Um, Maggie? I don't know if you were able to resist looking at any records of what happens with your life, but—"

She cuts me off. "Land sakes! I don't want to know!"

"Got it. Yeah, I wouldn't want too many spoilers either. So I'll just say that if 'someone' was worried about returning in time and doing something with her newfound, um, *revelations* that might disrupt the history books in some way, then I would probably tell that person, whoever she might be, that she shouldn't be worried about that. At all. I'd tell her that maybe she's on exactly her right path."

She gasps and covers her ears, but then she lets her hands fall away and smiles softly. "Thank you, Hannah."

I nod, and we share a smile before she asks, "And you? How shall I picture you?"

I grin. "Kicking butt and taking names, of course." But then I get more serious. "Remember when we were talking the first time and I was saying that stuff about women in my time having equal rights on paper but not necessarily always being treated that way? I was thinking that if you're going to be working so hard here, maybe I could do some stuff on my end to keep it going. You work on the laws and I'll work on the hearts. I can't let all your future efforts count for nothing, right?"

I give her an exaggerated wink, and she grins. "I like that." Our smiles fade as we stare at each other for a second, taking mental pictures. I swipe quickly at my eyes, then take a deep breath. "I think it's time. Are we ready to do this?"

She nods formally. For just that second I can see what she's probably like here, when she's being all "young lady of the house."

I bite my lip and put my fingertips on the glass. She tilts her head, then smiles and fits her hand to mine.

"It was nice to meet you, Margaret Dunlap," I say.

"Rock on with your bad self, Hannah Jordan," she replies.

Before I can even open my mouth to ask where she learned *that* expression, Maggie drops her hand and then her face becomes blocked by the back of the frame settling into place over the age spot. Then I'm falling, falling, falling.

I wake up on the floor, my feet in flip-flops, and my hair—*my* hair—in a ponytail.

I breathe in the quiet museum air.

It worked. Oh, wow. I jump up and race to the mirror. I edge the portrait gently out of the way, and my heart falls. There's no Maggie on the other side. Not even a shimmering behind the glass. In fact, it looks like the most ordinary mirror ever. My fingers fly to where the key-shaped age spot was—but it's gone! Completely, as if it never was there to begin with.

I let my hands fall to my side, and I take a few more deep breaths before slowly turning to face the empty room. I take it all in, a grin spreading across my face. Never have I been so happy to see velvet ropes or the blinking light of the security system.

"Hannah?" my dad calls from somewhere in the house.

"I'm here. Coming!" I call back.

I'm home.

I'M HOME!

NEWPORT GAZETTE DAILY NEWS
Century-Old Portrait Recovered,
Mysteries Remain

By Harold Mathews, City Desk

An unsolved art heist dating back to 1905 still puzzles investigators, but the missing portrait at the center of the theft has been safely returned to its rightful hanging spot at The Elms, onetime home of Gilded Age socialites Edward Julius and Herminie Berwind, now operated as a museum by the Newport Antiquities Society.

In fact, it appears that the long-lost portrait of the Berwinds' niece, suffragist Margaret Dunlap, painted by famed Impressionist artist Mary Cassatt, never left the home.

The artwork was recovered on Monday from its apparent century-long hiding space, a sealed room discovered off a tunnel that had been installed to facilitate delivery of coal into the house in The Elms' early days of operation.

"We're thrilled to have such an important piece back where it belongs, and we're excited to delve further into the mystery of how it came to be hidden right under our noses for all this time," says Antiquities Society president Barnaby Drumworth.

The discovery was made by Hannah Jordan, the twelve-year-old daughter of the property's caretaker. Earlier this week Jordan, who resides in an apartment on the museum's third story that once contained the home's servant quarters, discovered a piece of paper under a floorboard in her bedroom closet.

"I was packing for a trip to California we were supposed to take—before all this happened—and the handle of my duffel bag was caught on this piece of floor. So I got a flashlight, and I was on my hands and knees trying to push the board back down, when something underneath it caught my eye," Jordan told reporters at a press conference yesterday. "I got it out, and it was this note that talked about a secret door in the tunnel and a key to the door hidden in a chair in the drawing room. Basically, it was like a treasure map, and I was so, so psyched!"

Although the chair Jordan references had been sold at auction in the 1960s, she was able to track down the new owners with the help of museum volunteer Florence Ensminger-Burn, who herself has ties to the painting as the granddaughter of Margaret Dunlap, the portrait's subject.

"It ended up being way easier than we imagined. We made some phone calls, and by the next day I was holding the key in my hand. From there it was just a matter of unlocking the room and grabbing the painting," Jordan says.

She's being lauded as a hero for helping shed light on a heist that has baffled historians and museumgoers since the night the portrait went missing, at an elaborate Venetian ball thrown by the Berwinds in honor of the portrait's unveiling.

Still a mystery is how the painting ended up in the hidden room and who placed it there.

At the time of the theft, officials charged a twelve-year-old servant, Jonah Rankin, who worked in the home's kitchen, but he evaded authorities and was never heard from again. Historians long asserted that Rankin fled with the painting, but they couldn't explain how it never surfaced in any private art collections. Many had abandoned hope of ever laying eyes on it again. It is unclear whether Rankin was the author of the note retrieved under the floorboards, particularly given the fact that he was known to have been illiterate, and no records exist of his handwriting for comparison. Early analysis indicates that the note may have been written by a female.

Margaret Dunlap, who posed for the painting as a twelve-year-old, went on to make a name for herself as a prominent suffragist, using her position in society to rally influential women to the cause and gain audiences with politicians. She is pictured above at the August 18, 1920, ratification of the Nineteenth Amendment to the US Constitution, which awarded women the right to vote.

After restoration experts clean the recovered portrait, The Elms will celebrate the return of the famed piece by hosting a fund-raiser this fall, a Venetian ball that will mimic the 1905 event where the portrait was to have been unveiled.

Jordan, who has lived in The Elms since infancy and has been tapped to help create a Life of Children in Gilded Age Newport Tour of The Elms to debut at the holidays, spoke at the press conference about the significance the painting has played in her life. "I grew up looking at the reproduction of Maggie hanging on the wall, listening to tours discuss the theft, and researching the house's history for myself. The past has always come alive for me, but especially with that portrait. I just can't believe I got to be such a big part of setting things right with history. It's really so, so cool. . . . I mean, you almost can't make this stuff up!"

T HE *ART OF THE SWAP* IS BASED ON very real people. Not just famous historical figures such as Mary Cassatt, Elizabeth Lehr, and Alva Vanderbilt Belmont (who commissioned a fabulous "Votes for Women" set to serve tea on), and the original occupants of The Elms—Mr. Edward J. Berwind; his wife, Herminie; their niece Margaret Dunlap; their butler, Ernest Birch, etc.—but also the more recent occupants, a father and a little girl who was raised on the third floor of the museum, enjoying free rein of the mansion whenever it was closed to the public. In fact, a magazine article about caretaker Harold Mathews and his daughter Tara's experience growing up at The Elms was the spark that got our imagination going on this story.

In all cases we beg forgiveness for any liberties we've taken as we've reinvented these people to suit our fictional needs!

But while many of the people are/were real, the story

is not. There is no Mary Cassatt portrait of Margaret Dunlap and, therefore, no art heist and no Jonah Rankin. (If there's a magical mirror that makes time travel possible, we have yet to discover it but plan to never stop searching!)

While we took license with some things, wherever possible we tried hard to make sure that the physical descriptions of The Elms and the ways of life depicted for its occupants (the owners, their guests, *and* those who served them) were accurate reflections of the time period. Fun fact: all the ball details, from the floor-trailing diamond to the man who believed he was an English prince to the man who ordered an egg at parties, were all borrowed from actual Gilded Age–era Newport balls and residents.

The Elms is open for public tours, and we highly suggest popping in if you ever find yourself in Newport, Rhode Island. Harold Mathews remains the caretaker, though his daughter is grown and has moved away. There is an excellent Servant Life Tour that will even offer you a glimpse of the coal tunnel that plays such a big role in this story. Though, to our knowledge, there is no secret room inside it. However, in the adjoining furnace room there is an opening three quarters of the way up a wall, and Harold claims that this has never been investigated. Sequel?

For more on The Elms and the Gilded Age, we recommend the following resources:

- To plan a visit to the Newport Mansions (including The Elms) and to view pictures of their jaw-dropping interiors, go to www.newportmansions.org. This site also offers teacher resource guides on the architecture at The Elms, as well as other guides relating to the additional museums in the area, such as Marble House, The Breakers, and Chateau-sur-Mer.
- Meet Samantha: An American Girl is a series of books (and a movie) about a privileged girl living in New York State in 1904. She and Maggie likely would have been finishing-school friends!
- *The Art of the Swap* Classroom Discussion Guide (aligned to Common Core standards) and a related activities guide themed to Women's History Month are available at

www.simonandschuster.net/books
/TheArtoftheSwap.

One of the most compelling aspects of this story for us was writing about how the role of girls changed from Maggie's time to today. And while we both, as Hannah would say, "fly our feminist flags high" and are thrilled at all the freedoms that women and girls now claim, we worked on this book during a time in our own history when women's rights have once again come to the forefront of a national conversation. So in addition to including resources so that you can study more about how the women's suffrage movement gained momentum through the work of women who would have been Maggie's contemporaries, we're including resources on how we can all continue the march toward full equality. There's so much more we can achieve for all the girls and women around our world! Go, Girl Power!

To learn more about them, read these books:

- *Alice Paul and the Fight for Women's Rights: From the Vote to the Equal Rights Amendment* by Deborah Kops
- *Failure Is Impossible! The History of American Women's Rights* by Martha E. Kendall

- *If You Lived When Women Won Their Rights* by Anne Kamma
- *Origins of the Women's Rights Movement* by LeeAnne Gelletly

To get involved now, read these books:

- *Good Night Stories for Rebel Girls: 100 Tales of Extraordinary Women* by Elena Favilli and Francesca Cavallo
- *She Persisted: 13 American Women Who Changed the World* by Chelsea Clinton
- *Strong Is the New Pretty* by Kate T. Parker

And visit these websites:

- Black Girls Rock! Inc. at www.blackgirlsrockinc.com
- Girls for Gender Equity at www.ggenyc.org
- Girls Inc. at www.girlsinc.org
- Girls on the Run at www.girlsontherun.org
- Girl Scouts of the United States of America at www.girlscouts.org
- Girls Write Now at www.girlswritenow.org
- National Organization for Women at www.now.org
- Women's Sports Foundation at www.womenssportsfoundation.org

And watch these documentaries (these films are all unrated; please check with a parent or guardian before viewing):

- *Diamonds Are a Girl's Best Friend*
- *Half the Sky: Turning Oppression into Opportunity for Women Worldwide*
- *Miss Representation*

Acknowledgments

WE LOVE THAT GIRLS RUN THE WORLD over at Simon & Schuster, from CEO Carolyn Reidy at the tippy top right on down to the fantastic "Swap-esses" who worked on this book. Big thanks to publisher Mara Anastas, cover illustrator Julie McLaughlin, art director Laura Lyn DiSiena, managing editor Chelsea Morgan, production manager Sara Berko, copy editor Bara MacNeill, and the entire sales and marketing teams (which, of course, include men—to whom we're equally grateful!).

Our biggest accolades are reserved for Amy Cloud, the best editor two girls could ask for. You saw right to the heart of our story and encouraged us to add *even more* to our Girl Power subplot, and we love you for that. And a bonus thanks to Tricia Lin for all your added help!

Harold Mathews and Tara Kaukani, we are grateful for your willingness to share a window into your lives at The Elms. Hannah and her dad really came alive for us after hearing your anecdotes about living in Newport.

Alison Cherry, yours were the first set of eyes we trusted with this story, and you didn't let us down. Your notes and insight were amazing. Thank you!

Julia, Isabelle, Nora, Samantha, Nina, Jillian, and your moms: thanks so much for making an early version of *The Art of the Swap* a selection for your mother-daughter book club. Your feedback was beyond helpful!

And to all the girls reading this: keep demanding, keep dreaming, and keep bringing your brand of caring to the world . . . and we'll all be just fine!

Kristine wants to thank:

Kathleen Rushall, the best agent ever—cheerleader, support system, and friend. Thanks for believing in all my ideas and pushing me to be better.

Jen Malone—writing this book with you has been an amazing roller coaster. I've loved our brainstorming sessions, our coffees "midway," and all the joys of a shared file in Google Docs. I can't imagine writing this with anyone but you. I'm so glad we decided to drive to New Jersey together in June 2015. I can't wait to see Maggie and Hannah take on the world!

Pam Vaughan—for being my sports guru, and for helping to get Maggie's soccer game just right.

Katie—the first person in the whole world who believed in the idea of a story about a kid living in a mansion with her dad, the caretaker; and who is never afraid of asking a question, no matter how hard. I love you to the Lost Moon of Poosh and back.

Phil—for indulging me in my little "hobby" and for always giving me the time and space to write, even if it means the living room isn't vacuumed and dinner is takeout.

Jen wants to thank:

Holly Root, I'd never swap you for anyone else's agent (the pun trend continues uninterrupted!)—you are magic and that is all.

Kris—I think we make a better team than even Maggie and Hannah. Writing this with you has been so much fun!

J., B., and C.—thanks for accompanying me on research trips to Newport and letting me see The Elms through "kid eyes" (and for all the hugs and meals you deliver to my writing cave). I love you mostest mostest.

John, ten books in, and there are no words left at this point. But you already know them by now, don't you? SHMILY.

KRISTINE ASSELIN is the author of several works of children's nonfiction as well as the YA novel *Any Way You Slice It*. She loves being a Girl Scout leader and volunteering with the Society of Children's Book Writers and Illustrators. She is a sucker for a good love song (preferably from the eighties) and can't resist an invitation for Chinese food or ice cream (but not at the same time!). She lives in central Massachusetts with her teen daughter and husband and spends part of every day looking for a TARDIS to ~~steal~~ borrow. You can find Kristine online at kristineasselin.com.

JEN MALONE once traveled the world and planned movie premieres for Hollywood stars but now caters to far more demanding clients: her identical twin boys and their little sister. Luckily, her husband handles all the cooking! She lives outside Boston and loves school visits, getting mail, and hedgehogs. Jen's middle-grade novels include *The Sleepover*; *At Your Service*; *You're Invited*

and *You're Invited Too*, cowritten with Gail Nall; and *Best.*
Night. Ever., which was cowritten with six other authors.
She has also written the YA novels *Wanderlost*, *Map to the*
Stars, and *Changes in Latitudes*. You can visit Jen online at
jenmalonewrites.com.